# Recovery

When we are too broken to heal. When darkness overwhelms and all seems lost.

May the glimmer of light that is always there, come into view.

## J.M. Sins

Copyright © J.M. Sins 2025

All rights reserved. No part of this publication may be reproduced, stored in a retrieval system, or transmitted in any form or by any means without the prior written permission of the copyright owner.

Contact: jmsinsauthor@gmail.com

**recovery**

noun (ri-kuv-uh-ree)

1. the process of healing physically or mentally following a traumatic event, returning to a healthy state.

2. the action of being returned to the afterlife when recovery from traumatic events is not possible. Or, being returned to the afterlife when there is no further growth to be achieved in that lifetime.

# Prologue

## Monday 12th December 2022

THUD. The sound of the car slamming into my side, forcing me from the ground, was deafening. Then there was nothing but eerie silence as I sailed over the car, the flight momentarily freeing me from my imminent fate. Another sickening thud and cracks as my body hit the floor behind the now stationary metal assassin. Someone screamed, piercing my eardrums like a knife. Perhaps it was me. Pain was everywhere and everything.

A young boy, maybe eighteen, rushed to my side, crying and shaking, touching my face and pleading.

"I'm sorry, I didn't see you, you were just there in the road. Shit… shit, I didn't see you in time," he blathered, slumping to the floor beside me.

But I was not panicking. It was strange to lie in such pain and yet feel so utterly calm. No, not calm… acquiescent. An elderly couple approached us; it was them again, and now I was certain this was more than a coincidence. The man extended his hand, coaxing the boy back to his feet.

"It wasn't your fault, son, she just stepped out." His face was kind, only it was not the boy he watched as he spoke. His eyes focused on the beautiful goliath of a man whose grasp I had been escaping when I stepped in front of this damned car. The man who looked at me now with as much pain in his eyes as I felt in my wrecked body. The elderly man continued.

"My wife and I, we were on the other side of the road waiting to cross. We saw you coming, but she… she kept walking, didn't even look up to check for cars. Too busy looking at her bloody phone. You couldn't have known."

His words had not reassured the boy. He was panicking, not for himself but for me. So, leaving him in the hands of a passerby, the old couple walked away to someone else who had been there the whole time. Someone whose clothes and face had become familiar. Was it… no, it couldn't be. Could it?

Voices were shouting and my heightened senses could hear everyone at the same time. A panicked voice instructed me to lay still, as though I could have moved had I the strength to try. Another recalled the accident, presumably to someone on the other end of a phone.

"Yeah, she's conscious…. Yeah, she's breathing but it looks labored. She's been hit by a car, went right over the top. There's blood coming from her head and her legs look bad, she's lying awkwardly. You've got to get someone here. Please hurry. We're outside The Dog and Ferret on the corner of Collingwood Lane…"

But the voices and the light were fading, the pain was fading. What a strange feeling; while the panic and the noise continued, quiet peacefulness consumed me, and as my final breath slipped into the ether all I could see was him. I acquiesced.

\*\*\*

"Everything had been in place last night. He would have been recovered and order restored, had you not intervened. There will be consequences, Thomas. It is not for you to decide who lives or when recovery occurs. We warned you many times and gave him many chances to remember, but you have interfered, and the consequences reach far beyond your own."

In the midst of the chaos, the panicking passers-by, the girl laying helpless in the road and those trying to save her, the elderly couple calmly confront the one to whom their fight is, for now, lost. You see, there is a system in place, a system that has been effective for longer than can be measured with time. But every once in a while that system is disrupted, despite the efforts of those who maintain it.

They had indeed warned him, but today he had succeeded in outwitting them. For this, the consequences would not be his alone. They had reached those for whom the journey was almost complete.

# Chapter 1

## Monday 31st October 2022

## **Maya**

Totally Coffee isn't exactly a career defining choice, but feels somehow destined, should one believe in such a thing. I had been on my way to the job centre, parking on the high street and walking the rest of the way to enjoy the warm Autumn sun that was bright and low in an almost cloudless sky. Many of the Woodbridge High Street shop windows were decorated for Halloween, but something about Totally Coffee's display caught my eye, making me stop and look.

That was when I saw the piece of paper taped to the inside of the window between the wonderfully realistic witch and the glistening spider-infested web hanging from the roof of her hut. The display was outstanding, but the job advertisement a crude juxtaposition, handwritten on a piece of lined paper, cut on the skew from a larger sheet, simply reading:

*Full-time serving staff required. Enquire within.*

So I did. A large oak counter, matching display cabinets and tables made the place feel warm and luxurious. Modern metal-frame chairs with oak seats were tucked under the tables. One wall boasted bare, reddish-brown brick, the others were half panelled in oak and half painted in mid-tone grey. Flashes of greenery in cleverly placed planting added touches of living nature to the abundance of wood. It had none of the commercial vibe given by the big chain coffee shops. It was warm and cosy, the sort of place you might want to stay a while.

I received an impromptu interview in a room accessed from behind the counter by an unhappy looking lady called Ruby. It felt awkward, partly because Ruby seemed cross and partly because the room was cluttered with boxes of stock and a coat rack overloaded with bags and jackets. Seated at a table strewn with paperwork and interview forms, Ruby proceeded to ask questions. I was not the slightest bit prepared and she had seemed unimpressed by my lack of experience. So imagine my surprise when she rang the next day offering me the job.

Since leaving school I had explored nursing, psychology and even counselling, but none of them sated my want to help. None of them felt right. No matter what I learned, I became no clearer about who I was. All my friends and Sissy had known exactly what they wanted to do even before leaving school, but I had a feeling there was a purpose to my life, a way I could help people, I just couldn't seem to discover it. But at twenty-three it was high time I stopped searching for it and started earning some money.

\*\*\*

Today was my first day of full-time employment. The staff were nice and Ruby was okay, just older and more sensible than the rest of us. I got the impression that perhaps the others hadn't given her a chance. They told me she was married with young children and that her husband was mean to her. Her limp, greasy hair with no particular style and tired, make-up-less face made it clear she didn't prioritise taking care of herself. I wondered what this husband looked like.

I shadowed a boy called Harry, who was nice, although I won't be busting out any flirting moves for him. He was nineteen, boyish in appearance and with large, black-framed glasses that consumed far more of his slim face than was necessary. Flirting moves! Who was I kidding? If my flirting moves had any credibility, I wouldn't still be single at twenty-three.

Mum gave me the Spanish inquisition when I arrived home.

"How was your first day? Was everybody nice to you? Did you get enough break time to eat?"

Poor Dad will suffer all her fuss when I am gone, but I can't live here forever. It killed her when Sissy moved out, and I was sad too, of course; she is my sister and we've always been close. Mum wouldn't have coped had we fought; she wants everyone to be happy and nice to each other all of the time. She loves her family with every ounce of her being and we are lucky to have her. I am lucky to have them all.

She asked if I'd met any potential boyfriends today, her pretty face transforming from optimistic to disappointed when I told her "no". She gently reminds me every now and again that she was already married and had Sissy by the time she was my age. Thankfully, Sissy has a husband and they are trying to get pregnant.

Mum and Dad have always been deeply in love; that's what I want and won't settle for less. Sissy and Henry are happy but in a contented way, no flame ignites in their eyes when they look at one another. He's a good man and she's a good wife, but I see no passion between them. I want passion too. Mum and Dad still have it after all these years, connecting with one another in a way they don't connect with anyone else. That's what I am holding out for, my forever.

## Blaine

I wasn't prepared for her, for her eyes, the palest ice blue. Exposed, paralysed in her glance, I couldn't speak or move, just stared like I was retarded or something. And it was only a glance, but it changed something. Maybe everything.

She illuminated the place like a thousand watts of light radiating into the atmosphere. It had never been so bright in there. I did eventually speak and say what I wanted, but my presence clearly hadn't affected her the way hers affected me; she just carried on like I was nothing. I am nothing. But my god she's something.

Rob said he didn't see what I saw. And he didn't let me forget it for the rest of the day either, taking cheap shots at every opportunity. None of them too creative.

# Chapter 2

## Tuesday 1st November 2022

**Maya**

Mum and Sissy visited this morning on the premise that they happened to be passing and in need of coffee, but they were definitely checking up on me. Only I'm not fooling anyone; mastery of the menu and till is not coming naturally. Everyone is kind and patient, claiming to have been the same when they started. But could they really have been this bad?

Mum looked proud when I took her order, but not so much when I had to call Ruby over to clear the mistakes on the till. She is patient with me too and, despite what the others have said about her, seems to like me. Between customers she talked a little about her children and home life, referring quite bitterly to her husband during one such conversation. She is nice but most definitely not happy. I would rather stay single than feel that way.

Conversation soon returned to work and my slow progress. She assured me that I'll be fine and shouldn't worry about getting things wrong for now. It's early days after all. But I will need to learn the different roles and should try table waiting soon. I fear she's just had enough of rectifying my mistakes and hope there's less to get wrong in carrying people's orders to their tables.

## **Blaine**

I was sure I'd distorted the memory, made them out to be more than they were. But they're just as I remembered: ice blue, beyond normal. Portals to somewhere I don't want to go, somewhere dangerous.

Yesterday she was an unexpected shock, today I was hoping for her but still went into the same pathetic state of paralysis, unable to speak. What the fuck is going on? It's like when you learn French at school and have to think really hard about every word to be sure it's the right one. That's what it's like.

I was so nervous I dropped my coins on the counter, most of them bouncing in her direction. *Idiot*. Next time I'll use my card. Her face turned sympathetic and she shot me a smile as impressive as her eyes. I didn't notice her lips yesterday; they're perfect, like poster lips. In fact, her whole face is perfect. Pale, unblemished skin, the blondest hair, loose strands softly framing her beautiful face, the rest of it tied back. I don't even go for blondes.

Rob's having a field day over this, took the piss the whole day again and I have no excuses. I'm pathetic. I need to calm down the next time I go in there. I need at the very least to act normal, maybe introduce myself and find out her name.

## Chapter 3

## Wednesday 2nd November 2022

### **Maya**

Ruby kept me behind the counter with her again. Amber served with us and is everything the others described her as being. Outgoing and confident, a little bossy but in a good way, knows what needs doing and is not afraid to ask somebody to do it, even Ruby. She has a son, Rupert, and explained how his father "shit himself and did one" when she announced the pregnancy, her words not mine. But her boyfriend, Drew, who has been there since Rupert was a baby, loves him like he is his own. She said if all babies were like Rupert she would have ten.

The big guy who threw coins at me yesterday came in again today. He would have blended in with all the other customers had he managed to pay for his coffee without incident. But the coins slipped from his hands, cascading across the counter, making him stand out from the rest. Today he looked as though he wanted to talk but after a short and awkward silence, during which he stared at me intensely, he said nothing other than what he wanted from the menu. His friend, being considerably less awkward, said hello to Ruby, then to me, and ordered as normally as you would expect a man to order his coffee. I assumed they work in one of the garages around here, given their matching greasy blue overalls. Ruby chats with the regulars as though they're well acquainted, some on first name terms. Her tone is stern, yet they seem mostly comfortable with her just the way she is.

It's been an age since Rebecca and I caught up, so her visit tonight was overdue. She's one of those people who knew her career path before we were fifteen and has pursued medicine tirelessly since we left school. One day she'll be a surgeon, and a great one I would wager.

She quizzed me about my love life, or rather the lack thereof. She and Daniel have been together for three years now; he's a patient man and knows he must wait for marriage and children. She has never made a secret of how important it is that she achieve her goals before becoming a wife and mother.

I wished I had more to tell her. How uninspiring my life must seem compared to hers. She reminded me that Daniel still has a few single friends she could set me up with. I declined the offer, suggesting instead that she gather them all together in some sort of pressure-free social gathering so I could choose which ones to talk to. She gave me her all-too-familiar eyeroll and said, "And that, missy, is why you are still single. Too bloody picky."

# Chapter 4

## Thursday 3rd November 2022

### **Blaine**

Maya. Today, a name badge was pinned to the black uniform shirt that makes her skin look almost vampire white. I could entertain that as a theory if the stuff I've watched on TV is to be believed. I could assume her beauty is a trap to lure me in. The eyes a weapon to compel me. She'll turn me and we'll live forevermore in a heightened state of murderous passion.

Maya: the name's as perfect as her face. I didn't manage to introduce myself, but I did say her name, out loud, when I saw the badge. She responded with a tone of familiarity, like she remembered me. Not that she'd forget the weirdo who stares and throws money at her, I guess. She cracked an embarrassed half-smile before asking if I wanted anything else. But I just stared, my head silently saying what my lips wouldn't dare. "I want you, Maya, and I don't know why. And I don't know why I'm paralysed every time I see you."

I turned around as I was leaving to take her in one more time, but her and that Ruby were looking straight at me and laughing. Rob asked if I even knew if she was single, but what does it matter? It's not like she'd be interested; she already thinks I'm a joke. Who could blame her? I wouldn't inflict me on someone like her and I'm sure she's too good to just bed. Imagine being brave enough to try.

Anyway, Hannah's coming round later. That'll get my head back on planet earth.

## Maya

Garage guy, the money thrower, seems to be a daily frequenter. He's dark skinned, his hair is short on the sides, but just long enough on top to make out the Caribbean curl. He's distinctive looking being both tall and well built. Tattoos peep over the neck of his overalls and from out of his cuffs, covering the backs of his hands. As he reached his card across to the card reader, no doubt avoiding using coins, I noticed the skull on the back of his right hand, a snake weaving in and out of its face holes. His appearance contradicts his demeanour. He looks as though he should fear nothing, yet behaves as though he fears everything, including me.

Ruby is growing on me by the day. We get along just fine but she speaks as though the excitement of existence has been drained from her. Prior to the money thrower's arrival she presented me with my Totally Coffee name badge. He ogled it and said my name aloud before giving me a real hard stare as he asked for his skinny caramel latte. He looked embarrassed as soon as he had spoken the words, and I wasn't sure whether to laugh or look away, settling instead for an awkward smile while managing to poke the correct buttons on the till. When I asked if he wanted anything else he stared hard into my eyes, then shook his head. I wondered if there might be something wrong with him.

As he walked away from the counter I glanced at Ruby to see if she had witnessed the awkwardness. Her sideways stare and one raised eyebrow said she had and we both laughed just as he looked back over his shoulder at me. Poor thing will probably be too embarrassed to ever come in here again.

According to Ruby he's been a regular for some time but says very little and she has no idea what his name is. She told me the considerably less awkward guy he often comes in with is Rob. He's quite handsome but apparently not single, and a grease-covered mechanic to boot.

## Blaine

I regretted having Hannah over soon after she arrived. We smoked and watched TV, I half-listened until I could half-listen no more and pulled her up off the sofa, telling her to take off her clothes. She obliged the way she always does, standing there in skimpy black underwear that leaves little to the imagination, looking at me with come-to-bed eyes. Brown, ordinary eyes.

Her long, dark hair, big fake boobs and tiny waist look good. And she's covered in sexy inkings, apart from a patch on one of her thighs, like she's saving it for something. She demanded I take my clothes off too but

I wasn't into it like I normally am and told her to take them off for me. She obliged again, pulling my t-shirt over my head and unbuttoning my jeans, then got down on her knees and took me in her mouth. I was hard and could've carried on like that but I'm not a total pig. Picking her up from the floor and putting her on the sofa on her back, I looked at her face while sliding inside her, but I started losing it. I closed my eyes and that's when it happened, Maya's face appeared in my mind as clear as day, and there I was, hard as a rock again.

For the first time since we started sleeping together, however long that is, I didn't fuck Hannah tonight. It was Maya's face I saw and it didn't feel like just sex. I pictured her skin, pale and pure, untainted by the ink Hannah's covered in. I pictured her white-blonde hair splayed out beneath her, her breasts smaller and natural like they should be, and I pictured those eyes looking at me like she wanted me just as much as I want her.

But when it was over and I opened my eyes, disappointment quickly followed. Hannah got the wrong idea, saying I've never fucked her like that before, that she felt "it" from me tonight. Whatever *it* is, it wasn't meant for her. I lied, told her I didn't know what she was talking about and that it was no different to how it's always been. She got the hump, said stuff I can't now remember, so I asked her to leave. If she'd stayed any longer I might've said something I'd regret.

I have never had sex with her like that before, but I wasn't about to tell her I was picturing someone else. I'll stay away from Maya tomorrow, get her out of my head. This isn't good for me, especially if she thinks I'm a joke. I'll ring Hannah instead and apologise for tonight, see if she wants to go out for dinner or something. She didn't deserve that.

# Chapter 5

## Friday 4th November 2022

### **Maya**

Mum and Dad are discussing holiday destinations. Not abroad for the usual winter sun because, and I quote, "we don't want to spend our life savings on it, what with everything being so expensive now". But we will all appreciate the time together, even if it is cold and wet.

Dad is thankful for Henry; the son nature denied him. None of us could imagine not having him around, least of all Sissy. They're made for one another, always knowing what the other needs, always together and having little need for time apart. Yet still the lack of heat between them bothers me.

I have asked Sissy if it bothers her, but she believes there is more to a relationship than sex and passion. That you can't maintain the excitement felt in the early days forever; all relationships settle into more comfortable routines as time passes. Not that I would know. According to Sissy, that's how you know you truly love them, when your heart no longer skips a beat at the sight of them, yet you cannot imagine a life where seeing them is not an option.

Perhaps Mum and Dad's passion burnt out for a while and what they have now is a deeper love born out of years of being there for one another, years of sharing life experiences and growing together. Mum never wanted a career, embracing instead the role of stay-at-home wife and mother. Dad earned plenty to keep us all comfortable and probably preferred it that way; he took pride in providing for us all. Mum loves nothing more than keeping our home nicely decorated and spotlessly clean, and keeping us all well fed. And even though we are all grown up and Sissy no longer lives at home, not coming together for dinner every Sunday would crush her.

***

Ruby decided I can work the tables on Monday, admitting to keeping me on the till all week because she enjoys my company. She talked about her marriage again over lunch; her husband sounds like a pig of a man, but she stays for the children. She showed me a picture of him taken at a family gathering; he was unshaven in an unbecoming way. He looked ragged and dishevelled, his hair, although thin on top, looked in need of a good wash and cut. His face was round and full, a cold look occupied his eyes. Perhaps it was a bad photo, but I would cross the road to avoid him, even in daylight. Ruby said that once upon a time they were closer. Now she thinks he resents her for always being busy with the children, work and the house, even though he does nothing to help out.

Minutes after our lunch break ended, a man entered Totally Coffee and Ruby well-nigh launched me out of the way to serve him. Clearly familiar with one another, they slipped comfortably into conversation. She was different in his presence, more alive, more animated, and wore none of the usual look of defeat on her face. I stood back to watch the interaction with fascination.

"So, who's the mystery man?" I asked when he'd left.

"That's Dale, he works at Yardley's Motors down the road," she replied, her expression a mixture of the light she emitted while talking to him and the returning sadness she wears ordinarily. Adding that although she finds him utterly gorgeous, he most likely wouldn't take a second look at her, the remaining light leaving her face completely as she spoke. Poor Ruby.

Changing the subject quickly, she informed me that from next week my shifts will be spread over five days out of seven and will include one weekend day each week. Sunday is paid at a higher hourly rate, but I'm not sure Mum will be too pleased about me working instead of being at home with everyone.

So now I have two days off with no plans, other than Sunday dinner with the family when Mum wants to talk holiday destinations. She has busied herself researching places and claims to want everybody's suggestions before getting too carried away on her own. She says that every year yet still picks the destination herself regardless. I assured her I'll be happy wherever we go, it will just be nice to get away. It would also be nice if there was a spa close by for a pamper day in the absence of sun.

## **Blaine**

Keeping away from Maya didn't keep her from my head, and taking Hannah out to distract myself failed miserably. I tried, I really did; I took her to the Italian on the High Street, but all I could think about was Maya seeing us together. Which she didn't. And why would it matter if she did? She doesn't know I can't stop thinking about her, she doesn't even know my name.

We ordered our food but awkward silence followed. So I asked her stuff like "When did you realise you wanted to be a tattoo artist?" And "How come you've not settled down or got married yet?" But it felt weird and forced and the rest of the questions were just as lame. Luckily her enthusiastic responses filled the silence; the girl can talk.

I half-listened to most of what she said, but her stories don't interest me. She's a nice girl but she's not *the* girl, not even close. She's a pretty face and a good fuck but that's it. Sat there in a little skirt and low-cut top, all legs, tits and make-up, but it doesn't make me want her. My head drifted off, wondering what it would feel like to sit there with Maya, listening to her tell me about her life. About her family. About her. She'd be wearing something tasteful, something that doesn't scream "fuck me".

I asked for the bill as soon as we finished eating, I was all out of questions and couldn't sit there much longer. Then she said, "Let's walk to the seafront".

Why did I think taking her out would be a good idea? And as if the evening couldn't get any more awkward, my hand accidently brushed hers as we walked, and seizing the opportunity, she wrapped her fingers through mine, holding my hand tight. It felt wrong but she was smiling, she looked happy. I couldn't bring myself to pull away and ruin it for her, not after the other night, so I pretended I was cold and ready for a smoke and led her back to the car where she finally let go of my hand.

I drove to her place, at least that way I could leave when I'd had enough. Back in my comfort zone, behind closed doors, she put on some music and we smoked. Then she decided she wanted to know stuff about me, said she'd done enough of the talking and now it was my turn. I didn't know what else to do but kiss her to shut her up. It worked; she was all over me and it was okay. She smelled nice and looked better without the slutty clothes on. She did all the right things and before I knew it I was hard and it was easy.

We slid off her sofa, sinking to the floor, dragging a thick fleecy throw down with us. She fumbled around, pulling down cushions, placing one under my head. Then she was on top of me and I was inside her, and there was Maya again, in my head as clear as day. Her face, those eyes, her soft blonde hair. I could hear her voice in my ear saying she wanted me and that was it, it was all over. I couldn't look at her, at Hannah, or finish her off, and now I feel like an arsehole.

I couldn't say anything to her, I couldn't justify why it ended so quickly, so I held her because it was easier than having to speak. She took it, just laid there in my arms with her head on my chest. No more questions, no more talking, just laying with her arm across my ribs. I wanted to run but I couldn't put her through that, so I laid there until she fell asleep on that makeshift floor-bed of a throw and cushions, wishing she were Maya. Then I slipped out from under her and left before she woke.

# Chapter 6

## Sunday 6th November 2022

### **Maya**

Sundays are the best days. The house is full of laughter, everyone together, Mum smiling as though she's won the lottery. She spends most of the day cooking a roast dinner, everything cooked from scratch and always perfect. No one is allowed to help; it's her time to look after us all.

She made apple crumble and custard for pudding, the apples picked fresh from the tree in the garden. Grandad bought it when Mum and Dad first bought the house, before Sissy and I were even born. It was an infant tree then but is fully grown now. In the spring it bears beautiful pink blossoms, followed by enough fruit to keep us in pies and crumbles until the following year.

She tried making a strudel with them once and has never lived it down. Despite her amazing cooking skills, she never mastered pastry and the strudel ended up a soggy, greasy mess that no amount of her world-class custard could disguise. She was devastated, vowing never to make either pastry or strudel again. Thus far she has been true to her word.

Over dinner, Dad inquired as to whether I would be saving for my own place now I was working. Mum scowled at him over the top of her wine glass, clearly appalled at the prospect of an empty nest, and he stopped talking. Maybe he was looking forward to rekindling their pre-children relationship, feeling more youthful and a bit less responsible again. He's earned that. Or maybe he's having a mid-life crisis.

Mum quickly changed the subject to the holiday. It seems Somerset is the favourite destination thus far with four out of five of us agreeing on it. I suggested Wales for the stunning green scenery but was vetoed on the grounds that it will most likely be too wet for a winter holiday.

## Chapter 7

### Monday 7th November 2022

**Maya**

Amber and Ruby worked the counter while I took care of tables. My tummy had fluttered with nerves but carrying trays from the pick-up point to a table is, as hoped, easier than taking orders. The only difficulty I had was finding the correct tables; apparently it's frowned upon to shout the table number while you're looking for it. Amber had warned me that it's not the look Totally Coffee aims to achieve. Servers should know their coffee house like their own home, and that's all well and good, but for me this is day one on tables and I'm not so familiar with this place.

I missed having Ruby by my side, but other than the snooty couple who huffed at me after their paninis completed two rounds of the place before I located the correct table, I seem to have fared much better than on the till.

Ruby sent Amber and I for lunch together. She talked mostly about Rupert, showing me photos on her phone of his nursery drawings. We talked a little about holiday destinations too. Amber's favourite place is Scotland; although cooler in the summer than here in the south, the scenery is apparently breathtaking. She also told me the money thrower came over this morning, barely taking his eyes off me whilst she served him. I quickly retorted that such a man is just not my type: garage grease and overalls are no match for a good suit and prospects. Besides, I had been too busy trying to deliver orders correctly to notice anyone who hadn't claimed a table.

But I did notice when he returned after lunch, staring directly at me, our eyes locking briefly. It was intense but flattering; he's good-looking, even if he's not my type. Amber saw him too, glancing over at me and raising her eyebrows as though to say "see".

Next at the pick-up point was a skinny caramel latte for table five. I knew even before working out where table five was that it was his. Suddenly I was nervous and struggling to maintain composure as I walked towards the table, looking anywhere but at him, aware of his eyes boring into me the whole time.

Walking became an unnecessarily conscious act, my feet suddenly feeling double their normal size. Prematurely relieved I had made it to the table without tripping over, I leaned forward to place down the tray, only I slammed it down hard, as though someone had nudged me, sending the top half an inch of latte froth spilling over the side of the tall glass mug. My cheeks warmed and we both reached for the serviette on the tray at the exact same moment. Instead of my hand landing on the serviettes, though, I grabbed the back of his skull-tattooed hand. My cheeks burned and my heart raced. I didn't know where to look. Then he spoke.

"It's okay, Maya, I've got it." His voice was warm and gentle, not at all like the awkward man who threw his money on the counter just a few days ago.

"Oh god, I am so sorry," I replied, finally looking up at him.

Now I was the one being nervous and clumsy in his presence. But he was smiling, his eyes looking intensely into mine. He turned his gaze away to wipe down the side of his mug before looking up and speaking again.

"I'm Blaine… and I think you just got me back for throwing my money at you."

His eyes flashed a cheeky glint and I couldn't help but laugh back at him. Not an alluring feminine laugh, more of an ugly snort. Well done, Maya, very attractive. I was already walking away when he spoke my name again, making me look back.

"Thank you… for the coffee, I mean. Not for spilling it or for holding my hand."

He cracked another smile, exposing slight dimples in his cheeks, and I could feel the warmth returning to mine. It was that very moment that I noticed his intense eyes were a beautiful shade of green. I nodded in response and wished the heat in my cheeks would subside.

As I walked back to the pick-up point, my feet a normal size once again, I realised Amber and Ruby had been observing the encounter like hawks homing in on their prey. I couldn't resist looking back at Blaine one more time. He was no longer "the money thrower", but he was still watching me. I was both flattered and unnerved.

The final part of the process of serving tables is cleaning them down as soon as they're vacated to ensure no customer arrives at a dirty table. Some customers had left a tip on their tray among the empty cups and plates; some left a mess on the table. Blaine left a smiley face doodle on the bottom of his receipt. I don't know why but I picked it up, folded it into a neat square, being careful not to fold across the doodle, and put it in my uniform trouser pocket.

## Blaine

My heart sank when she wasn't behind the counter. I wanted to say something sensible, change her perception of the ridiculous version of me she'd witnessed so far. But it was Ruby and the other girl. Then I saw her, half the room away, her eyes ripping up the space between us to tear at my soul. My heart thumped. I wanted to sit down so she'd have to bring my coffee to me, no Ruby listening to every word, only Rob had asked for one too. I couldn't let his go cold and I couldn't get back in the queue after I'd sat in to drink mine. Then the girl was asking what I wanted and out came, "a regular Americano and a regular skinny caramel latte to go, please". And coffees in hand I walked out, my chance missed. She didn't even notice me.

Rob called me a lame prick and reminded me how I don't have a problem ringing Hannah when I want my end away but can't even talk to this girl. He says me and Hannah don't bother him but there's something in his eyes when we talk about her. They've been mates forever; he clearly cares about her.

It was while I was chatting to Rob that she messaged, like her ears were burning. I'd forgotten to reply to her last message, too busy thinking about Maya and how I couldn't stay away from her if I wanted to. Hannah doesn't serve as a distraction; she seems to make it worse.

*Had a really good time Friday*, with a winky face emoji, then, *I wish you'd still been there when I opened my eyes Saturday morning.*

So now I feel shitty. I shouldn't have taken her out, I wasn't thinking about her, I just wanted Maya out of my head. That failed miserably and now Hannah's reading too much into it. I didn't tell Rob about the message or about taking Hannah out. I didn't reply to that message either. What could I say? *I hated every second of it, Hannah. You're a nice girl but I feel nothing for you. Oh, and there's this girl who's driving me nuts and every time I'm with you all I think about is her.* She's a decent girl, she doesn't deserve that.

I thought of nothing but Maya all morning. My hands going through the motions, but my brain struggling to keep up. Thankfully, everyone else was too busy to notice. Early afternoon I made my excuses and left. I don't know what I was thinking. I remember telling Rob I was popping out and wouldn't be long. I don't remember crossing the road or even opening the door, I just remember seeing her. I remember that she looked up when I walked in and looked me right in the eye.

The next thing I remember is asking the girl for my coffee to drink in and the look she gave me. I get coffee almost every workday but never sit in. She handed me a slip with a table number on it and asked me to take a seat, staring at me all the while. Ruby was there too, looking at me like she wanted to take me down. She usually says hello at the very least, but not today. Just a dead-pan stare was all I got.

Table number five. I was sitting, waiting, terrified and relieved at the same time. She looked angelic and completely oblivious to my presence. I couldn't take my eyes off her. She saw me walk in but must have assumed I'd taken my coffee and left. Or maybe she presumed nothing at all because she has no reason to think about me.

I watched her approach the pick-up point; next was my tray, but she stopped when she saw it. She paused, like she needed to think about it. She didn't do that with the previous trays, just picked them up and walked. But there she was, like she was composing herself before bringing it over.

It seemed like she was trying hard to look anywhere but at me as she walked to my table, and when she arrived she thumped that tray down, spilling my coffee, instantly blushing. We both reached for the serviette to clean up, but I got there first and she grabbed my hand instead. I don't believe in supernatural beings, but I'd imagine that's how being touched by one would feel if they existed. A combination of heat and chills simultaneously, electricity pulsing from her fingertips through my skin.

Her cheeks glowed redder and seeing her vulnerable made it strangely easy to speak. I told her I'd got it and finally she looked at me, straight in the eyes. I can't help it; I'm obsessed with a girl I don't even know. I managed to introduce myself and tell her she'd got her revenge for throwing my money at her. That's when she did this weird snort thing through her nose. Any other woman and I'd have run in the opposite direction. But it's Maya, I don't think anything could put me off.

She was walking away when I called her name, a knee-jerk reaction because I didn't want the encounter to be over. She turned around and in the absence of any sensible conversation starters I thanked her for the coffee and cracked a joke about her grabbing my hand. But she just nodded and walked away. It was over. That spot she touched on my hand felt more alive than the rest of my whole body.

I watched as she served more tables, wishing I was at every one of them, having another chance to speak with her and look at those eyes. But I was out of both coffee and valid reasons to sit there watching her any longer. She didn't see me take the pen from my overall pocket and absent-mindedly scribble a smiley face on my receipt. And she didn't notice me leaving.

Shit, I didn't leave a tip, just a stupid doodle. Great, so now I look like a skinflint. Well done, Blaine. Very attractive.

## Maya

What was left of the shift passed without incident and my first day on tables was a comparative success. I had faced an inquisition following the Blaine encounter, Amber asking the questions, adding, "He's gorgeous, Maya," and "Just think how beautiful his children would be." But Ruby was quiet, a strange disapproving air about her.

Blaine. The name suits both his face and demeanour, manly and a little out of the ordinary. I wouldn't have expected to be so nervous around someone like that, him being the very opposite of what I desire, yet I found myself weak at the knees. I told Mum all about it when I got home. She laughed and hugged me and said, "It's about bloody time." I insisted that nothing was going to occur, but her expression suggested she thought otherwise. Dad piped up from behind his newspaper, jumping to my defence.

"He doesn't sound good enough for my girl." Thanks, Dad, exactly the point I was making.

He continued that while there was nothing wrong with being a tattooed mechanic, he expected me to be with someone who earned a better living and had prospects, someone who could take care of his little girl. And while I'm not a little girl anymore, I do agree with all that he said. So why I am secretly hoping he comes back tomorrow?

The truth of it is I felt something when I knew it was his coffee on that tray, when I touched his hand and when he spoke to me. I felt something when I looked into his eyes, something I haven't felt before. I will refrain from telling Dad about that. There's no need to tell Mum, she seems to have sensed it.

I felt something tonight too, when I pulled from my uniform pocket the smiley-face-embellished receipt. What I felt was a flutter in my heart, as though it had missed some beats. It made me light-headed, forcing me to sit on the edge of the bed to gather my senses. I should have put it in the bin, but I folded it neatly back up and put it under a book in my bedside table moments before Mum entered my room and sat on my bed beside me.

"You know, Maya," she said, "sometimes you don't get to choose who you fall for, sometimes the universe chooses for you. And when it does there is usually a reason why."

With that, she wrapped her arms around me, kissed my forehead and left my room.

## Blaine

Rob rang, said Hannah's been round telling him how I'm falling in love with her and that he's coming over because he wants an explanation. She's his best mate, it's understandable he's pissed off. I apologised, repeatedly; I don't love Hannah, but I can't stand the thought of hurting her.

I couldn't find the words to tell him what's been happening in my head, but he barked my name, said he was done waiting for answers. Only I can't explain this obsession with Maya, it's knocked me sideways. I told him how I'd tried to make more of an effort with Hannah to take my mind off Maya, but not only did it fail, it gave her the wrong idea.

He knew about my visit to Totally Coffee, how I'd sat at a table so she'd have to serve me. Ruby told him. Then he said, "You must have it bad." Like you wouldn't believe, mate. I asked him not to tell Hannah about Maya; there's no point rubbing salt in the wound. But it's too late, he already told her, just not who the girl in question is.

I wanted to tell Hannah how sorry I am. I never meant to make her feel like this, but going to her would only make things worse — or is that an excuse because I don't want to feel worse than I already do? The trouble is all I can think about is Maya. I want her to touch me and look at me again. She saw me today; I mean really saw me. I've been cold for so long and suddenly a fire grows inside me every time I see her or even think about her.

Rob left and shortly after Hannah sent a stream of messages telling me how much I've hurt her, how she thought I really wanted her. I can't just leave her after what I've done, so I replied, telling her I'm coming round, but her battery must have died because it didn't deliver.

## The Elders

"We are still deciding whether we must take him. He has neither remembered nor progressed, just as you did not. We cannot meddle or manipulate; it is for him to resolve. Alone."

"But what if he cannot? What if he allows my wrongs to control him?"

"That does appear to be the path he is choosing. At every opportunity to progress he fails. You know we must recover him if he endangers someone so close to joining us."

"But he has not harmed anyone."

"Yet. It is not your purpose to manipulate the system for your own gains."

"The gains are not mine. My time is spent, ruined by my own fear. I cannot allow him to do the same."

"He is not your responsibility. We will continue to monitor and act where and when appropriate. We will continue to monitor you also. Your progress here is as vital as his progress there."

# Chapter 8

## Tuesday 8th November 2022

### **Maya**

I awoke at 3:10 a.m. with a vivid dream fresh in my memory. A man had stopped me on the street, his face obscured as though looking through fog. With a tone of desperation he told me everything was his fault, that he could not take back his depravities but I could help to make it better. I ran but he gave chase and was almost upon me when he shouted, "It will all make sense, Maya," and with his outstretched hand just millimetres from my arm he faded into thin air.

My bleary eyes searched the room but only the outlines of my wardrobe and the window were visible through the darkness. I was too rattled to go back to sleep and when I entered the kitchen Mum was already there with the kettle on.

"Strangest thing," she said, "but I woke up fifteen minutes ago and knew you needed me, so I came down here to wait for you."

After I shared the dream she decided her motherly instinct must have sensed it. She has always been in tune with Sissy and me and seems to know what we need from her. While chatting over our tea, Mum brought up Blaine. Apparently, Dad is worried because he has high standards when it comes to us girls, but she knows matters of the heart better than he does and insisted I don't let his advice overshadow my decisions. Only I know what's right for me. She said we can have checklists as long as our arms, but our heart's desires do not come with a tick list of pros and cons. Then giggled as she said, "Listen to me, suddenly a love guru!"

We ended our tea and chat, returning to bed around four a.m. I fell quickly asleep but another dream played out: Blaine this time. I was serving him at a table, just like yesterday, but he stood up as I turned to walk away. Reaching for my arm he pulled me towards him and kissed me, slowly and passionately; I did not resist. Pulling away, he looked deep into my eyes, the green of his as clear as day, and now here I am, wide awake again.

## Blaine

The quiet streets were a stark contrast to the inside of my head when I left Hannah's last night. Internal noise and self-loathing overwhelmed me. I shouldn't have gone; it made neither of us feel any better. She doesn't want my apologies; she wants her heart unbroken. Rob knew about the visit and politely asked me to back off to let her get over me. I don't get why she'd be so hung up on me, someone who can't offer her a damn thing.

Driving home in the darkness I found myself wondering where Maya lived. Not in the terraced houses or flats in town, somewhere grander, one of the big houses on the outskirts. Maybe with a boyfriend, not a husband; she doesn't wear a ring. If she's already taken I'll concede, buy my coffee elsewhere. But I have to know.

Today she was back behind the counter, no Ruby beside her. Her hair was strikingly blonde against the black uniform, and her eyes — well, they looked tired actually. She held my stare until the corners of her mouth turned up into an almost smile. But yesterday's confidence was long gone; every part of me wanted to shut down rather than risk repelling her by saying something stupid. We were staring, neither speaking for I don't know how long. Eventually she said, "Hello, Blaine."

The sound of her voice speaking my name sent a ripple through my chest. She asked if I was okay, but like the idiot I knew I'd be I told her she looked tired. Just what every woman wants to hear. She explained how a dream had woken her in the night. Then she blushed and her eyes disconnected from mine. The last thing I'd wanted was to make her uncomfortable. I seem to be perfecting the art of making women feel bad.

With the warmest expression she assured me no offence had been taken, that she felt as tired as she looked, then asked if I wanted my usual. And out it came, I asked her out, like it's completely normal to ask out someone you don't know. I was so caught up in our first real conversation that my guard just fell. And surprisingly, she didn't say no. She didn't say yes either, just shook her head softly and said, "I don't know."

Does that mean she's single but not sure about me? It's certainly more promising than a flat-out "no, thanks, I'm already taken". She apologised too. I've not witnessed a kinder rejection. So I told her I'd just have my coffee for now. Then Ruby was hot footing it towards us with a box full of something in her hands. I drew a sad face on my receipt and pushed it back across the counter towards her, took in those beautiful eyes one more time and walked away.

## Maya

His eyes fixed on mine and my tummy fluttered. I couldn't decide whether I wanted to speak to him or run away. Only running away was not an option, so there I stood looking back at him, noticing the lines on his furrowed brow, the almost pained expression on his face, his broad physique and height — he must be six feet — and the dark tone of his skin.

Ruby had stepped out the back to fetch biscuits for the grab-snacks display, leaving me alone. My stupid heart thumped hard as he neared the counter and I was certain I would say something idiotic or snort again. With just the counter between us, we stood in awkward silence until I could be quiet no longer. His back arched slightly and he shuddered when I said hello; it was subtle, but I saw it. For a moment I feared my voice had repulsed him, but when I asked if he was okay he replied, "I'm good."

The lines on his brow softened and he was smiling, telling me I looked tired. I was waffling about the dream that had woken me when I remembered the other dream: Blaine pulling me towards him and kissing me, his strong arms rendering me helpless. His big, tattooed hands holding my face, his lips pressed onto mine. I stared at his full, plump lips, which looked as though they might feel exactly how they did in the dream, wanting him to kiss me right there over the counter. My cheeks burned with embarrassment. He apologised, saying he hadn't meant to pry, but I had to look away; it was all too much. I asked if he wanted his usual to get the encounter over with and could not believe my ears at his reply.

"I want to take you out, Maya."

I looked back at him in shock. I spontaneously shook my head, and out of my mouth came, "I don't know. I'm sorry," the words creating a confusing mixture of relief and disappointment.

"Okay, just the coffee then. For now," he replied, looking as disappointed as I felt.

Ruby appeared as if from nowhere, clutching a box of biscuits, looking at both of us in turn and asking if I needed any help. I reassured her we were fine, only his face said otherwise as he took a pen from his overall pocket, drew another face on his receipt, a sad one, and pushed it back towards me. With one last intense look into my eyes, he collected his coffee and left. Ruby was on me immediately.

"What did I miss?" she asked.

"Oh, not much, he just asked me out."

"He asked you out?" she exclaimed, but the realisation that the drawing of the sad face meant I must have declined dawned on her.

In front of Ruby and without a shred of embarrassment, I carefully folded the receipt and tucked it into my trouser pocket.

He said, "For now."

## Chapter 9

### Wednesday 9th November 2022

### **Blaine**

Everything feels upside down. I can't ask Hannah to come round. I no longer see nothing when I close my eyes, and I feel things I don't want to. Eleven days ago everything was easy, I'd go to work, get rid of everything I felt at the gym, see Hannah when I needed to, and in between I'd smoke and numb whatever was left my head. Easy.

Now I go to work knowing all the while that Maya's across the road. I go home and smoke but instead of being numb I see her in my mind's eye, I picture being with her. And not sex, just being with her, talking to her.

The gym did nothing to help last night; without Rob distracting and challenging me I thought of nothing but Maya. He stood me up for Hannah, saying she needs him more than I do right now. Then today he tells me it's over with Beth, after nine years together. She's always been jealous that him and Hannah are best friends, so when Hannah announced she thought

I was falling for her, and Rob told her that's impossible because I'm clearly falling for someone else, well, Beth lost it, assumed he just wanted Hannah for himself and kicked him out. I had no choice but to offer him a roof over his head. All of this is my fault.

No matter how hard I pushed myself her face and those damn eyes wouldn't vacate my head. So I made up my mind, right there in the gym: I'll ask her again and this time I'll tell her I might just stand there until she accepts my request. After repeating it in my head, scripting my lines so I wouldn't fuck it up, I had it down to a tee, but when I opened the shop door this morning she wasn't there. Ruby and one of the other girls were behind the counter, their eyes on me while my own searched the place. No Maya. Ruby asked what I wanted but the other girl, Amber according to her name badge, stepped in, saying, "It's okay, Rube, I've got this one." Ruby walked away and Amber asked what I wanted, but when I placed my order she replied, "No, I mean, what do you really want?" For a moment I thought she was flirting, until she said it was obvious I wanted Maya. What could I say? I couldn't deny it, but I was so taken aback I couldn't respond either.

"You know she's single right?" she added. And suddenly everything seemed possible. That's why she didn't say no. I asked if she knew why Maya had turned me down.

"Because she's an idiot!" she replied. "She doesn't know what she wants, that's why she's twenty-three and still single. She thinks she wants someone who wears a suit and tie and works in an office… but where's the fun in that? And besides, you guys all look the same underneath your clothes." Then she said, "So, a skinny caramel latte to take out, right?" I nodded. "Don't give up on her, she just doesn't know what she wants. Maybe you could show her you're what she needs. She's off today because she's working Sunday. You don't work Sundays, do you?"

She was grinning, like there was more to the sentence but she wanted me to figure it out for myself. I started to ask what she was implying but her attention had already turned to the next customer, like I was no longer standing there. So I took my coffee, walked back to the garage and told Rob what had just happened. He thought it was obvious, at least to him: Amber was implying I go in there Sunday when I'm not in work overalls. That must have been what she meant.

## Maya

Another broken night's sleep spattered with dreams, most of which had escaped my memory by morning's arrival, had left me with a headache. But one remained as clear as day: that faceless man again, chasing me, insisting I say yes if I want to know how everything is his fault, if I want anything to make sense. I would have preferred to dream of Blaine again.

I'm beginning to wonder if anything makes sense anymore. I can't sleep for strange men chasing me, and I can't expel a strange man in dirty overalls from my waking mind. I needed a distraction and when I entered the kitchen looking somewhat dishevelled in my dressing gown and pyjamas, Mum suggested a day of retail therapy. Sissy was free to come too. I still had to break the news to Mum about working on Sunday and figured that might be easier over lunch with a few bags of goodies under the table to soften the blow.

I can't be certain whether it was Mum's breakfast pancakes, the paracetamol or some new clothes that did it, but the headache soon lifted. I found the perfect little grey dress, one to put by for the right occasion: smart-casual, dressy but not over-dressy. Sissy talked Mum into having a make-up trial at the department store; she looked so pretty when it was done and I wondered how Ruby might have looked if she were here to join in. The next stop was lunch, where I broke the news about working Sunday. Mum must have felt as good as she looked because she simply said, "That's okay, darling, we can eat later. Will you be finished by four?"

We had almost finished lunch when Sissy asked about my new job. I told her in detail about the lovely staff and what the job entailed, but she continued staring at me as though waiting for more, for something specific. Mum glanced at both of us in turn, giving the game away.

"Have you told her… about Blaine?" I asked Mum.

With that, Sissy grabbed my arm and hung off the side of her chair, giving me an excited if not awkward hug, saying she had waited for this moment forever. My demeanour shifted to stiff and embarrassed; Sissy looked worried at having said the wrong thing, explaining how Mum said I had met someone rather dishy at work. Mum looked suddenly uncomfortable and gave me a sorrowful look.

"I'm sorry, Maya," she said, "I just thought it was significant; this man clearly has you rattled and that kind of attraction doesn't come along every day."

Sissy agreed and I was at a loss for words. She was kind, asking what I felt about him and listening intently as I described the brief encounters we'd had so far. That's what I didn't understand, I told them, I'd only seen him a handful of times and we had spoken just a few words to one another, so how could the attraction be so intense? How could he possibly know he wanted to take me out when he had no idea who I was? And how could I be so bothered about turning him down when I had no idea who he was?

He's not what I desire in a man, never have I imagined myself being with someone who works in a garage. Sissy suggested I relax; nothing had happened yet and I was under no obligation to do anything I didn't want to. But that's the trouble; I do want to. I described the dream in which he had kissed me and how I wanted to do it for real when I saw him yesterday.

With my emotional knickers well and truly knotted we paid our bill and left the restaurant to continue shopping and discussing my dilemma.

## Chapter 10

## Thursday 10th November 2022

### **Blaine**

Rob had retired to bed after several whiskeys and a pasta dinner, leaving me drinking alone, my head swimming with Maya and Hannah and now Beth kicking him out. I was grateful he hadn't been chatty; I had no words of reassurance about everything working itself out anyway. Shit happens, you have to forget about it and move forward. He'll find his feet again. I tried recalling the words I'd scripted for Maya, but the whiskey had me and I couldn't recall a thing. I'll let instinct freewheel when the moment arises.

I watched her glance over here on her way in this morning, but the sun hid me from view, shining on the office window. She must have been looking for me, why else would she look over? The thought of it gave me a surge of confidence and when I opened the door of Totally Coffee she was behind the counter looking straight at me, red-cheeked before I'd even reached the counter. The top button of her shirt lay open, exposing pink-white flesh, a fleeting image of a diamond heart flashing in my mind. I could feel adrenaline in my veins, like when you're in the middle of a good workout, feeling alive, charged and ready. And bingo, Ruby was distracted talking to someone else.

## Maya

Blaine returned to my dream. Nothing extraordinary, no kiss this time, just Blaine on the garage forecourt looking at a car, oblivious to my presence. I looked for him this morning in case the dream had been an omen, only he wasn't there. And I had hoped to be serving tables; speaking would be easier without Ruby by my side. But I have a feeling that's exactly why she kept me behind the counter, to protect me from whatever it is she believes he might be.

She was especially flat in her mood this morning and between customers explained how she and David had argued last night. Moments later, Dale walked through the door. Her face immediately softened and her eyes sparkled with life.

"This is how a man is supposed to make you feel," I whispered, then pretended to be busy, turning my back so Ruby could flirt, as best she does, in private.

It was while she was occupied with Dale that Blaine opened the shop door. My cheeks flushed hot, my heart pounded and my feet spontaneously moved me further down the counter, away from Ruby. When my brain caught up with my feet a state of panic arose within me, but he was standing in front of me; there was no time to run and not a single word graced my tongue.

He wished me good morning and ordered a flat white, not the usual skinny caramel latte. So, finding my tongue, I asked if he was sure. With an expression as serious as any I have ever seen he insisted he wouldn't ask for something he wasn't certain he wanted. Quickly deciphering the meaning behind his words I was about to respond when he said, "Maya, I know you don't know me, and I don't know what this thing is between us, but it's there and I'm sure you feel it too." I did feel it but stood there in stunned silence while he continued.

"Let me take you out to dinner to find out who you are. If you say no, well, I'll just have to stand here until you change your mind."

Out came another of those awful snorts but, seemingly unperturbed, he just stood, waiting for an answer. And once again I declined his offer with a shake of the head and an apology, the words falling from my mouth in a rush of nerves and indecision. By now Ruby was looming behind me and Blaine, clearly under the pressure of her glare, made light of the situation.

"Okay, maybe I won't stand here until you change your mind, but I will ask again."

With that he said goodbye and walked away from the counter, but not before pushing another sad face on another receipt towards me with his hulking great hand. Ruby picked up the receipt and handed it to me.

"That's also how a man is supposed to make you feel," she said, before barking at one of the boys to take over the counter so she and I could take a break while it was quiet.

In the privacy of the staff room Ruby asked if I liked Blaine as much as he seemed to like me. I admitted I did, but that he was not what I had spent my life dreaming of being married to. And I wouldn't indulge in brief encounters to sate my lust. Neither Mum nor Sissy did that; they were teenagers when they met Dad and Henry and knew it was right straight away. I want that too, and Blaine is not that person. She asked how I could be so sure; well, of course I couldn't be completely sure, but he's a mechanic, with tattoos and once or twice he'd come in wearing a baseball cap. I mean, come on!

Ruby erupted into uncontrollable laughter. I had never seen her so amused and was offended that she found my dilemma so hysterical.

"Maya," she said when she had calmed down enough to speak, "you are a beautiful soul, but you really are a snob." Then laughter overwhelmed her again. She was right. I've based my assumptions of how a suitor should look without regard to what makes my heart beat faster or fills me with desire. What else could I do but laugh with her?

Back behind the counter, Ruby insisted she wasn't telling me to give in to him, that only I knew if something felt right, but that apparently, during a recent conversation with Rob, he had told her that Blaine was a good guy, reliable and trustworthy. I wondered how that conversation had come about, if Ruby had been probing, concerned for my welfare.

After each stream of customers slowed to a lull my thoughts returned to Blaine. I pondered what it might be like to share a life with someone like him. The truth is, I look at people like Blaine and wonder why they are single. Were they simply not lucky enough to meet their perfect match at a young age? Or can they not commit to one person long-term? Can they not provide security for a partner and children and so sail through life mostly alone? Then I realised that I hadn't met my perfect match in my teens or married and had children in my early twenties. Maybe I'm afraid to commit to someone in case it is not as perfect as the relationship I aspire to.

"I really am a silly snob," I said to Ruby as we cleaned down the counters and machines at the end of the shift. She gave me the briefest of hugs before replying.

"I think you're just cautious and that's not a bad thing. I wish I'd been cautious." And now I like Ruby just a little bit more.

Blaine was on the garage forecourt when we left the shop. He looked over, raising his hand in acknowledgement of Ruby and me. We both giggled as we returned the wave. Inside my car I slid my hand into my trouser pocket to make sure the sad-face receipt was still there. It was.

## Blaine

I needed the gym and suggested Rob join me. He must have had some crap to thrash out too. Today saw another refusal from Maya, but I see the way she looks at me, the way she falls silent like her nerves have caught hold of her. I see her talking to other customers and the words come all too easy. She feels something for me, I'm sure of it. And I can hear the other girl, Amber, telling me not to give up.

Rob said Ruby quizzed him about me because she's worried for Maya, said he'd told her I'm a good guy and she's no need to worry. His words made my head spin, my hands lost their grip, the weights crashed to the floor and my body dropped to the weight bench. He threw his energy drink into my lap and a few mouthfuls sent the feeling away. Ruby wouldn't have quizzed Rob if she didn't think Maya felt something.

***

He hadn't told Hannah that Beth kicked him out yet, he didn't want her feeling worse than she already did. "You know, because of Beth's jealousy towards her," he added quickly. But I knew what he really meant and it was okay, I know how much I hurt her and I hate myself for it. She didn't deserve that; I shouldn't have used her as a distraction and if I could change what I did then I would. He said he'll see her tonight to make sure she's okay.

# Chapter 11

## Friday 11th November 2022

### **Maya**

Ruby announced my allocation to tables with a playful gleam in her eyes. Half of me wanted to thank her and the other half wished I had called in sick. I knew he would come and was certain he would take his coffee at a table when he saw me serving them.

It was almost eleven a.m. when I collected the skinny caramel latte for table number five and set off, tray in hand, willing myself to be confident. Instead of avoiding his gaze, I looked him dead in the eye, holding his stare until I reached the table, carefully setting the tray down, all the while thinking, *Say yes this time, Maya. Say yes.*

"Hello, Blaine, one skinny caramel latte."

He thanked me and inquired as to how my morning had been. Holding my nerve I told him it had been just fine, quietly hoping it was about to improve significantly. But then I remembered the dream kiss again and warmth flooded my cheeks. He smelled divine, even from a few feet away; I thought about kissing him for real and my cheeks flushed even hotter. I stood there too long, waiting for his next move and suddenly it was awkward. He was not asking to take me out, he was smiling but not threatening to sit there until I said yes. For want of anything to say I asked if I could get him anything else, but he simply replied, "I think I have all I need, thanks, Maya."

Confused and disappointed I walked back to the pick-up point to await the next order and the cooling of my cheeks. Blaine sat at that table for almost thirty minutes, sometimes looking at his phone and sometimes watching me, smiling each time our eyes met.

With every passing minute I became increasingly rattled. Why hadn't he asked me out? Why was he just sitting there watching me? Perhaps he was a lunatic and I'd misread his intentions. But then I looked back at table five and he was gone. My heart sank a little — okay, a lot. I rushed to clear his tray and look for the receipt that was neatly folded in half, held in place by his empty coffee mug. No face this time, just the word "Sunday".

Sunday? What the bloody hell was that supposed to mean? Was he coming back to ask me again on Sunday and this was a forewarning, time to consider my response perhaps? How could he even know I'd be here on Sunday? I could feel eyes on me again, only this time they were Ruby's. She looked equally confused when I described what had happened, or rather not happened.

I guessed that would be his only visit for today and was disappointingly right. I looked up every time the door opened but it was never him. Most of the faces were happy, but none of them the face I wanted to see, and by mid-afternoon I wanted the shift to be over. I was lonely out there on the floor without Ruby, and when the day finally ended I made the most of the clean-up time to chat with her and the others about all the things I had missed behind the counter. I could tell Ruby was pretending to be okay after her recent fall out with David, but it was obvious she was not.

Neither Blaine nor his car were on the forecourt when we left Totally Coffee, denying me one last glimpse. Why did he bother taking his coffee to a table with no intention of asking me out? And what did he mean by "I think I have all I need" and "Sunday"?

The new receipt was added to the growing pile in my bedside table drawer and I told Mum about today's visit from Blaine. She found it odd too and was at a loss to offer any possible explanation. I checked that she hadn't somehow invited him here for Sunday dinner without telling me. Of course she hadn't; Mum will always guide us with the kindest of words but would never interfere in our lives.

## Blaine

I was ready for third time lucky when Ruby greeted me at the counter, nodding across the shop to where Maya was serving a table. "You'll be drinking in today, will you?" she asked with a smile. This was a whole new side to Ruby I'd never known existed. Rob's always said she's alright, but our conversations had never extended beyond "what can I get you?" and "a skinny caramel latte please" before. Maybe Rob putting in a good word had paid off.

"You know Maya thinks she needs a man who wears a suit, works in an office and earns enough to support his family?" Her words echoed Ambers.

"The total opposite of me then?" I replied.

"Yes, but that's only what she thinks she needs. Do you have a suit? I'm sure if you turned up in one she'd realise that the clothes on the outside don't make the man on the inside. A man in a suit might still let you down, while a man in dirty overalls just might treat you like a queen," she added.

I knew then that today was not the day to be asking her out, but it was too late to take my coffee to go; the skinny lad with big glasses was already traying it up. So, I thanked Ruby who continued smiling at me while passing me a number: table five again.

Taking my seat I watched Maya collect my tray. She looked over, holding my stare as she walked then carefully placed the tray on the table. For the lack of knowing what else to say I asked her how her day was going. She blushed as she answered then stood looking me straight in the eye. Was she waiting for more? Did she want a conversation today? I didn't know what else to say; I'd already decided not to ask her out and was formulating a plan in my head when she asked me, red cheeked, if there was anything else I wanted. But there wasn't, I had all the information I required and just needed to act upon it.

She walked away, back to the pick-up point. I ached to talk to her and look at her face for longer. Instead, I drank my coffee, watching her drift from table to table, glancing at me occasionally. I ordered myself a new white shirt with next-day delivery from my phone while I sat there. A decent one, no expense spared for this.

I hadn't expected to hear from Hannah any time soon, but she texted while I was admiring Maya, saying she wasn't angry with me and hoped that one day we could be friends for Rob's sake. He'd got enough on his plate without being stuck between the two of us. All I could do was tell her again how sorry I was and that I really never meant to hurt her. She replied with a thumbs up. Looking back at the beautiful Maya I was certain I could never have felt like this about Hannah. This was something more. Something I couldn't explain away.

I didn't tell Rob about the message; he'd only tell me how I missed something good with Hannah. The thing is, I never doubted her, I just never felt anything more for her. I never wanted to. But she had a big heart to be able to tell me she wasn't angry with me. Rob's a lucky guy to have her watching his back.

## Chapter 12

## Sunday 13th November 2022

### **Maya**

It is Sunday. Saturday, by comparison, had been uneventful. I cleaned my room, relaxed with Mum and Dad and read in front of a roaring fire. Mum told Dad about the receipt. "What if he's an axe-murderer, Maggie? Or a stalker?" he declared, dropping his newspaper into his lap. "I don't think this is normal, Maya; your mother would have run a mile had I tried wooing her like that."

Mum disagreed, insisting she would have been enchanted and, somewhat disgruntled, Dad picked his newspaper back up, retreating behind it. Mum quickly added, "Not that there was anything wrong with our courtship, darling, you stole my heart and have treasured it ever since." He looked at her, eyes full of love and adoration and responded with a strange snorting sound. So that's where I get it from. How had I not noticed that before?

Sunlight streamed through the crack in the curtains when I woke this morning; my eyes squinted in the harsh light before the realisation that whatever Blaine was forewarning was happening today forced them to adjust. My heart danced in my chest. I wanted to stay in bed and hide, but I also wanted him to come strolling through that door to make a date proposal I would be brave enough to accept. I would have been brave enough on Friday had he asked.

It was dry and sunny with a cold bite on the breeze when I left home. Autumn had been kind thus far, but the temperature felt less stable now. I wondered if winter might be harsh this year. I would love to see snow that actually sticks and looks as pretty as a Christmas card.

Parking close to work was easy what with it being Sunday; most of the other high street shops were closed, including the garage. But still I looked over in case he was there. Having Amber or Ruby by my side would have been a blessing today, my nerves craved their reassurance. Amber would have equalled my excitement and Ruby's composure would have grounded me. Instead, I had but a handful of faces I'd barely worked with. Ruby, however, had left a shift plan assigning me to tables, clearly a strategic move to ensure privacy and the chance of a conversation when he came in. I felt nervous again, and excited. But mainly nervous.

## Blaine

It's Sunday. Broken sleep spattered with endingless dreams left my head feeling heavy, all of them leaving me frustrated. I'd tried explaining my reoccurring TV dream to Rob yesterday after falling asleep on the sofa full of roast dinner, then flinching myself awake, but it had sounded silly saying it out loud. They're always in a different context but with the same theme. I'm watching a film, something is happening, most often something bad, but I don't get to see what it is.

It was nice having Rob around to help me prepare for today. He talked about Beth, said he couldn't go back and try again, he doesn't love her, just feels a growing animosity born out of her jealousy of Hannah. He's been putting up with the status quo for an easy life. Apparently the happiest he's seen Beth recently was when Hannah went round and told them she thought I was falling in love with her. That lasted all of ten seconds before he informed her that I was falling for someone else and Beth's face returned to its normal sour state.

He apologised for bringing it up but it's okay, it's the truth. I deserve to feel uncomfortable. My discomfort is probably nothing compared to what Hannah feels. And then she's big enough to message and say she hopes that one day we can be friends, for Rob's sake. It's a wonder those two didn't end up together.

## Maya

I hadn't expected so many customers. Whatever happened to Sunday being a day of rest? Only none of them were Blaine. On tenterhooks all morning, I checked that door every time it opened and by eleven a.m. it felt as though I'd been there ten hours already. How could the time drag so much?

A smartly dressed man of slim build, fair skin and polite manner came in and asked why a girl like me would work in a place like this. Ordinarily, he might have been just the kind of man whose attention I would welcome. But he was not Blaine either and I found myself telling him that I was waiting for the man of my dreams to arrive and that it didn't look as though that was going to happen today. He didn't utter another word. Poor thing.

My lunch break arrived but I was impatient to return, wondering if I might have missed him, eating my sandwich in record time and getting straight back on the floor. With no Ruby or Amber to report back, he may have taken his coffee and left in my absence. Curiosity gnawed at my stomach as I delivered tray after tray to table after table with one eye on the door.

The afternoon dragged on and my disappointment grew each time the door opened and a stranger entered. Taking my afternoon break at one of the tables, I sat facing the door and took my phone from my bag. Mum had messaged saying, *Well?* Well, there was nothing to report and I replied explaining so. She messaged again, *Oh darling, there's still time.* But time was running out with only an hour left of my shift.

And it was sod's law that the final hour passed at lightning speed. All too soon it was four o'clock and one of the boys was locking up, standing on door duty to let the remaining customers out. The day was over. He had written "Sunday" but had not appeared. I had no clue how this man had got under my skin the way he had, but when the last of the customers left the shop and the door was locked for the final time, I was more disappointed than I could have imagined.

I had been disappointed when Lee Clark dumped me in year seven for the pretty Lucy Littlemore following a whirlwind three-day romance, during which we swapped biros and shared a packet of Starburst. But it was not like this. I was disappointed when Daniel Wirrell, year nine, asked another girl out before realising I existed. And I was heartbroken at sixteen when my eight-month relationship with Jacob Lanning ended because he pushed for sex before I was ready. I couldn't determine if that had felt worse than this or just different. I wasn't attracted to those boys in this way. Maybe that was it; they were just boys and I just a teenager. But I'm twenty-three now and my heart works differently.

With the clean-up finished, everyone left the shop. The sun was still shining but hanging just shy of the horizon, casting long shadows on the ground. The air was marginally warmer than when I'd arrived this morning. Zipping up my coat I turned towards my car and there, twenty metres or so down the road, was Blaine, leaning against a pristine black VW Golf. Not just Blaine, but Blaine in a crisp white shirt that clung to his now-visibly muscular body, revealing what the loose-fitting overalls did not and accentuating the darkness of his skin. Well-tailored grey trousers hugged his thick thighs. He wore black shoes in place of the usual dirty work boots. The shadow of stubble on his cheeks and chin was a contrasting edge to the smartness of his clothes. He looked devastatingly handsome without the overalls and grease. My heart danced in my chest once again. I had waited all day for this and was suddenly panicked at what *this* might be.

Standing to attention when he saw me, our eyes locked and he stepped forward. This was it. I hadn't moved an inch while he continued towards me, never breaking eye contact, and when he was right in front of me he reached out, taking my hands in his. They were warm and big against my small, cold fingers. My heart turned cartwheels; still I hadn't moved or spoken a word. I simply stood, looking hopelessly into his eyes, noticing for the first time flecks of gold and brown in the green. Then he spoke, fear and vulnerability present in his voice, a total contradiction to the big, rugged appearance of the man.

"I want to show you something. Please, give me this moment. If you don't like it I promise I'll bring you straight back."

Did he want me to get in his car with him? What if Dad was right? This man who was practically a stranger, this man who smelled heavenly and looked divine, why would he even be interested in me? It occurred to me that I had not said a single word, yet I had promised myself that today I would say yes to Blaine, but here I was frozen in trepidation. He spoke again, his voice deep and soft and afraid.

"Maya, please, just give me this one chance." So I did.

Abandoning caution, I followed as he led me past his car to the turning that leads to the park behind the high street, my right hand in his left the whole time, his palm warm and exciting against mine. I knew this park well; we came here as teenagers. It was full of trees and life in an area that was otherwise buildings and concrete. At its heart was a pond with a wooden bridge and ornate wooden railings. The pond was small enough to walk around and I always thought the bridge was unnecessary yet beautiful.

Through the thin white cotton of Blaine's shirt the outlines of many more dark tattoos were visible on his arms and across his chest. He returned my gaze, asking if I was okay. "I think so," I replied nervously, caught directly between the vision of him kissing me in my dream and fearing for my life.

Rob was standing by the bridge as though waiting for us and I started to think I shouldn't have gone with him, but it was too late for regret and I took solace in the presence of other people strolling and walking dogs. He nodded at Blaine then walked away across the park; a sense of relief surged through me. Then I saw it. The bridge was lined with thick candles twinkling in hurricane jars, maybe ten on either side, an assortment of flowers placed loosely around them. He had done this for me. I had barely said two words since he took my hand and now we were standing on this beautiful bridge, surrounded by the candles and flowers he had placed there, all to impress me. I took a very deep breath as I took it all in.

"You did this for me?" I asked. He took hold of my other hand again and stood face to face with me.

"I know I'm not what you're looking for," he replied, "but please believe me when I say I feel something for you that I can't explain." He was looking so intensely at me as he spoke that I was by hypnotised him. "I'm certain you've felt something too," he continued. "All I'm asking is for you to give me a chance, otherwise I fear I'll have to pursue you until the end of time."

Passion and longing were swelling inside me and before my head could formulate a response he pulled me gently towards him. When our bodies were an inch apart he placed his hands lightly around my face. I was powerless as he pressed his lips gently onto mine. My head spun and my knees felt weak. His fingertips slid through my hair as I breathed him in and reciprocated the kiss. My arms wound around him and I could feel his muscular body pressed lightly against me. His arms encircled me in return, holding me as though I were glass, as though I might break should he hold me any tighter. Time seemed to freeze into a beautifully warm eternity until he released me from his embrace and looked deeply into my eyes. His expression changed from one of longing to one of fear and, stepping away from me, he said, "I'm so sorry. I didn't mean to do that, not yet. I just wanted to talk and tell you what I've been feeling these last couple of weeks since I first saw you."

"Please," I cut in, "don't be sorry. I wanted you to do that, I'm just not very good at this." He protested, assuring me to the contrary. The awkwardness and uncertainty seemed to slip away and, taking his hand again, I shook it as though meeting him for the first time.

"Nice to meet you Blaine, I'm Maya Caley," I said.

He told me his name was Blaine Thomas Farriner, but recoiled a little as he said it, his head moving slightly in a jerk-like motion, adding that he prefers not to use his middle name. I told him not to worry; my middle name is Elizabeth, after my nan, which is hideous. Again, he protested, insisting it was perfect and repeating it aloud.

"Maya Elizabeth Caley, if I'd known this would be so easy I probably would have slept better last night."

Suddenly talking to him was easy and my heart resumed its normal rhythm. I expressed my disbelief that he would go to such lengths for me, but he pulled me towards him again and softly said, "I would have moved a mountain if I thought it was the only way."

Brushing the strands of hair from my face with a warm fingertip he pressed his lips onto mine once more. He was slow and purposeful and smelled so good. I breathed him in again and felt his energy filling my body. I thought about doing things I have never wanted to do with a man before. It was almost painful to let go of him, but I remembered Mum, Dad, Sissy and Henry all waiting for me at home before they could start serving up dinner.

It was almost five o'clock already and I knew they would be wondering where I was. Taking my phone from my pocket I saw the missed calls from Mum and Sissy. Apologising sincerely, I told him I had to go. His soft expression turned to one of panic until I explained about my family and how they would be waiting for me. I rushed a text to Mum saying, *On my way.*

As he escorted me back to my car I asked, "What now?"

"Well, I've got some candles and flowers to clean up, but you need to go home and be with your family. I'll come into work tomorrow if you're going to be there," he replied.

At my car he pulled me into one last embrace. I didn't want to leave, I wanted to stay in those strong arms, breathing him in, finding out who he was. It felt as though walking away might drain me of all my energy. He told me my eyes were the most beautiful he had ever seen, then kissed me passionately before bidding me farewell, until tomorrow.

## Blaine

Rob reminded me how it took Andy weeks to convince me to wear a shirt and trousers for his wedding and here I was doing it voluntarily for a girl. He followed me on his bike and helped set everything up then stood sentry while I walked to Totally Coffee, to Maya, and somehow convinced her to come with me.

That feeling when her lips touched mine, what the hell was that? I knew who I was, how I functioned. I trusted the life I've carved for myself. But now I was… fragmented, a jumble of pieces that wouldn't fit back together. She did exactly what I wanted her to, she came with me, she liked what I'd done, she didn't reject me. But instead of being happy I now feel disjointed, like I need another fix of her, of that feeling.

Only I let her walk away. What if she wasn't expected at home? What if she'd said that to escape me? I returned to the bridge to clear away the candles and flowers but what I really wanted to do was follow her to see where she lived. It was almost dark; night had fallen quickly and the candles looked even better than they had fifteen minutes earlier. Blowing them out one by one until I was surrounded by a shield of darkness, then packing everything back into my boot, I headed for home.

I wanted to be alone with her, I wanted to be inside her and couldn't think of anything else. But I'd already let her go and now I'd have to wait until tomorrow to see her again. A whole night of aching for her. Tomorrow I could take her to dinner, a real date. I couldn't bring her here, I couldn't risk going too far and scaring her off, not now I was so close to getting her.

Thankfully, Rob was out when I got home. I didn't want him seeing me like this, I wanted to lay undisturbed and play what happened over in my head, over and over and over. She kissed me back; I felt the essence of her seeping into my veins. I hadn't believed it would work, but I'd had to try. I imagined chasing her forever and that seemed ok, safe somehow. And I hadn't meant to kiss her, but there she was in front of me, looking up at me with those eyes, hair blowing across her face in wisps, a magnet drawing me in. But she kissed me back and now I'm filled with a pain I don't understand. It's not in my bones or my muscles, it's in my veins, in my blood.

Hannah was easy; we got together, watched TV, smoked and had sex. That was it. Never anything to think about, never anything to feel. I never pined for her. But this, this is excruciating, and it's been barely two weeks since I first laid eyes on her. Maya Elizabeth Caley.

## Maya

"Maya Elizabeth, where on earth have you been? My potatoes are almost ruined, get your bottom to this table immediately," Mum called from the kitchen when I floated through the door in a dream-like state. She and

Henry had been busily salvaging potatoes from the roasting tray and draining vegetables, but she stopped to face me.

"Oh, darling, he showed up. And you said yes, didn't you?" That intuition again.

The potatoes were the same crispy perfection they always were, far from ruined, and dinner quickly became a Spanish inquisition, all four of them bombarding me with questions about Blaine, about what had just occurred. Mum and Sissy gushed more with every detail imparted, while Dad and Henry looked increasingly concerned. Mum gave them a telling off; he clearly had good intentions to have gone to all that trouble and not been the slightest bit put out when I ran home to my family. Then, after deciding I should have brought him back here for dinner, she told Dad and Henry off again because it wouldn't kill them to surprise their women with candles and flowers every once in a while. Their faces resembled two naughty schoolboys being reprimanded for bad behaviour.

I thought of Ruby, of what she might say about it all. I already knew she would keep me behind the counter with her to hear about his Sunday plan. She would have to retract her snob accusation now.

Sissy and Henry loaded the dinner things into the dishwasher while Mum served coconut sponge and custard for desert, over which she announced that our holiday destination was decided. Despite her attempt at democracy, none of us had any say in the final choice. Apparently, my recollection of the conversation with Amber about holidaying in Scotland had led her to research destinations there; that was how she discovered Hamlet-Noel, a Christmas village within the Cairngorms. It would be perfect for the time of year. She asked that we all book the second week of December off work so she could go ahead and book it and described what she had seen on the website. It boasted a Christmas market, quaint village shops and a choice of self-catering cottages or all-inclusive hotels. It was so festively decorated it looked as though it might have been the north pole. Amongst many other attractions there was a festive forest light trail, an ice-skating rink and food kiosks in a square at the heart of the village where carollers serenaded the guests.

It sounded fabulous but the thought of not seeing Blaine for a week made my heart sink. Mum must have sensed what I was thinking and asked if I wanted to invite him. But that would be ridiculous, all we had shared was a kiss and our last names. I declined the offer; it was far too soon for that. Sissy agreed and Dad and Henry looked rather relieved.

Mum stayed with me in the kitchen while the others took a glass of wine to the lounge. She was happy for me and somehow knew this was right. She had no idea why, but from the moment I mentioned Blaine she knew we would be together and that he would make me happy. I admire her optimism, but it's too early to determine our future. Then she asked what it was like. I blushed and she smiled warmly.

"It was like something I thought I would only ever dream about," I told her. "He was warm and gentle and smelled so good. And he did all that for me."

She told me he did "all that" because he recognised my value, because he knew he had to do something special to win the heart of someone so precious. And now I'm lying in my bed remembering those kisses. Remembering the warmth of his hands and body, the intricate colours in his eyes and the smell of his cologne. Remembering how those muscular arms held me as though I were glass. Regretting not swapping numbers so we could talk or text. I have so many questions to ask him. My head is full of Blaine Thomas Farriner. But until tomorrow all I can do is remember.

## The Elders

"A trigger can be something simple, something unexpected. The reaction latent, inevitable. The subject might be naïve to what will be unleashed. We are neither inexperienced nor naïve, we have amassed our knowledge by living these scenarios countless times, experiencing and overcoming. That is how we have arrived here, the destination of our long journey.

"It is our duty to recover those who experience yet fail to overcome. We allow for mistakes; they are, after all, experiences and opportunities, an essential means by which to grow. But for some the cause was lost before they began, as though it had been written in the stars for them to fail. Not because they are bad, rather because bad things happened, their own order disrupted beyond what they could recover from.

"We have observed Blaine for many years for this very reason. His path was always going to be a difficult one. He believes he knows how to overcome, but his method is foolish and somewhere not too far beneath the surface he is aware of this. But he is scared. Justifiably so. We have pondered and questioned his case; should we take him, thus affording him the opportunity to start afresh, or do we grant him the opportunity to make right the damage? But now there is a complication. A possibility that might force our hands."

"We must all agree on the course of action. It must be unanimous, there simply cannot be a hasty decision."

"And that may be our failure."

## Chapter 13

## Monday 14th November 2022

### **Maya**

Each time sleep overwhelmed me he appeared, his warm hands holding my face as he kissed me. And each time he kissed me I awoke hoping to see his eyes looking back into mine, but there was only darkness and a longing to see him.

I had not anticipated him waiting for me on the high street, back in the greasy overalls but looking divine, nonetheless. In his hand was a single white Gerbera I recognised as one of the flowers from the bridge. From a distance his expression looked pained until my movement towards him caught his attention and his face illuminated, like a spotlight being switched on above a work of art.

He strode towards me, reached for my hand, pressed the Gerbera softly into it and invited me to dinner this evening. He wanted me to decide where, promising to come over soon for my decision before leaning in to kiss my cheek. My lips burned to press into his; I inhaled deeply, capturing the scent of his cologne. As he walked away, my tummy tied itself in knots. I watched him until he reached the garage where he looked back at me and winked; my tummy tightened all the more.

Ruby was waiting with bated breath to hear everything that occurred. I described it all, everything he had done, everything I felt. She asked if the flower in my hand was from yesterday, a memento I had not yet been able to part with. When I explained that he had been waiting for me outside she sighed, drifting into a silent reverie, and I wondered if David had ever done anything like that for her.

It was around ten-thirty when Blaine entered the shop. He smiled warmly and his eyes seemed to change as they fixed on mine, that light switching on again. Ruby said, "Wow, it looks like you two are going to need a minute!" before walking away.

I suggested The Dog and Ferret just on the edge of town for dinner. It serves the best home-cooked food and offers cosy, intimate seating, perfect for a first date. It's Dad's favourite pub, but I didn't tell Blaine so. Stating that it was in fact our second date, he reminded me how I had run out on our first, looking teasingly woeful whilst clutching his heart. He asked if I would allow him to pick me up from home at seven.

The receipt for his latte rolled out of the till and he watched while I wrote my address on the back, coupled with a smiley face, and pushed it towards him. Covering the back of my hand with his he looked intensely into my eyes and said, "Maya Elizabeth Caley, I will see you at seven on the dot."

To which I replied, "Blaine Thomas Farriner, shall I book us a table?"

He did that uncomfortable thing with his head again.

"Yes please, but let's just keep it at Blaine," he said, lifting the back of my hand and kissing it gently before setting it back down on the counter and smiling warmly.

## Blaine

I was still on the sofa staring at the ceiling when Rob came back in the early hours. He assumed by the look on my face that it had gone better than expected and asked what I was planning on doing with the boxes of candles on the lounge floor. Maybe I'd use them for her again somehow. He was worried about what was happening to "Mr Detached". I wished I could answer that. He said no more and disappeared to bed.

Instead of sleeping, I laid awake, wondering how best to play today, deciding to wait for her outside work. But my anxiety grew as I stood there waiting. What if she'd changed her mind and didn't want to see me? What if my coming on strong yesterday was too much? What then? Anxiety gave way to anger at myself for being weak-willed, for not going slower. But when I looked up she was walking towards me, smiling like she was happy to see me. Relief rippled through my body. My feet took over and before I could stop them I was in front of her and she was gazing up at me with those ice-blue eyes, agreeing to have dinner with me. I told her to choose a restaurant, that I'd be over later for an answer. I wanted so badly to kiss her lips and taste her to sate the craving, but held my nerve, kissing her only on the cheek.

By mid-morning I was done waiting. My eyes never forget how beautiful she is but every time I see her it hits me all over again; a wave of something new and unrecognisable courses through my veins. Ruby was next to her, looking at me with that warmth again, then, saying something quietly to Maya, she walked away, leaving us alone.

Maya had chosen a pub for dinner and I knew the place, The Dog and Ferret. It's never busy, just perfect to sit and chat. And she's letting me pick her up from home. She wrote her address on my receipt and passed it to me, saying my full name again. His name.

## Maya

Before the workday ended, Ruby made me promise to fill her in on tonight's dinner date tomorrow. My last two dates were disastrous, both set up by Rebecca with friends of Daniel who turned out to be single for sound reasons. One had been completely self-obsessed, continually changing the subject back to himself, incapable of listening to anything I had to say. The other, despite wanting to know all about me, could not believe how little I had accomplished thus far in my life by comparison to his own extensive achievements. Both dates ended without an exchange of numbers or the promise of a second date.

Mum asked how I was feeling. I had butterflies in my tummy. What if we had nothing in common? A kiss, no matter how good, is not enough to assume we are a match. She cursed herself for making me think about it, assuring me that my nerves were perfectly normal under the circumstances. And the circumstances themselves are enough to assume something will grow.

She reminded me that nobody knows if something will last forever, not her and Dad, not Sissy and Henry, not anyone. They were just lucky enough to meet someone it did last with but could not possibly have known that at the beginning. And even they can't be certain it will last forever. The only thing you can do is work hard at keeping it alive. Some give up easily and others stay and fight, and that, she thinks, is the difference between those who succeed and those who fail.

I shuddered at the thought of Mum and Dad or Sissy and Henry parting ways. But just because they are strong now doesn't guarantee they will always be that way. They all just took a chance that has thus far paid off. Now I must do the same.

Mum interrupted my thoughts, asking what I was planning to wear, agreeing the jumper and trousers were perfect for the choice of eatery and the time of year. She believed he would think me beautiful should I arrive in a potato sack and wellington boots.

Dad was in the lounge with his newspaper, catching up on the world's events. He looked up and smiled, telling me I looked fit to date a king rather than a mechanic, but Mum overheard from the kitchen and shouted at him. He winked at me and reminded me to stay in public places until I knew for sure who he was. When I reminded him that Blaine was picking me up in his car he grimaced, insisting he would worry about me until I walked back through the door, so woe betide me if I was late coming home and caused him undue stress. Mum shouted again.

At six fifty-nine the doorbell chimed; Dad and I exchanged glances and I don't know who looked more nervous. Mum appeared in the doorway, motioning with her head for me to answer the door. It was too soon to inflict the pair of them upon him, so I opened it just far enough to slip out without him seeing them or, worse, them saying something completely embarrassing to him.

He was wearing another shirt, the palest of blues, pristinely ironed and clinging to his muscular arms and chest just as the white one had, only this one was thicker, concealing the tattoos beneath.

Clutching a bouquet of beautiful red roses, he held out his other hand to lead me to his car, where he held open the passenger door and then closed it behind me. Climbing into the driver's seat he handed me the flowers, which smelled almost as good as him, and told me I looked beautiful. Only I felt considerably underdressed in my choice of outfit and told him so. He disagreed and said he could not imagine an outfit I would not look perfect in. My mind's eye created a picture of the potato sack and wellington boots.

Mum and Dad's silhouettes loitered in the lounge window, most likely checking him out. I could only imagine what they were saying about this hulk of a man with thighs and arms the size of tree trunks, dark skin and stubble. He was no Henry, but Henry is no Adonis. My inner snob was relieved he had worn a shirt and trousers for their first glimpse of him and not the greasy overalls.

Small talk flowed during the drive to The Dog and Ferret. We discussed our days, how he had bought the shirt especially for tonight, and then he tried convincing me his thighs were not made for trousers. He could not be more wrong. The trousers made them look masculine and shapely in a way loose overalls did not. I confessed to recycling an outfit, but it is one I only wear for special occasions, which this was. I also confessed to how nervous I had been, and he admitted he was too, but I couldn't believe someone of his stature could possibly be intimidated by the thought of spending time with someone like me.

I didn't wait to see if he would open my door again when he parked in the car park; I did not want him thinking I had delusions of grandeur. But still he walked around to my side of the car and took my hand, slipping his fingers through mine. I felt a million dollars; this gorgeous man was publicly displaying his commitment to me, however new or short-lived it may have been, he clearly wanted the world to see that we were together.

I'm certain every head turned when we entered the pub. Every woman eyed him from head to toe, probably wondering what he was doing with someone like me. Even the men glanced at him. Never have I made such a statement simply entering a building, but there we were, the odd couple, approaching the bar to ask where our table was. It must have been an omen because it was table number five, set in the quietest nook of the whole pub and next to the open fire beside a window that looked out onto fields and the woods beyond. Perfect.

# **Blaine**

It became obvious when I pulled onto the driveway that she had either won the lottery or lived with her parents. The large, detached house with its stone-clad walls was surrounded by mature trees; large flowerbeds punctuated an impressive, perfectly maintained front garden. It was stunning. Through a sizeable lawn, a path lead to the generous wooden front door, which opened just a little, revealing the girl who dominates my every thought. She is small and fragile like a mouse yet fills my mind as though she's as vast as the universe. She slipped out of the partially opened door, clearly shielding me from her parents on the other side. Or maybe them from me.

Inside the car I handed her the flowers I'd picked up on the way and she lowered her head to inhale their scent. Even that, the way she can appreciate the beauty in something as simple as a flower. She's a goddess and I cannot fuck this up.

I didn't ask too much about her yet, we talked about work and our choice of clothes for the evening. She felt underdressed and guilty for recycling an outfit when I'd bought a new shirt, so I explained how shirts and trousers are not my usual attire; I don't go anywhere often enough for this kind of dress code: work, the gym and dossing around at home all require no more than casual clothes. And anyway, these thighs were not made for trousers. She blushed, telling me that, on the contrary, the thighs were perfect for them. I might have blushed too.

Walking into The Dog and Ferret with Maya I remembered how I felt walking into the Italian restaurant with Hannah, like I wanted to be anywhere but there, with her. And here I was walking into a pub with Maya, wanting to be exactly there, with exactly her. Wanting everyone to see us and know we were together, that this beautiful woman was giving me a shot and I'd do everything in my power to make her want me just as much as I wanted her.

Our table was in a corner by the fire, cosy and intimate with two wooden chairs on one side, a padded bench seat against the wall on the other. I pulled out a chair for her, but she motioned with her head for me to follow her around the table to the bench, where we could sit side by side. Then, taking me completely by surprise, she pinched the front of my shirt between her fingers, pulled me towards her and kissed me, without a care for who might see. A chemical reaction in my blood rendered me speechless and she apologised for her forwardness. I adore this girl already — she's incredible — and the most amazing thing is that she wants me. Me. "Mr Detached", as Rob kindly put it. The man who doesn't fall for anyone.

Of course I gave her permission to kiss me as often as she needed to; I'd never object. So she did, holding me there even longer. I didn't care who saw, I wanted everyone to see. Kissing Maya is like dancing with angels. Imagine being caught in a moment where nothing else matters or exists, you're weightless and every deadened cell in your body comes back to life. Then she pulled away, but the feeling remained because she was still there, looking at me with eyes that are bluer and paler than ice. This girl was everything, yet still I knew nothing about her.

A waiter interrupted us to take our order, greeting Maya as though they were familiar. He looked embarrassed but I didn't care; I couldn't have felt prouder. Conversation flowed effortlessly over dinner. She told me about her parents and her sister and brother-in-law, the whole family sound kind and pure, like there's so much love between them. She told me how she aspires to have the same relationship as her parents and as a result it's kept her single. I asked why she gave in to me, of all people. Apparently, her mum told her to listen to her heart not her head, that it desires what it desires and there's nothing she can do about it. I need to shake that woman's hand for making her take the chance on me.

She confessed to having a dream where we kissed before we actually had and knew right then that she wouldn't be able to resist me for long. Then she asked how I knew I wanted her despite knowing nothing about her. So I told her how she mesmerised me the moment my eyes fell upon her, how I had to know her even though she rendered me incapable of speaking like a normal human being. She found that part amusing, saying she'd never had that effect on anyone before. Well, she had that effect on me.

The pub turned out to be her family's local, not quite on their doorstep but it's their favourite place. When eating was done we continued to sit and talk, mostly light-hearted stuff about things we liked, places we'd been, that sort of thing. I told her about my time at the gym and how it keeps me focused and positive. She didn't really have any hobbies but enjoyed reading and learning; she'd done various courses since leaving school but hadn't found the one thing she wanted to do with her life yet. When I told her I was glad she got the job at Totally Coffee she explained how she saw the ad for the job in the window as she walked past. Like it was fate. Like someone brought her to me.

I found myself telling her about Hannah. I didn't want her finding out later down the line that I'd been seeing someone else when we met. I wanted her to know that whatever else came before her, nothing would come between us now we'd found each other. She looked hurt, or maybe confused, but she has nothing to fear, my intentions towards her are pure. She has to know I mean that.

When dinner was done I wasn't ready to let her go, but I also didn't trust myself to be alone with her at mine. Maya's the kind of girl you treat with respect, so I suggested catching a film. She agreed on the condition she chose it. I wasn't about to argue.

## Maya

Blaine was perfect; his eyes never straying from me, not even to the two pretty women at the bar, one displaying ample cleavage in a low-cut top. Even Dad would have risked a peek had he been here.

And he continued being the perfect gentleman, pulling out a chair for me, but the far side of the table had a bench and I wanted to sit close enough to smell him and touch him. Seated side-by-side, my usual inhibitions vanished and I gave in to my urges and kissed him. But my forwardness seemed to stun him and now it was me apologising. He assured me I could kiss him as often as I saw fit, so with a newfound confidence I kissed him again.

As we ate and talked, he claimed his cooking was as good as the food we had ordered, he the steak and I the lamb, and was looking forward to cooking for me one day. This was an exciting revelation, a man that cooked and claimed to cook well. Mum would be impressed.

I confessed to kissing him in my dream and how it made me want to do it for real. He appeared rather pleased, admitting to being mesmerised from the moment he saw me, being rendered speechless in my presence. I remembered the awkwardness of the initial visits, how he looked as though he wanted to talk but said so little. His admission made perfect sense. He said he had never seen eyes like mine, eyes that looked through him as though I could see his soul. Eyes that haunted him, but in such a manner that he couldn't look away. I couldn't imagine any man I'd ever spoken to saying such a thing.

Then he admitted to being involved with someone when he first saw me, claiming it was never serious, that he never wanted a relationship with her and had believed she felt the same. Only it transpired that she wanted more from him. He felt terrible for hurting her but couldn't force himself feel something he did not. But this thing between us, he could not ignore it. He said it was completely over with her and that he had no doubt that he wanted only me.

It was a lot to take in for a second date. Pangs of jealousy at the thought of him being with someone else gnawed at me; kissing her the way he kissed me and being intimate with her when I had never been intimate with anyone. I realised then the chasm of experience that separated us, this man had lived while I existed in my sheltered little life trying to find myself as an adult and not really succeeding. He put his arm around me, holding the small of my back with his hand.

"Maya, please trust that my intentions towards you are completely pure. I won't hurt you or even consider being with someone else. I simply can't see anyone but you. You have to know I mean that. You have to know how beautiful you are."

And just like that, I believed him. The way he looked at me, his eyes speaking straight to my heart, it was not the look of an incongruent man. Mum was right, the heart desires what it desires, there is nothing we can do to change it. I have to take a chance on him. We cannot change what has gone before and we should not let the past cloud how we think the future might pan out. And looking into his eyes, I didn't feel as though I had any choice in the matter. I couldn't have walked away from that table, never to see him again. My heart had decided what it desired.

He asked if we could catch a film before calling it a night. I could think of nothing worse than leaving him to go home and agreed. The waiter brought the bill and without hesitation Blaine snapped it up and paid it. I protested that I should pay my half, but he simply responded, "No, you shouldn't."

He took my hand, helping me from my seat, and held it tight as we walked back through the pub, his fingers woven through mine. Again, people looked at us and I gripped his hand a little tighter. I don't know how I knew, but I just knew this was right.

## Chapter 14

## Tuesday 15th November 2022

### **Maya**

I awoke disoriented, engulfed in darkness; it was after six a.m. and message notifications waited for me on my phone, messages from Blaine. The faceless man had visited in my sleep again. Standing side by side in an unfamiliar house, we watched a woman sleeping on a bed. Her dark face bore purple-red bruises, her left eye was swollen, bloodied, yet she looked peaceful in her slumber.

"Once upon a time he saw only her. Now he sees only you, Maya, and you must make him show you who he is. I could show you myself but that won't help him." He looked sorrowfully at the woman. That was it, the whole dream.

I had fallen asleep thinking about the mystery girl Blaine had dated. What was so repellent about her to prevent him from wanting a relationship? Why would anyone be with someone they didn't see a future with? I fought pangs of jealousy by recalling his speech about his intentions towards me. I had believed him so easily, his warm voice and intense stare making it difficult to take his words as anything other than sincere. I concluded that if there were still anything between them he would surely have kept her existence a secret.

When my eyes had adjusted to the harshness of the light I read the messages that waited patiently for me.

*Good morning beautiful*, sent at five a.m.

*So, you're not an early riser? Shame, I wanted to tell you how much I enjoyed last night. I'm not usually up this early either but I can't stop thinking about you*, sent at five-thirty a.m.

*Just had an epiphany… You took a chance on me. I'm the luckiest man alive. But I'm going to stop messaging until you reply, I don't want you thinking I'm some weird stalker type. Until you wake…* sent at five-fifty a.m.

I replied: *I've always fancied having a stalker. Am bitterly disappointed to discover you do not fall into this category of human being. However, I really enjoyed last night too, so providing you are willing to work on your stalking skills then I think we have a chance.*

I had hoped he might be sitting, phone in hand, eagerly awaiting my response, but after several minutes the message remained unread and my head drifted to last night. We had left The Dog and Ferret with all eyes on us. Being with him and holding his hand fed my soul. I felt like the woman I had dreamed of being; desirable, mature, capable of winning the affection of a handsome man.

He had led me through the darkness to the car, opening the passenger door for me, but before I could get into the car he turned me around to face him and with his hand on the small of my back, pulled me into his body. He pressed his lips onto mine, kissing me with a passion I have never experienced before. An icy breeze blew against my skin but the heat from his body negated the cold, leaving me hot to the core. His strong hands explored my back and neck as I dissolved into him. I wanted that moment to last an eternity, but my ears had detected voices talking from somewhere around us and he was loosening his hold on me, he was pulling away. I didn't care if anyone saw us. Gripping him tighter I pushed myself harder into him. He responded by momentarily pulling his face away from mine, just enough for me to glimpse that serious, almost pained expression, just enough for him to look deeply into my eyes and silently confirm that he didn't care about the presence of others either, before he kissed me again.

The voices were gone, or maybe still present but inaudible over the wind in the trees and my thumping heart. Cold evening air mixed with the scent of his cologne; I could feel his heart beating too, or maybe it was mine. The heart desires what it desires and there is nothing we can do about it. I surrendered every one of my expectations about how my perfect man is supposed to look and the job he should have. This man made me feel more than I had ever dreamed of feeling.

Our lips parted and, taking my face in his hands, he kissed my forehead lightly then looked into my eyes, no words, his face still etched with that pained expression. I asked what was wrong and he replied that everything was very much right, then gestured for me to get into the car.

By the time we arrived at the cinema the last film had already started and, feigning relief that he didn't have to suffer a chick flick, Blaine suggested the bar at the top of the high street instead. It should have been quiet on a Monday night, the perfect place to continue getting acquainted, only fate had other ideas. My eyes fell upon Amber and her boyfriend, Drew, cosied up at a table as we entered. She spotted us too, leaping from her seat, beckoning us to join them. I wanted nothing more than to be alone with Blaine and looked up at him, awaiting his response.

"Well, it would be rude to ignore her," he said with a smile.

And just like that we were double dating. Amber wanted all the details up to now, how and when did I say yes to the date, listening to every answer with bated breath. It seemed Amber had a hand to play in encouraging Blaine to pursue me. I pretended to be cross with them both for conspiring but could not hold the face for long.

A message alert jolted me back to the here and now, and my hands scrambled through the duvet for my phone.

*Damn, I must have got in the shower just as you replied. I'll work on my stalking skills, but this is new territory for me, you'll have to be patient. I feel you're worth the effort. I just hope I am worth the patience. How did you sleep?*

## Blaine

Maya didn't know Amber had given me the heads-up about her being single and working on Sunday, but when we joined them at their table I was pretty sure she was about to find out. The bar's one of those smart places with coloured LED lighting, a mix of high tables with bar stools and low coffee tables with purple velvet sofas either side. It was busy and heads turned to look at us the way they had in The Dog and Ferret. We're together and it appears everyone's taking notice. I'd pay to hear what they're thinking, if they're admiring her beauty or wondering what she's doing with someone like me.

Maya had looked dubious, but how could we ignore them when Amber was in favour of this happening. She introduced us to her boyfriend and pressed to hear how we ended up here together. It wasn't long before she was hinting at her part in this. Maya eyed us both questioningly so I explained about Amber's intervention while Drew got drinks. Her eyes sparkled as I told her the details and Amber was elated when Maya told her what I'd done on Sunday. Drew returned to a playful slap on the leg from Amber, who told him he could learn a few things about being romantic from me. The irony's nothing short of ludicrous: me, romantic? But this girl commanded pulling out all the stops, without actually demanding a thing.

The rest of the evening was exactly what you'd expect of an evening with friends, even though I know nothing of the people I spent it with. Even Maya. Amber and Drew are nice people and seem like a solid couple. Drew talks about Amber's son with love; I respect that, it's not easy raising another man's son, a boy that embodies genetic traits of his biological father yet loving him unequivocally.

Last orders were eventually called and Amber was quick to request we do this again soon. Nobody disagreed; we'd swapped stories and laughed and the time had flown by. My only regret was having to share Maya, but I'd enjoyed feeling like a couple, not two virtual strangers on a date.

In the car Maya looked woeful, exhaling a gentle sigh. I didn't need to ask what was wrong; she didn't want the date to end either, but I wasn't prepared to take her back to mine and risk overstepping the mark. This girl had an innocence about her. I could tell she had standards and boundaries; she was the type you go slowly with. I knew this, even though every part of me wanted to feel her bare skin against mine, to wake up next to this beauty and slide into her before my eyes had even adjusted to the new day.

Lights were still on in the house when we pulled onto the drive and I was conscious that her parents could be watching. It felt like being a teenager again, exciting and new. In the privacy of the porch we swapped numbers and kissed, that chemical reaction reoccurring in my blood as her lips touched mine. She was like heroin and I was addicted. It seemed as though neither of us could pull away, until a noise from behind the front door killed the moment. Then the words I'd been dreading.

"I should go," she said. And with a last glance, "Message me." Then she was gone.

Back in the car I picked up my phone and typed, *How soon is too soon?!* Her reply was instant. *It is never too soon.*

# Maya

There are few things of which I am certain. I am certain my family will always be my greatest supporters. I am equally certain that one day my life will end, hopefully when I am old and have amassed a wealth of happy memories to take to my grave. And now I am certain that Blaine will be everything I dream of.

*I slept well but missed you,* I replied.

*How could you know you missed me? You were sleeping*, he answered.

*Because I was relieved when I opened my eyes and saw your messages. I think I would have been sad had you not been waiting for me on my phone. Is it too soon to feel like that?*

*It is never too soon.*

Flattered and giddy from his response, I wondered how he must look in the shower, water flowing down his muscular physique, pictures adorning his flesh. Like a god, I imagined. I wished to be there with him and wondered if I might feel terribly self-conscious being naked in his presence; I was hardly shapely or voluptuous. What if he was repelled by my childish form?

Stripping off my pyjamas I studied my pubescent-looking, barely B-cup breasts in the mirror. I had no curves of any description. My clavicle and hip bones protruded like razors, ready to tear through the flesh of any man who dared intimacy with me. How could I possibly bare this body to him?

Mum knocked on my door as I berated myself. Throwing on my dressing gown I invited her in and shared my fear about how Blaine might perceive my immature body. Of course, she thought I was being ridiculous, that I had a body any man would desire. Well, we were going to have to agree to disagree on that one.

She continued, hoping I was not planning on baring myself to him so soon; he should work for the privilege, earn my respect and trust, and she was relieved to hear I have no such intentions. I just fear that against his masculinity my childish body might disappoint when the moment arrives.

I had savoured every moment of last night; the time spent with Amber and Drew turned out to be as good as the time spent alone with Blaine. It was easy considering none of us were too well acquainted. I had worked only a handful of shifts with Amber, had never met Drew and despite my attraction to the man, I had no idea who Blaine truly was. Come to think of it, he learned considerably more about me last night than I learned about him.

He listened intently to every answer I gave about me and my family, each answer inspiring more questions. I had asked about his job, his home, and felt embarrassed that I live with my parents while he owns a flat. He talked of school bullies who forced him to stand up for himself and mentioned his mum when talking about his alleged cooking skills, but little else. Perhaps I stopped him giving more of himself away by interrupting with stories about Mum's cooking.

He did say he would like to cook for me. A date at his. The thought both excited and unsettled me. I remembered how uncomfortable Jacob made me feel when pushing for sex; I was younger then but am no more experienced now. How would I feel if Blaine pushed too? How would I reject his advances without hurting his feelings? What if he didn't want to wait? It would be Jacob all over again. Only I couldn't imagine walking away from Blaine.

Ruby was waiting for the details of my date when I arrived at work, unaware yet that Amber had been a part of it. Her demeanour changed when Amber announced how much she enjoyed double dating with Blaine and me; she suddenly looked as though she regretted not delegating tables to Amber.

Ruby quizzed me just as Mum and Dad had last night. Dad disapproved of how long it took me to get through the front door. Mum tutted, reminding him that I am a grown woman and he must accept that I am as entitled to a good snog as every other woman on this planet, including her. His face was a picture. Poor Dad.

Ruby revelled in every detail, clearly yearning for romance herself, and when the subject of last night was all but spent I told Amber about Mum choosing Hamlet-Noel for the holiday. She was thrilled to have been a contributing factor in the decision and will await my appraisal before considering it as a surprise for Rupert next year.

A message from Blaine awaited me when I took my break. I had hoped he would visit first thing but there had been no sign of him.

*You are cordially invited to a lunch date, at a time of your choosing, on the bridge where it began. RSVP ASAP with your ETA so the host can be suitably prepared.*

I showed the message to Ruby who insisted I accept the invitation and take an extra fifteen minutes to make the most of it.

*The invitee accepts the invitation and will arrive at twelve-thirty p.m. The invitee advises the host to ready himself for the snogging of a lifetime. Not only has it been almost twelve hours since this last occurred but he seems to have stirred something within the invitee, making her think of nothing else.*

Embarrassment coursed through me as soon as I pressed send; it sounded ridiculous. But the message showed as read immediately it delivered. Too late to delete it and send something more sophisticated.

*Marvellous. I'm providing the main course and it seems you're providing dessert! Wrap up warm, it's chilly out there,* came his reply.

The following hour dragged painfully as I dreamed of breathing him in while his strong arms held me. Just two weeks ago I could not have imagined even being attracted to this man. Rob came in for coffee before lunch and asked how it was going with Blaine, but before I had a chance to answer he added that he had never seen Blaine like this and that I clearly had a profound effect on the man. I blushed.

"Well, it looks like that makes two of you," he said, rolling his eyes in jest.

Rob has known Blaine for a few years and although Blaine is not the most open of people, he trusts him; he has always been true to his word and treated Rob with respect. He laughed at himself for asking me a question and not allowing me to answer. I told him it's early days, but that it's good so far. And I told him about the lunch invite; he nodded, making an "ah" sound as though something now made sense.

I had not factored in the time it would take me to walk to the park and across the grass to the bridge when I replied with my ETA. He was tapping his watch and shaking his head in mock disappointment when I approached. I hung my head, returning a look of mock shame. He reached out his arms, wrapped them around me and lifted me off my feet, planting his lips firmly against mine. The scent of his cologne mixed with the smell of oil and grease from his overalls and my head fought between indulging in the kiss and worrying about the smell of garage spoiling my coat and uniform.

My feet landed back on the ground and I could feel him releasing his hold. Pulling him back into me, I stood with my head against his chest for a few moments more before he asked if the smell of his overalls was a turn off. I could not deny that engine grease is not my favourite aroma, but fortunately the smell of him from beneath the overalls was good enough to counteract the effect.

He confessed how both Amber and Ruby had told him I prefer my men in suits and ties, that he had bought a new shirt for each occasion as they aren't something he ordinarily wears. I fought my disappointment as he explained how he usually wears hoodies and jeans. I wanted to keep seeing those muscular arms squeezed into shirts that clung to the contours of his flesh, especially the white one that teased a glimpse of what laid beneath. But I did not want to be that snob. He was gorgeous and made me feel good; what did it matter what he wore?

Taking my hand and leading me to the bench beside the pond, he unpacked lunch from his rucksack, placing it on the tea cloth set out between us. He looked rightfully proud of his efforts, only I wanted to skip first course and go straight to dessert. He noticed my dreamy expression, reached across and pulled me gently towards him.

He kissed me then said, "Now stop thinking inappropriate thoughts and eat."

Out came one of those hideous snorts; I was caught in the act. Only this morning I feared my pubescent body would send him running for the hills and there I was wishing I could tear off my clothes, and his, and throw caution to the wind.

We ate his beef and horseradish sandwiches and chatted as easily as we had the night before. He asked a multitude of questions as though soaking me up. Pausing to unpack the next course, I jumped in and asked, "So, what about you? I don't know half as much about you as you do about me."

"What do you want to know?" he asked.

"How long have you lived in your flat?"

"About four years."

"Where did you live before that?"

"I rented."

"Does it bother you that I live with my parents?"

"No."

I attempted to justify why I had not left home but he said I shouldn't be embarrassed, rather that I am lucky to have great parents and so much love in my family, that I should cherish being there. He pulled out two slices of shop-bought cheesecake and handed me a spoon.

"Can you not make cheesecake?" I asked in jest.

"No," he replied, pulling a woeful face.

"But you can cook a good steak?"

"Yes. Along with lots of other things. Puddings have just never been my forte."

"And it was your mum who taught you to cook?" I wanted to hear about his family after he had said how lucky I was to have mine.

"Yes," he replied, offering no more.

"Tell me about that," I probed.

"She's an amazing cook, puddings too, but I was more interested in dinners so that's what she taught me."

I started telling him about Mum's puddings but realised I had pulled the conversation back to myself again. He was listening intently when I stopped in my tracks and said, "What about your dad?"

His expression changed from one of interest to one of distance as he looked away from me.

"He's rubbish at cooking, Mum did it all," was all he offered.

"Same, my dad would need a map just to find the cooker. What does yours do?" I asked.

He was staring at the floor, not speaking, and after a long moment I poked his leg to remind him I was still waiting for an answer.

"Mechanic, same as me. That's why I got into it. He had me tinkering with cars when I was a teenager. I guess I liked it enough to pursue it as a job. And it's done me alright."

"Are you close with your parents?" I could tell from his face I had asked a difficult question.

"They're good people and I'm grateful for everything they've done for me. But I probably don't see them as much as I should."

"Any brothers or sisters?"

"Yes, one of each, Luke and Lucy. But it's my turn."

He questioned my previous relationships and a wave of embarrassment washed over me. This would be the moment he realised how inexperienced I really am. My turn to hesitate and his turn to poke me for an answer. My cheeks warmed and he looked concerned as he said,

"Please don't say you're with someone else."

"Quite the contrary," I replied.

He looked as relieved as I was embarrassed when I described my abysmal dating history and failed dates. I felt ridiculous next to this Adonis of a man and found myself trying to justify things again. His interjection was a welcomed interruption to my rambling, and I can't describe my relief when he said, "My relationship history isn't great either. I feel like I've always been waiting for you. I just didn't know it. I can't really explain it any better than that. The day I saw you for the first time... something happened inside me that I had no control over, like you commanded me to feel this way just by looking at me. Everything changed in that moment."

The funny thing was, I felt exactly the same. I was waiting for my perfect man when out of nowhere came the very opposite of what I dreamed of. Everything I believed to be right for me was suddenly wrong and I found myself feeling things I had never felt.

I do not recall if any more was said or who instigated it, but suddenly we were kissing, more passionately than was appropriate in a public space. I could smell him and feel him, every breath I inhaled breathed him deeper into me. I did not want to stop, I wanted his flesh in my hands, not the thick, rough material of his overalls. I pulled away from his lips and with my hands still wrapped around his neck the words "I want you, Blaine" fell from my mouth. He replied that he wanted me too, but I told him that is not what I meant. I meant I want you, now. Staring hard into my eyes, he explained he was not willing to mess this up by going too fast. He kissed me again and again, and in between kisses told me he would not risk this being anything other than perfect by being impatient.

This morning I had been concerned about rejecting his advances and pushing him away, and there I was making the advances and he the one resisting. I had one final question before time forced me back to work. "So, when will you cook for me at your place?"

But he was not silly; he was reading my intention and suggested I cook for him at mine first. He didn't seem the slightest bit phased when I pointed out that would involve meeting my parents. He told me he would like nothing more than to shake the hands of the beings who created me.

And that was the end of our lunch date. He pulled me up from the bench, held my face in his hands and kissed me on the forehead.

"What have you done to me?" he asked.

Taking my hand in his, he slid his fingers purposefully through mine and as we walked across the park I noticed that other people had been there too. Teenagers in school uniform sat on a bench, parents watched their little ones in the playground at the far side of the park. An elderly couple threw balls for two small dogs close to where we had sat. I was wondering how long they had been there when the woman glanced over, a look of concern on her face. Clearly it had been long enough to see us getting hot under the collar and she looked as though she did not approve.

I had not noticed any of them until now. All I had been able to see was Blaine.

# Blaine

I woke early, the words "it is never too soon" circling in my head and picked up my phone to message Maya. No reply. I messaged again, then again, before worrying she might think I was stalking her. I wondered what she looked like when she was sleeping and if she'd think of me when she woke. Then Hannah popped into my head and I hoped she was okay. She would be now Rob was moving in with her; he announced it this morning over our bacon sarnies. But I was pleased for them; she needed him and I didn't need him here.

I wondered who might be in Maya's past. My gut wrenched at the thought of someone else kissing her, waking up with her and worse, being inside her. I wondered how it would feel to lay in bed together, exposed and vulnerable. I couldn't imagine there'd be a single tattoo on her body, just pure skin, nothing fake or added. Every part of her as striking as her eyes. Then I showered to cool off.

I decided I'd invite her for an impromptu lunch in the park. We could meet on the bridge; I'd provide the food, nothing fancy, just a few sarnies and something sweet that I could pick up on my way to work.

From the shower I heard my message alert and rushed to finish. She missed me. I didn't understand why but I'd take it. After a short exchange of messages and a round of sarnies for lunch bagged up, I agreed to drop Rob at Hannah's after a gym session later and left for work. Rob had an appointment mid-morning, something to do with the house; he was gone from work for over an hour and when he returned I left, arriving at the bridge early.

Maya was two minutes late, but her smile as she walked towards me shone through the gloom of the cloudy day, my own personal sunshine. Lifting her off her feet, I kissed her. A move that left me worrying about the smell of my overalls, the last thing I wanted was to put her off.

Over lunch she asked questions, but I had questions too and turned them back on her. It turned out that not only had this girl not been snapped up already, which was hard enough to believe, but she hadn't had a serious relationship either. Her only actual relationship lasted just a matter of months, ending because he pushed for things she wasn't ready for. And there it was, the confirmation of this girl's standards, she was not to be rushed. She'd dated since then but nothing that evolved into anything serious. She was a free agent with no baggage and that was music to my ears.

We ate and talked and somewhere in that conversation I told her what meeting her had been like, how I think I've always been waiting for her. Her eyes bore into mine, then she was leaning into me with a determination that commanded a response. We kissed like something had been declared, like a forever-connection had been made. Then she said she wanted me, there and then, and I was not expecting that. She was caught in the moment but I wasn't prepared to fuck this up. I imagined losing her, my whole future playing out in front of me. Living my lonely existence, getting older and lonelier with nothing but weed and the gym for company because I fucked this up. Well, that was not happening, and I told her so. This guy would be doing everything the right way with her.

She asked when I'd cook for her, a cheeky ploy to get us alone no doubt, one she might live to regret when push comes to shove, so I suggested she cooked for me at hers instead. I'm sure she wouldn't risk anything like that in the presence of her parents. Besides, I want to meet them and let them know I'm deadly serious about her. They must be wondering about me and my intentions towards their girl.

She neither declined nor accepted my proposal but rolled her eyes, knowing she'd been rumbled. And that was the end of our lunch date; work beckoned and we parted ways outside Totally Coffee. As I looked back over my shoulder she mouthed "message me" before disappearing through the door. I was high on her when I walked back into the garage. Rob took one look at me and said, "Good god, man, you look like you just got laid." But the truth is I got so much more than that.

After the gym we loaded his stuff into the car, he thanked me for the temporary roof and suggested a last smoke before we left for Hannah's. He'll probably be back for something decent to eat by the weekend.

All I wanted was to see Maya again, take her somewhere nice, hold her, feel her against me, but I'd returned to the flat alone and was cooking some dinner when my phone pinged. It was Maya inviting me to dinner tomorrow, only her Mum would be cooking. Now this will be out of my comfort zone, attempting to make good first impressions with the most important people in her life. I'll need to bring my A game, another new shirt and trousers for sure. And I mustn't panic and say something stupid or say nothing at all.

Somewhere in my musings I acknowledged I was stoned and wondered what I'd do if she wanted to see me unplanned one day when I'd been smoking. Or turned up here unannounced. I'll have to quit, but that's okay — she gives me a better high than anything I could smoke.

I turned in early for bed to get some sleep and give myself a better chance of making a good impression tomorrow. But as I laid there in the darkness all I could think about was saying the wrong thing and fucking it up, or her parents taking one look at me and saying, "Nope, you're not right for our Maya." I convinced myself I wasn't right for her; we were too different; I'd lived a life she couldn't imagine. And the weed, there was no way she'd approve.

After an hour of torturing myself I got up and rolled a joint, a strong one to knock me out.

## Maya

Thoughts of Blaine consumed the afternoon and I wished we had plans for tonight. Instead, I'll be spending time with Mum and Dad, bringing them up to speed. Mum will be thrilled he wants to meet them; I'm not so sure about Dad. His expectations of his girl's suitors are much the same as mine, and probably the reason I had those expectations in the first place. Blaine will be as much of a shock to Dad as he was to me.

I tried picturing Blaine talking with Dad and Henry but couldn't imagine a single conversation they might have. Neither Dad nor Henry have ever lifted a car bonnet; they have people to do those jobs, and Blaine is one of those people. Dad doesn't come from money and once upon a time he was a Blaine, just not so big or tattooed. He worked hard for what he has so should at least appreciate Blaine's work ethic and that he owns a property. Still, I'll speak to him to ensure he behaves himself and makes Blaine feel welcome.

His car was already gone when I left work, depriving me of one last smouldering look before the day was over. I was sure he would message before long and made my way home, happily reminiscing about our lunch date. Mum stopped cooking to hug me when I arrived.

"Maya Elizabeth, I can smell him on you. Have you even been to work today?" she asked.

I told her about the lunch date — well, most of it — and she looked delighted when I announced that Blaine wanted to meet them both. She called Dad in from the lounge, demanding he put down his newspaper as he needed not concern himself with matters of the world right now because Blaine wanted to meet them.

"Already! You're not pregnant, are you?" Dad replied.

I snorted and told him that really would make the news considering we'd not even had sex. His face relaxed before he winced a little, the thought clearly too much to bear.

Mum insisted we invite him for dinner tomorrow; she said she'll cook to prevent scaring him off, and they will be here to meet him but not to dine with us, so as not to overwhelm him. Dad was instructed to flex his credit card and take her somewhere nice for dinner to give the two of us some privacy. I revelled in the vision of being alone in the house with him, curling up in front of the fire, lying in his arms.

I messaged to check he was free before I got carried away. He accepted the invitation and sent me a picture of the dinner he was preparing, revealing a glimpse of the kitchen beyond the food. Charcoal grey cupboards and a steel worksurface lined the wall, an island unit with bar stools stood in the centre. Everything looked impeccably clean and tidy and my curiosity to see where he lived peaked.

Retreating to my room to be alone with the memories of our lunch date, I stripped off my uniform. The smell of Blaine's cologne filled my nose as I pulled my shirt over my head. I breathed in deeply to inhale as much of him as possible.

In the shower I could think of nothing else; the hot water made my skin tingle. I slid my fingertips between my legs, rubbing them gently backwards and forwards, then around in circles, the whole time thinking of Blaine, imagining him here with me, his hand between my legs, his other arm outstretched, hand pressed against the tiled wall as he leant into me. I thought about him kissing my neck, then my lips. My knees buckled as I let out an involuntary groan so loud that I was suddenly conscious of Mum and Dad's presence in the house.

## Chapter 15

## Wednesday 16th November 2022

### **Blaine**

The film played out on an old wooden box TV set. A western set in a town where wood-frame buildings lined dusty streets. In the blinding sun three cowboys stood, each pointing their gun at one another, each of them a target. One of them looked like me, another could have been a woman. A stalemate seemed to have been reached; no one was shooting, no one lowering their weapon.

The camera panned away as a gunshot rung out. The thud of a body hitting the ground was clear but I didn't see who'd fallen or who'd fired the shot. The screen flickered furiously before turning black and I hit the side of the TV with a balled fist. I woke up sweating and confused, still laying on the sofa. That joint really knocked me out.

It was after seven thirty a.m. and I was late getting up for work. No time for breakfast today, the perfect excuse to visit Totally Coffee for a drink and some food, and of course to see the most extraordinarily beautiful girl.

Rob was working on an exhaust when I pulled up on the forecourt. "You're late, Farriner. Can't live without me, huh?" he shouted. I patted my heart and pulled a sad face like I was lost without him.

Totally Coffee had only just opened but there she was, looking radiant. Like a magnet pulled towards her I would have climbed over that counter to kiss her if Ruby hadn't been standing in front of it, filling up the biscuit stand. She saw me first, greeting me with enough volume to garner Maya's attention. The smile and the light in her eyes were all I needed; I didn't care if it was too soon. I was falling for this girl.

Maya had clearly informed Ruby of tonight's date as she asked if I was nervous to meet the in-laws. It was a little soon to be calling them that, but yes, I was terrified. They laughed in unison at my discomfort. I was glad she'd warmed to me; it was a vast improvement on the ambivalence of before, but it would have been nice to speak to Maya without her standing beside me. Anyway, Maya said she'd be expecting me at seven and I explained that I'd be using today's lunchbreak to buy a new shirt and trousers.

"You really are trying to make a good impression." She smirked.

Of course I was, I needed them to see me as suitable for their girl. I'd heard the way she spoke about them; it was clear how important they were to her. And I'd seen where they live and the cars parked on their drive. I couldn't be turning up to meet them in anything less than well-tailored trousers and a good shirt.

So lunchtime saw me entering the menswear shop in town, the one I hadn't ventured into since Andy's wedding, and being fitted with a smart pair of grey trousers and a thicker white, long-sleeved shirt. I didn't want all these tattoos visible the first time they saw me. And in the hope that this became a regular thing, I bought a second pair of trousers and another shirt.

*** 

The reflection in the mirror was saying "he's made an effort but still looks like a thug". In my mind's eye I pictured them slamming the door in my face, dragging Maya to the attic and locking her away to keep her safe. A little dramatic perhaps.

The shirt and trousers were a good fit though; the thighs didn't look like they were trying to break free but at the same time the material clung nicely, and the shirt covered most of what it needed to. A few sprays of aftershave later and I was ready — nervous as hell, but ready.

Every second of the drive was spent torturing myself. It felt like everything rested on this meeting, on being accepted, and I wondered why I'd suggested this in the first place. Ah yes, so she wouldn't come to mine where we'd be alone, where I might do things I'd regret and lose her.

The front door opened, revealing Maya in a short grey dress with long, blousy sleeves that cuffed at the wrists and flat, grey, ballet-pump-style shoes. Her hair hung loose around her shoulders, soft and wavy, shining in the light of the generous hallway chandelier. Her legs were bare and inviting. I held my breath for a second to take her in. No scooping her off her feet or long passionate kisses this time; I knew the parents would be lurking somewhere close by.

As it turned out they were right behind the door. I kissed Maya on the cheek but my hands were too full of the flowers and wine I'd picked up on the way to hold them out to Richard and Maggie to shake. I handed Maya the red roses and she tip-toed to kiss me quickly on the lips before I handed Maggie the other bunch. I had no idea what they were, just mixed flowers, not romantic looking. She gave me a hug, short but warm, and said, "It's lovely to meet you, Blaine."

She was as kind and pure-looking as Maya, her hair just as blonde and her frame as slight. Her eyes were blue, but a normal blue. Richard eyed me silently; I could guess what was going through his head. Holding out the wine I said, "I hope you like red, it's a good one." He scrutinised the label and agreed, thanking me, holding out his hand to shake. I didn't grip it too tightly; I wanted him to feel like he'd got the upper hand. He did have the upper hand — she's his daughter.

Maggie led us to the kitchen, saying she hoped I liked the lasagne she'd made and that she and Richard were going out for their own date so as not to overwhelm me. Giving me a playful smile, she added that there was plenty of time for that. I liked her, she had a welcoming warmth about her. Putting both bunches of flowers in vases of water she set them in front of the big kitchen window.

"The postman will think Richard's done something wrong when he sees all these through the window in the morning," she joked.

The Caley's kitchen was as impressive as the outside of the house; solid wood worksurfaces, an abundance of cream-coloured cupboards, a huge wooden table with eight chairs in the centre of the room and a big double oven with plenty of rings for cooking big family dinners. I could picture what it must be like here when they all got together. Maya is a lucky lady.

Richard entered the kitchen, pulling up a chair at the table with us. I'd already offered to help Maggie but she'd declined assistance; I was a guest and would be treated like one, was her response. Maya advised it was better to just give in.

I complemented Richard on his beautiful home and he responded modestly that he'd been lucky to fall, unskilled, into a job that paid good money and to have met a beautiful woman who made a beautiful home for him and their beautiful children. He beamed with pride at his family. Maggie looked at him dewy-eyed and blushed. So that's where Maya gets it from. He attributed the interior design to Maggie, saying she had impeccable taste when it came to décor. Maggie insisted Maya give me a tour of her impeccably good taste before I left.

Maya poked Richard, telling him Maggie probably needed some help; he rolled his eyes, realising he'd overstayed his welcome at the table and asked if there was anything he could do. She instructed him to light a fire so we could sit in the lounge after eating and off he went.

Maggie asked questions while she dished up; nothing too personal, making it easy to answer without being evasive. I thanked her for cooking and when I said I'd like to return the favour one day she suggested we team up and cook together. I hadn't imagined feeling so welcome here.

I pleaded with her not to clear anything away, that was the very least we could do after all her effort. She conceded and stepped away from the sink, wished us "bon appetit" and left the kitchen. A few minutes later the front door closed and we were alone.

Maya was the perfect dinner date again, telling me all about this amazing house. Both she and her sister were born here, Sissy accidently when she came so suddenly there wasn't time to get to the hospital. Maya's home birth was planned since the first had been so successful.

She asked questions about Luke and Lucy, about whether we were as close as she and Sissy were. I didn't want to lie so I answered what I could then suggested she give me that tour, particularly of her room. I had no dishonourable intentions, just curiosity.

The house was stunning, Richard wasn't wrong about Maggie's eye for décor, it's like something out of a magazine. Not over the top, just perfectly homely and of beautiful quality. Solid wood floors in the hallways, warm deep pile carpets in the rooms. The occasional touch of wallpaper gave character and depth to a wall. Family photos decorated every room; they were on every surface and leading the eye up the wall of the curved staircase. There were pictures of the girls as babies, throughout their childhoods and into their adulthood; photos of Sissy and Henry's wedding, Maya a bridesmaid in an elegant dusky pink dress; pictures of Richard and Maggie on their wedding day, looking younger and fresher and every bit as happy as they had tonight. Richard was a good-looking guy who'd matured well. He was grey now but once had a mop of fair hair.

A glimpse into Sissy's room revealed a shrine to the child who had flown the nest. An elaborate desk, probably used for studying once upon a time, was home to framed photos of a younger Sissy with friends. A large collage of similar photos hung on one of the walls, another framed photo of Sissy cheek to cheek with a smartly dressed Henry on one of the bedside tables. Maya said Sissy and Henry still slept here when alcohol had been consumed and driving wasn't appropriate.

Maya's room was everything I'd expected it to be, soft pinks and creams, elegant and feminine just like her. Everything in there from the carpet to the wardrobes, the bed to the dressing gown hanging on the back of the door, looked and felt luxurious. No expense had been spared to make it a room fit for a daughter valued like a princess. Somehow this girl had grown up so loved and privileged, so indulged, and yet she was kind, caring and humble, all the things I wouldn't expect someone who'd had so much to be. Now I was intrigued to meet Sissy; they couldn't have achieved this perfection twice.

I suggested checking on the fire but she tugged at my arm, making me sit on the bed, pulling pieces of paper from her bedside drawer, handing them to me with the instruction to open them. They were the receipts I'd drawn on. The first with the smiley face, two with sad faces and the fourth that said "Sunday". She'd kept them, like taken them home and put them in a drawer kind of kept them.

Again, I was reminded of the purity of this girl. She'd folded them up and taken them home, even that first one. I remembered the way she seemed awkward when she brought my coffee over that day. I knew she'd felt something and clearly I wasn't wrong. Why else would she have kept that one?

We sat for a moment staring at each other. It was a moment I won't forget because I could hear her even though she wasn't speaking. She felt exactly the same as me. She was in deep too.

Inappropriate thoughts crept into my head; I needed to leave her room but she stood up and came at me, half standing, half leaning over me. Her hands were on my neck pulling my face into hers. I reacted instinctively, standing up to stop her, sending her off balance. I caught her as she wobbled and kissed her beautiful face, trying to make light of the circumstances. I kissed it over and over again, then her lips, but she pulled away saying, "I get it, you don't want to muck things up by going too fast. Neither do I, but I feel things that are hard to resist when I am with you."

Scooping her up in my arms I carried her downstairs to the fire waiting in the lounge, and there we sat, cosied up together, until Richard and Maggie returned and joined us.

## Maya

The day passed quickly despite the fact I hadn't seen Blaine since his early visit. He arrived at seven on the dot with flowers for me and Mum and wine for Dad, choosing well on all three counts. He looked divine in his new clothes. I was certain Mum inhaled a little deeper than normal when she hugged him and guessed by the slightly startled look on his face that he was not expecting such a display of affection. Dad kept a distance, eyeing Blaine from head to toe before stepping forward to shake his hand.

Mum put our flowers in vases and set about serving dinner while asking Blaine a little about himself. Once they had left for their own date, he relaxed into ours. He loved our home; his eyes lingered on the framed photographs and studied every detail of my bedroom. Reaching out, he felt the furniture, my dressing gown, even the wallpaper behind my bed. Pulling him down to sit on the bed I passed him the receipts from my drawer. "You kept them?" he asked, studying my face as though looking for a reason, and there it was again, that desire burning inside me just like yesterday in the park. I practically threw myself at him, only he stopped me again, and the more he resists the stronger my desire to be intimate with him grows.

He carried me effortlessly down the stairs to the lounge where the fire roared. I wanted to kiss him and see his body without the shirt concealing it. I can't explain this version of myself because I don't recognise it. I explained how yesterday he'd asked what I had done to him; today I was asking what he had done to me.

I think Blaine was relieved he wouldn't have to fight me off again today when Dad's headlights illuminated the window. They came straight to the lounge to join us; Mum described the lovely Italian they had dined at on the high street, and Blaine said was familiar with it. Before long Dad and Blaine were engaged in conversation, politics mainly, and that was a side to Blaine I had not anticipated; he really was quite knowledgeable about world affairs. Dad, clearly impressed, got up and declared that we should open the fine bottle of wine Blaine had provided, only Blaine declined because he had to drive home. Dad, looking even more impressed, opened the wine, filled his glass and took a big gulp. Sitting back in his chair he said, "Maya tells us you own a flat."

Blaine obliged, informing him how he bought it cheap due to its neglected state, brought it into the twenty-first century and should have a tidy lump of equity when he sells it. Dad asked when he plans to do so and buy a house. Blaine looked stumped; I could see he didn't want to ruin the good foundations they had laid. Mum must have sensed his concern also and intervened, telling Dad that was enough interrogation for one night.

"It's okay Maggie," Blaine responded, "it wouldn't be a bad thing to look at what I could get for it. I just hadn't had a reason to before. I've been enjoying the changes I made to the place while it suited my single lifestyle."

And there was the opening Dad had been waiting for.

"So, how long have you been single?" he asked.

Dad sees people like Blaine as people who jump from relationship to relationship, never getting serious with anyone. And even though things had been going well, it could all come tumbling down if Blaine said the wrong thing. In Dad's eyes, us girls were destined to be with loyal gentlemen: providers; honourable, hard-working men.

Mum leapt to his defence again, telling Dad not to pry, but Blaine, remaining seemingly unphased, reassured Mum that it was perfectly reasonable for a father to be concerned for his daughter. He explained how he has prioritised work and renovating his home. Then he told them how when he met me something inside him changed. That having met someone as beautiful as me, he knew he would move heaven and earth to win my affection. Concluding his speech he told them, and me, that he would continue to move heaven and earth to keep it.

Mum had that look on her face like when she was reading a Mills and Boon novel and let out a delighted sigh. We all sat in silence for several seconds; no one could top that or even knew how to respond. Until Dad got up, shook Blaine's hand once more and said, "Well, it looks like a welcome-to-the-family moment to me. We accepted Henry into our home and our family the very day Sissy brought him to meet us; if your intentions towards Maya are as you say then you are just as welcome here as Henry."

Blaine stood up respectfully, visibly honoured by Dad's declaration, returning the handshake and thanking him profusely. I'm not entirely sure, but I think he may even have called him sir.

By now Mum had teared up and was on her feet, waiting to embrace Blaine. She echoed Dad's "welcome to the family" and I wondered if this might all be too much for Blaine. She let him go and asked Dad to join her in the kitchen to make coffees, and I seized the moment to check he was okay. He took my hand and, sitting back down on the sofa, admitted he couldn't have wished for tonight to have gone any better, that I was one lucky girl to call these people my parents and all of this was why he refuses to move too fast and ruin things. He was right and one day I would be grateful he didn't give in to this silly girl and her urges.

At ten o'clock Blaine announced his departure and Mum and Dad agreed that time was getting on. I, however, did not want the evening to end; it had felt good having him here, like he was a part of our family.

Sissy had enjoyed this all these years whilst I had sat alone, wondering how it would feel to have a man of my own. I told him I would miss him again while I slept. He replied that because he could now picture where I slept, he would take happy thoughts home with him, then kissed me tenderly and walked away down the path to his car. I called after him.

"Tomorrow?"

"Of course," he replied.

Mum was waiting to pounce when I shut the front door, hugging me so tight I could barely breathe.

"Thank goodness you stopped trying to resist such a gorgeous man; you will be the envy of every hotblooded woman who sees you together," she said, quickly adding, "and he will be the envy of every hotblooded man, of course."

Dad hugged me goodnight and I thanked him for being gracious tonight before he disappeared upstairs, but I don't think he understood how much his acceptance of Blaine meant. Lying in bed I reflected on the evening, introducing him to Mum and Dad could not have gone better. Blaine could not be better. Mum's words made me think of all the looks we got from people in The Dog and Ferret and in the bar after; would people really have been looking at us with envy? I mean, he was another level of gorgeous, but I couldn't help but feel how out of place I must have looked beside him.

My phone pinged on the bedside table. It was Blaine, happy but apparently missing me.

# Blaine

I didn't need a smoke when I got home. I'd left here feeling like I needed Diazepam to calm my nerves but returned on a natural high. They liked me, Maggie somewhat more quickly than Richard, but even he'd got there by the end of the night. And Maya with those receipts.

Nothing mattered when I met her. Women didn't matter; they were replaceable. Jobs didn't matter; there were always other garages, always someone needing a car fixed. The only thing that mattered was this place because it was mine, but nothing else. And now Maya matters, her parents matter, keeping my job matters, looking good for Maya matters. Being good for Maya matters.

I messaged to tell her I missed her already. She replied saying she missed me more. I don't think it'll be too hard to fall asleep tonight.

## Chapter 16

## Thursday 17th November 2022

### **Maya**

A sharp intake of breath woke me. Faceless had been at my bedside, leaning over me as I lay, shouting something unintelligible. I tried rolling away, only my body wouldn't move. He leaned in closer until his breath blew the wisps of hair that rested on my face. I breathed in deeply to muster a scream for Mum or Dad, but the sound of my breath had woken me and I was alone.

It was three a.m. Isn't that what they call the witching hour? When spirits from beyond the grave contact the living. Thoroughly perturbed, I knew I wouldn't sleep any time soon and messaged Blaine to tell him about the dream and how I wished he could hold me. Seconds later he was ringing, my message having woken him.

He hated that I was scared and that he couldn't comfort me, and instructed me to picture him here, arms wrapped around me; no funny business though, said he knew what I was like. Had I been that bad? I loved talking to him like this, as though he was mine.

We had talked for almost half an hour when I realised I felt better and should try to sleep, him too, or we might not get up for work. He promised to visit in the morning to make sure I was okay and we hung up. The next thing I knew my alarm sounded and I wondered if the phone call been part of the dream. But my phone was still on my chest, vibrating with the alarm, just where I had left it after speaking to him. I checked the call log and there it was, twenty-seven minutes of conversation.

I hoped to catch a glimpse of him on the forecourt. Just a smile, a wink or that sultry look would have sated my want. But it was not to be. Ruby assigned me to tables, quietly admitting she would rather have me behind the counter with her but didn't want the others to think I was getting special treatment. Amber was allocated to order prep and I wondered if Ruby was peeved with her for being in the right place at the right time on Monday.

Each time I returned to the pick-up point for an order Amber asked questions about Blaine, soaking up the details. Drew had been pestering her to arrange another double date. It seems Blaine is Mr Popular with everyone.

It was not too far into the shift when my tall, dark, handsome man strolled through the door making eyes at me. He winked before turning away to order his coffee, making my heart flutter in my chest. I watched him walk to a table, number one today, the table in the nook: a little area of the café tucked behind a half-wall enclosing the end of the serving area.

I asked Amber to bang on the wall when the next order was ready to go and slipped around the corner to his table, placing down his tray without incident. Even from where I was standing I could smell his cologne and I couldn't help but lean over to kiss him. As I pulled away he reached for my arm, pulling me back to kiss me again, this time with heat. I managed a few minutes at his table, during which we agreed on a cinema date this evening and I asked how he was feeling after meeting Mum and Dad. He was more concerned about the effect it had on me, giving me bad dreams. I'm quite certain the two events were not related, but he took a little convincing. Then Amber knocked on the wall.

A tray of coffees and toasted teacakes were delivered to table four and I was back at table one, telling him about Drew and how he seemed to be working his charms on the men and the women. He argued that he possessed no such charms, but I had to disagree. Mum is as taken with him as Amber and Drew. And me of course. Even Dad had seemed impressed by the end of the evening.

When I returned once more to table one he was gone. I knew a receipt would be waiting for me and sure enough it was tucked under his coffee glass, folded neatly, an "x" drawn at the bottom with the words "until tonight" below it.

Today held little opportunity to speak with Ruby so I suggested taking our break together and she smiled for the first time today. I told her about tonight's cinema date, but she responded by telling me not to move in with him or have children if I want to keep the magic alive. I think she was joking but it was hard to tell.

# Blaine

She woke me, shaken by a nightmare. I wanted to hold her but turning up in the early hours probably wouldn't have gone down too well with Richard, so I remained in my bed, fighting the urge. This morning she was on tables and I was allocated a perfectly secluded seat, where I could kiss her, breathe in her beauty and secure her company this evening.

I'd wondered if Rob would still join me at the gym after work, now he has Hannah to play with, but he was keen to work on his chest and abs and was still going at it when I left to get ready for my date. It was a good session, both of us driven and working hard. I was focused on looking my best for Maya; I had no idea what had inspired Rob.

Maya had suggested the cinema for tonight's date, insisting she picked the film. I owed her that, and it wasn't a bad choice. I had her down as a chick flick kind of girl but she chose a thriller. I warned her she'd be on her own again if it gave her bad dreams. But she knew I'd answer the phone if she needed me.

I wasn't ready to take her home after, so we drove to the narrow road that spans the top of the hills overlooking Woodbridge. It's quite something at night when the town's illuminated, the perfect place to sit with someone you don't want to be apart from. A couple of metres from the side of that road the hills fall gradually away, down towards the outermost residential areas of town, a long gentle descent of grass, bushes and trees that creates the town's backdrop of greenery, apart from the one spot a good fifty feet wide — Hell's Mouth it's nicknamed — where the ground gives way to a sheer drop of a hundred feet or more. It's the site of a landslide over a century ago that wiped out an entire family who lived in a cabin at the bottom of the hill. It's reported they were crushed to death by the weight of earth and chalk as they slept.

We talked a little about my cooking prowess. I'd have liked to cook for her but she'd have to behave herself, no funny business because at some point I'd give in to my urges. She looked at me with those soul-piercing eyes, trying to pull a sad face, but her mouth turned up at the corners as she broke into a laugh.

"Honestly, Blaine, that behaviour is not like me at all. You just have this strange effect on me," she explained. Only I meant what I said about continuing to move mountains; I'll resist my urges until she's truly ready.

The time flew, it was soon gone eleven and reluctantly I drove her home. Her perfect face looked as disappointed as I felt when we reached her front door so I held her tight to my chest. After several moments the security light clicked off, leaving us in darkness. She always feels tiny and fragile in my arms yet has the power to make everything better. The feeling inside me when I hold her, it's like being invincible.

## Maya

The film was good but seeing it with Blaine was better. Holding my hand the whole time, he didn't talk through the film, one of my pet peeves. Sissy is terrible for it. Even Henry says it drives him mad. He sat, absorbed in the film, glancing down at me periodically and smiling.

Afterwards he parked on the road that runs along the hill above the town. It was the perfect view and he was the perfect gentleman to share it with. You couldn't be blamed for thinking Blaine wouldn't possess a romantic bone in his body. You certainly wouldn't assume he was capable of what he achieved on that bridge on Sunday, and I wouldn't have thought he would want to sit here with me, overlooking the town in which we have lived our separate lives all this time without knowing each other exist. And yet here we were, quite infatuated. Him doing everything it took to win me. He even wanted to cook for me at his place, but said I must behave, no lunging at him, no tempting him to do the things he is trying to resist for both of our benefits.

It was late when he took me home but Dad was up waiting for me. I assured him Blaine had been the perfect gent; he smiled, bid me goodnight, then disappeared upstairs. I went to the kitchen and sat at the table, smiling to myself and admiring the vase of beautiful roses on the windowsill. I knew I should go to bed, only I was wide awake, I wanted to see him already, I wanted to get into bed beside him and feel his skin against mine. A message alert sounded from my pocket, interrupting my thoughts.

*Let me cook for you tomorrow night?*

## The Elders

"Our duty is not to lead or advise but determine when one's autonomy is counterproductive. We need not justify why we must protect her, nor must we listen to your pleas for his salvation. We must do what is right.

"You are a threat to order, a threat to everyone, no matter where you are. You must heed this warning; do not interfere. Your own path is long and your interference will only serve to prolong your journey.

"Leave her alone, Thomas."

## Chapter 17

## Friday 18th November 2022

### **Maya**

I woke at eight despite having no work or plans, already eager to see Blaine. The thought of the two of us alone in his flat made me giddy. What if I got carried away, led him on and then got cold feet? What if he got carried away and I got scared?

When I ventured downstairs Mum was cutting vegetables, adding them to the lamb already in the slow cooker. Putting the skillet back over the heat and pouring three perfectly round puddles of batter onto it, she asked if Blaine would be free to come for a family dinner on Sunday. Sissy and Henry could meet him and he could cook dinner with her. I agreed to ask him later and told her about our date at his place. I can hide nothing from that woman, as she slid the hot pancakes onto my plate she asked what was worrying me. It was pointless hiding it from her, and Dad had already left for work so would not have to suffer hearing it. She explained that there was no wrong or right time for intimacy, providing we were both ready. He didn't strike her as someone who would take something so precious from someone who clearly meant as much to him as I did. I asked how she could be so sure.

"Oh, Maya, have you learned nothing from his eyes?" she replied. "A man who looks at a woman the way Blaine looks at you would take nothing he had not earned. He will hold you like fine china until he can trust that holding you any other way will not break you or risk never being able to hold you again."

Feeling reassured, I messaged him, *Cannot wait for tonight. Until then, I will be at work within the hour, just for a coffee, if you have five minutes spare.* He replied, *Just five? I'll take what I can get of those eyes.*

Mum had been peering over my shoulder and piped up, "See!"

With a burning urge to see him before tonight, I made myself presentable and set off for Totally Coffee. Ruby was there, and so was Blaine already. The two of them were so absorbed in conversation that neither saw me enter. I cleared my throat behind them, announcing my arrival. Blaine winked at me and said, "Oh sorry, I didn't see you there, I was too busy chatting up this beautiful lady."

Well, Ruby blushed all shades of red while Blaine leaned forward to kiss me in front of everyone. Amber cooed over how cute we looked while Ruby suggested we get a room. Blaine asked if I had any last-minute ideas about what I would like for dinner tonight, but I could think of nothing apart from how good the man smelled and that I would like *him* for dinner.

I decided to leave the Sunday dinner invitation until tonight; I would not want to put him on the spot in here. It was one thing meeting Mum and Dad but having a meal with all of us and cooking it with Mum was quite another. I would be sure to let him know that part was optional.

"Have a great day, ladies," he called out as he left Totally Coffee to return to work, shooting me an intense and lingering look with those beautiful green eyes.

Ruby had a glow about her following Blaine's compliment and I could not help but feel sad that her own husband did not make her feel that way.

Sitting quietly with a coffee I thought about Blaine and about tonight. I thought about the odd man in my dreams and as I did so I noticed an elderly couple walking past the shop window, looking in. It was the couple from the park and they were looking straight at me. I had not decided whether to acknowledge or ignore them when the lady gave me a wave. I waved back, awkwardly, before they moved out of sight.

Shortly after, Ruby joined me at my table, asking if I would mind the company while she took her break. I motioned for her to sit, and she told me how Blaine's words, however untrue they may have been, reminded her of an old flame with whom she had been very much in love. He would say similar things and make her feel wonderful. Apparently, she wore a face-full of make-up back then and weighed considerably less. I wanted more of a glimpse into her world and the factors that lead to the breaking of this lovely woman's spirit, but she decided she had said enough and should return to the counter. I pleaded with her to tell me more, but all she said was, "I didn't always look and feel this way. Once upon a time I was happy." As she stood to leave her sad eyes defied the smile she forced.

Poor Ruby. It's funny how when you meet someone you can assume they were never anyone other than who they are now, that there was never another way of being, thrashed out of them by their circumstances.

## Blaine

She couldn't wait for tonight, the message said, but I was scared witless. What if she got heavy again and I lost control? I wanted to impress her with my home, I wanted her to be impressed that I survived the evening without luring her into my bed. I didn't want to regret bringing her here. I hid the ashtray in a cupboard. At some point I'd tell her I smoked, or maybe I'd stop, then by the time it came up in conversation it would already be something I used to do.

She was calling into work and I wasn't about to miss the opportunity to feel alive in her presence, even if only for five minutes. Ruby was at the counter talking to Amber, who practically cheered as I walked through the door. I don't recall people noticing me before Maya. Now people smile and talk to me. I never knew I wanted this; I honestly thought I was happy being left alone.

Moments later, Maya arrived; she didn't have any requests for dinner so I decided on salmon steaks. I'd serve them with sautéed veg and sweet potato wedges. Simple, so there was no chance of mucking it up but it would still look impressive. And a good bottle of white and orange juice as an alternative. After work I prepped the veg and left the salmon marinading in the fridge; all that was left to do was shower, iron a shirt and wait.

I used to wait for Hannah. I'd feel numb, no excitement, no fear. Just the knowledge that she'd arrive, we'd smoke, we'd sleep together and she'd leave. It was enough. Now I'm full of excitement at Maya being here in my home and full of fear about how to behave. How far is too far? I want to talk and learn more about her, I want to feel her but not so much so that she doesn't come back.

The buzzer rang at seven. I'd reused the candles and jars from the bridge, placing them down the hall and in the lounge and kitchen. I'd bought table candles too and flowers and a vase for the centre of the table.

I took a mental photograph of her standing on my doorstep; she was here because she wanted me. She was smiling, her face illuminated because of me. Her eyes pierced my soul like I was seeing her for the first time yet again. Tonight would be challenging.

I gave her a tour of the lounge and kitchen, it was not the biggest of places, but it was all mine. She told me how she wished she had her own place; I responded with a gentle plea to appreciate what she had but she reminded me how I didn't see my parents as much as I should. She's right, they did something incredible for me, they loved me and showed a warmth most would struggle to show.

Maya declined the wine as she was driving, but the orange juice looked just as nice in the tall glasses Rachel gave me along with most of my kitchen accessories when I bought this place. I'd always assumed their support would stop when I left their house, but they were generous and carried on doing what parents are supposed to do. I really should see them more.

Maya watched as I cooked and seemed impressed with the meal. She filled me in on her uneventful day while I cleared the table and loaded the dishwasher, and when I pulled out the shop-bought roulade she told me how Maggie had invited me back to dinner on Sunday, only this time for a roast with Sissy and Henry too. A full-on family experience and she wanted me to cook it with her. So the pressure was on, but I was game. I wanted this girl and I wanted all the people who loved her to know I was serious about her.

We retired to the sofa with coffee and dessert and, noticing the lack of photographs, she decided that if she couldn't see pictures of my family then she'd just have to meet them in person. After all, by Sunday I'd have met all her nearest and dearest. But there'd be questions I didn't want to answer and an awkwardness I couldn't address.

Then, as though testing all of my limits simultaneously, she said it was only fair she saw my bedroom, as I'd seen hers. I pointed towards the door on the other side of the hall; I wasn't about to give her a guided tour and risk falling foul to my urges. She disappeared a short while before popping her head back around the lounge door. She wasn't expecting something so clean and well-coordinated for a man and wondered what it would be like waking up next to me in there.

My resolve was beginning to fail so I suggested a walk around the seafront. She knew what was going through my head — the same thing that was going though hers — and agreed. The evening air was mild and it was nice walking hand-in-hand with her. We walked the length of the harbour, past the pub I've drunk in alone many a time, and along the promenade, and as we walked she asked again when I'd introduce her to the people in my life. I had to tell her that except for Rachel and Warren, and Luke and Lucy, there weren't too many others. There was Rob of course, but I couldn't exactly take her round to see him now.

I hadn't told Maya about his friendship with Hannah or how they lived together and decided now was a good time to get everything out in the open. I explained how they'd been joined at the hip since they were kids, that he'd recently separated from his long-term girlfriend and, after living with me for the shortest time, he'd now moved in with Hannah. I reiterated that I felt nothing for her, I was never in love with her, we weren't even a couple, but it must have got under her skin because she asked if I was ever like this with Hannah. I pulled her in front of me; I had to make her understand, Hannah was nothing to me.

I want *you* Maya. Only you.

# **Maya**

Hannah and Rob were best friends, and they lived together. Did it matter if she was still connected to Blaine? He felt nothing for her. So why was she now in my head? Did she want him the way I did? He said she was hurt when she discovered he was falling for someone else... He said he was falling for me, on Monday when we were in The Dog and Ferret. I repeated the words back to him, asking if they were true.

"I'm beyond falling for you," he replied. "I've fallen. I know it's soon, but I've never been surer of anything." And that was good, but did he make her think they had a future too? Was he like this with her? His response came immediately.

"No, it was nothing like this." He never saw anything beyond each moment with her. He never wanted to know everything about her, nor had he any inclination to meet or be accepted by her family. They never went anywhere together, and when his feelings for me became so intense so quickly it scared him. Only then did he take her out, and that was merely an attempt to distract himself from this "crazy-beautiful" girl he had met. He insisted he had spent the whole time wondering what it would be like to be sat there with me.

Pleading with me not to stew on it, he admitted to feeling guilty for doing that to her, adamant he only realised how she felt when it was too late. And just like on Monday it was hard not to believe him; he speaks with conviction, with passion in his eyes and his expressions.

I would never have imagined him making such an effort for me. The candles in jars that had lined the bridge now lined his hallway leading to the lounge and kitchen. Fresh flowers sat at the centre of the table, which was laid for two, and tall, thin table candles made the flowers cast dancing shadows on the table.

He cooked an impressive meal and showed me his home. Everything was clean and tidy, obsessively so. The décor perfectly matched his masculinity. The kitchen was a well-designed space with room for a dining table and an island with bar stools for casual eating. The walls were all white, the cupboards charcoal grey with stainless steel finishes.

The lounge hosted a similar colour palate to the kitchen. The furniture and fittings, even the rug on the wooden floor, were all strong geometric shapes. His bedroom felt warmer, with accents of brown in the artwork on the walls, copper cylinders topped with glass beside the bed for side-tables, matching copper and glass lamps on top. These rooms were not thrown together, they were carefully thought out.

His bed was made of thick planks of wood, the mattress sitting central on top, almost a foot of wood visible on either side and at its end. A thick, heavy-looking headboard of the same wood dominated the wall it occupied. It was the most masculine and beautifully rustic bed I have ever seen. I imagined waking up in it and Blaine being the perfect host, bringing me coffee in bed. I wondered how long it might be before we crossed that line and how it would feel. Would I feel like a little girl, out of my depth with this man who would expect more from me than I could deliver? Was it possible for this silly inexperienced girl to please him? I would bet Hannah knew exactly what to do.

I was quietly relieved when he suggested a walk. The seafront was pretty, illuminated in the darkness, boats swaying gently on the water among flashes of reflected light. He held my hand tight as we strolled and I asked when he would introduce me to the people in his life. That was when he told me about Hannah.

Back at home and lying in bed, struggling to calm my busy thoughts, I picked up my phone to message him. *When will you introduce me to your family?* I wondered if he might have fallen asleep, but eventually his reply came.

*My family are different to yours. You'll meet them, I promise, but in time.*

He had told me a little about his parents and that he had a brother and a sister, but they didn't sound so different. He had changed the subject quickly when I asked about his siblings; maybe they didn't get along so well. Maybe he had secrets and was worried they might let them out. I read the message several times but could decipher nothing more from it.

*Okay. Are you sure you want to come here to cook with Mum and meet Sissy and Henry on Sunday? I would understand if you wanted to give it a little more time.* I replied.

But he responded immediately. *Absolutely. I'm looking forward to learning some new tricks in the kitchen and meeting Sissy. I need to know if they created a second human as perfect as you.*

Seconds later another message came.

141

*P.S. Wish you were still here. I'd never rush you, but I also wonder what it would be like waking up next to you in my bed. No woman has ever spent the night in there you know. You'd be the first… and the only.*

Now I could sleep.

## Blaine

I considered tonight a success. No lines were crossed and now I could trust myself to be alone with her. Hopefully Sissy and Henry would be as accepting as Richard and Maggie. But I was not ready for the questions that would follow her meeting Rachel and Warren; they didn't even know about her yet. They'd be happy for me but they'd also want to meet her, then I'd be getting it from both sides.

# Chapter 18

## Saturday 19th November 2022

### Maya

After every visit something in me lingers, the feeling that he might be real. I had been walking through the park, the old couple were there, only I was alone and when the old man turned around he was in fact faceless. This time it was he who watched me, speaking quietly as though he did not want his lady companion to hear, only I couldn't hear him either. I moved towards him, but in true dream style the more I walked the further away they seemed to be.

His blurred mouth kept moving, repeating a muffled, unintelligible sentence in the hope I might decipher his words. But I could neither decipher them nor read his distorted lips. And with each step the ground became progressively muddier and harder to traverse until my feet began sinking. I could go no further and had no choice but to retreat onto dry grass, but as I turned away from him he screamed out.

"DON'T GIVE UP, MAYA".

The dream ended suddenly and I awoke, not frightened but curious. Who was he? I told Mum about it over breakfast while Dad gazed at the open newspaper. Saturday was his favourite day — no alarm clock, although he still got up early — and nowhere to rush to.

"Dreams are just your brain's way of processing what it absorbs," he contributed.

Mum agreed that it was indeed peculiar to dream repeatedly of the same unidentifiable person. Even more peculiar was the dreams starting right after meeting Blaine. But Dad was certain they were merely my brain processing the fears and emotions of a new relationship when my conscious mind succumbed to sleep.

Rebecca rang, ending the discussion about what the dreams might mean, and invited me to catch up over dinner later. The thought of not seeing Blaine tonight twisted my stomach but I agreed, then messaged Blaine, hoping he would visit his favourite lady at work this morning. His response came quickly.

*Wild horses couldn't keep me.*

And they did not. Rushing through the door soon after I arrived, he was in no hurry to leave and feigned a look of sadness when I told him of my plans with Rebecca. I suggested he spend the evening preparing for the family battering he'd be receiving tomorrow; it could be a long day for him cooking alongside Mum and facing a barrage of questions equivalent to being in front of a firing squad. He lifted his arm, flexed his bicep, and joked that he was strong enough to take it.

Before leaving he invited me to take lunch with him; I could think of nothing nicer and suggested taking it in here. Cold wintery air had chilled me when I left the house this morning and I didn't fancy sitting in the park. I didn't fancy seeing the old couple after last night's dream either, as unlikely as that may have been.

Recalling my dreams to Blaine over lunch, I asked if he had ever experienced reoccurring dreams himself. It turns out he had, for as long as he can remember. In his dream, he is watching TV. The location and subject vary from dream to dream, but every one ends the same, without him being able to see the outcome.

He asked what I thought mine might be about but I had no clue, I didn't know the faceless man and I couldn't place the theme of any of the dreams against the circumstances of my life. He said the same and deduced that he probably watched too much TV. He also decided the faceless man was most likely telling me to surrender myself to Blaine. He gave me a look that was half joking, half serious. I pulled him towards me and kissed him; I did want to surrender myself to him. My body tingled; I wanted him again. I wanted to know how being as close as you can possibly be to someone felt. He looked at me hard, the way he does with those intense eyes. I stared right back at him, imagining how he looked beneath the clothes.

"What? What are you thinking, Maya?" he said, snapping me from my thoughts. My cheeks burned as his face illuminated and his mouth turned up into a heartwarming smile.

"You're doing it again, aren't you? Thinking inappropriate things in inappropriate places," he said. Guilty.

My lunch break ended with his demand that I not think inappropriate thoughts about anyone else and somewhere in the middle of the afternoon he messaged: *Still behaving yourself I hope young lady.*

*Naturally*, I replied.

When I left work this evening he was leant against my car, smiling heartily. Scooping me up in his huge arms he said he wanted to give me something to keep me going until tomorrow, and with that he put me back on my feet and planted his lips against mine, a kiss so passionate my best behaviour wanted to rebel once more. If it were not completely dishonourable I would have rung Rebecca to cancel dinner and go home with him.

He requested I dream about him tonight and would be expecting the sordid details first thing in the morning. I didn't want him to go; I wanted to invite him along for the meal but resisted the urge. He opened my car door and gestured for me to get in, bending to kiss me one last brief time before closing my door and watching me drive away.

*\*\*\**

When Rebecca had finished talking about her studies and experiences at the hospital, she asked how things are going with Blaine. I described my desire to be intimate with him. Her exact words were, "For god's sake, Maya, get those bloody chastity knickers off and do it. You could die tomorrow. Do you really want to die a virgin?"

I laughed so hard the snort appeared, sucking a piece of half-chewed pasta into my throat and making me choke. The offending pasta shot across the table and Rebecca pleaded with me never to do that in front of Blaine or any other man, or a virgin death would be a certainty. Having recomposed myself, I confessed it had already aired itself in Blaine's presence but that it did not seem to have deterred him. She thought I should just go ahead and marry the man if he could tolerate that and still find me attractive. Anyone who didn't know her so well might have been offended.

## Blaine

A pang of jealousy gnawed my stomach at the thought of her having dinner with a friend. Images of other men looking at her the way I do teased my head. Her flawless skin, the way her eyes drew you in. How could other men not see her the way I did? If only I'd known how today would end I could have spared myself the torment.

We had lunch together at a table in Totally Coffee. She told me about her dreams and I told her about mine. She kissed me then gazed at me in silence; I knew she'd gone to that place again and called her out. I thought about that kiss and what she might have been thinking all afternoon, then waited for her after work to hold her for what I assumed would be the last time today.

I rang Rachel as a distraction and told her about Maya; she sounded somewhere between sceptical and happy. I explained that it was early days, too early to introduce them yet, but that I would. She nagged in her loving way to make sure I didn't take too long about it.

I'd barely hung up the phone when Rob rang, asking if he could come round. Hannah was out on a date and he was bored. Well, that's what he said, but he was pissed off and didn't hide his annoyance too well, mentioning her every ten minutes, saying how she didn't even know the guy and now she was out god knows where, doing god knows what with him.

He was about to roll a smoke when I stopped him. His face was a picture, but I can't risk it being the thing that puts Maya off. "Who the hell are you?" he asked. I was just someone trying to get it right this time.

A while later Hannah rang Rob, asking him to pick her up. He didn't say much more, only that he'd see me at work on Monday then wished me good luck for tomorrow and left. I was alone, with no distractions, thoughts of Maya being out without me filling my head. I would have driven myself crazy just sitting there so I showered, letting the hot water run over me while I stared at the tiled wall, trying hard to think of anything but Maya. Think of work, Blaine, think of anything. I thought of Rachel; she and Warren are the kindest people I know, they loved me unconditionally, gave me everything they had, and I was repaying them with distance. I owed them more than that.

I was thinking about going to bed early and watching a film in the hope it would send me to sleep when the door buzzer went. Assuming it was Rob, back for something he'd forgotten, I threw a towel around my middle and answered.

# Rachel and Warren

"He's met someone, Warren."

"You mean a woman? He's met several of them."

"This sounds different. He doesn't usually ring to announce it. He rings to check up on us and make sure we're okay. He rings on the rare occasion he wants to come round. Then he mentions his latest conquest because we pressure him into telling us. He'll be okay, won't he?"

"What did he say about her?"

"That he's met a girl and that she's pretty special."

"Special?"

"Exactly!"

"What else did he say?"

"That we'll love her, but he's not ready to introduce us yet."

"You can't blame him for that, love. You don't know how much he's told her about himself. Bringing her here's a big step, one he'll have to talk about and let's face it, he's never been a talker. He'll do it when he's ready."

"I know. I just want to see him happy with someone. He was such a kind boy, all things considered."

# Maya

I can't explain what happened after leaving Rebecca, at least not from a rational perspective, but she was right. It was cold and dark; the roads were quiet and the moon shone bright over the houses and trees. There was only one place I wanted to be. I parked the car and stood at his door, an outstretched finger hovering over the buzzer. No thoughts, just a racing heart and the feeling of being present in the moment. I pressed the buzzer, committing myself to the impulse.

The door opened and he stood with confusion on his face. He was wet, just a towel around his waist, his chest and arms covered in tattoos, all of them as beautiful as his muscular body and dark skin. An intricately detailed eagle spanned his chest, its wings spread wide as though in flight, and pictures and patterns covered the rest of his flesh. There was so much to take in. I felt not an ounce of regret at coming here; I felt alive, I felt like a woman. He was beautiful and I was certain I was ready.

# Blaine

Hers wasn't the face I expected. I was naked except for the towel and we were alone. There were no words or explanations, she just walked in, slid her hands around my neck and kissed me. The smell of her coursed through me; the feel of her against me charged my skin like electricity.

A voice in my head screamed "stop"; I was supposed to be resisting until she was ready, only she looked and felt so ready. I responded to her kiss; it was deep and wanting, her hands were holding the back of my head, pulling my face into hers. We were in the open doorway, then we were ambling down the hallway towards the bedroom, wrapped in each other's arms. I pulled away, not to stop her but to make sure she wanted to do this as much as I did. She whispered into my ear.

"Please, don't stop. I want this more than anything, I want you more than anything."

We reached the bedroom where she unbuttoned her blouse and skirt, letting them fall to the floor, revealing mismatched underwear, a perfectly shaped body and pure, unmarked skin. Her breasts were small and perfect. Stepping towards me, she pressed herself against me, and I was harder than ever. She wanted me and I was incapable of resisting her.

## Maya

He did not resist my advances but pulled back to look at my face and ask if I was sure. The feel of his skin beneath my hands made me tingle all over; his muscular body, his arms powerful enough to lift me from my feet, yet so gentle they barely moved me. I was sure.

Engaged in a sensual dance down the hall and into his bedroom, we were locked in each other's arms and in the most passionate kiss. I had feared him being disappointed at the sight of my body, but now I wanted him inside me, even at the risk of it hurting.

Blaine guided me onto the bed as though I were made of glass, as though the slightest wrong move might break me. My heart was thumping hard when he placed his hand flat on my chest and asked why I was nervous. I told him this was my first time. He sat up, his head falling into his hands. He had no idea. I had thought my virginity was obvious when I described my abysmal dating history, but he looked back at me with the softest expression and said, "You're a virgin? And you want to do this with me?"

I had been quite convincing up to that point but felt like the silly girl out of her depth again. Nonetheless I wanted him and rose up onto my knees beside him. We were face-to-face and I had never been more certain of anything. I straddled his lap, insisting that my mind would not be changed, that I was falling fast and that his honest intent was enough to make me believe this would only bring us closer. We kissed again; his hands explored my body. We became a single entity. I pressed myself against him and all my fear was gone. I just wanted him.

His practised fingers made light work of my bra, pulling it from me before pushing me back just far enough for him to lower his head and explore my breasts with his mouth, his hand on the small of my back supporting me. Losing myself in the moment I pushed harder against him. He kissed between my breasts then up my chest to my neck. I felt him entering me. His eyes closed as he let out a groan. It didn't hurt as I had expected, rather a feeling of euphoria pulsed through my entire body. He held me still, unable to move, just frozen on him. Frozen with him. His hands ran through my hair then swept it away from my face to look at me.

There we stayed, moving rhythmically up and down, perfectly in tune with one another; I was drowning in him but in a beautiful way. I was overwhelmed with love and passion. I did not care that it had only been a week, it didn't feel cheap or rushed. It certainly didn't feel as though it was going to ruin anything. On the contrary, I knew then that Blaine was my forever and was certain I would think of nothing else from now on.

He was looking into my eyes when he lifted me off him with absolute ease, laying me down on my back, hovering above me, kissing me all over. His warm lips worked their way down my body until he reached between my legs. There he stayed until the most intense feeling rose in my groin. I pulled at his shoulders and he didn't resist, just worked his way back up the bed until we were face to face, then kissed me deeply as he pressed himself back inside me. His strokes were slow and gentle; my whimpers grew louder until the feeling inside me exploded. Burying his head in my neck he groaned, freezing deep inside me for the longest moment before pulling back just a little, his lips pursing to kiss my neck. I laid wrapped around him, still holding on tight. It was so much more than I ever dreamed it would be. In that moment I felt as though I never wanted to let him go.

A long and comfortable silence later he lifted his head, looked into my eyes and asked if I was okay while lifting rogue hairs away from my eyes. He looked worried, so I reassured him that I had never been more okay, and he rolled onto the bed, pulling my head onto his chest and my body close against his. With his arms around me, holding me tight, he kissed my head over and over and told me this was where we belonged, forever.

# Blaine

Taking a woman's virginity — every man's dream, right? Well, not mine. Taking something so precious is only for the worthy, surely. How could I be worthy? Yet she considered me so.

Every second we were in tune with one another, immersed in every single moment. This was my forever, there wouldn't be another after this. Maya was where my promiscuity ended. The thought of coming inside another nobody, that feeling of wanting them to leave, I didn't want that again. I remembered those final times with Hannah when all I could see was Maya. It changed how it felt, like the sex was better if I thought about Maya. But nothing compared to tonight.

I couldn't bear the thought of her getting up and leaving me. I wanted to feel her skin against me all night; I wanted her perfect face to be the first thing I saw in the morning, so I took the second risk of the evening and asked her to stay.

# Chapter 19

## Sunday 20th November 2022

### **Maya**

The perfect night rolled into the perfect morning. I would like to say I slept soundly all night, but I had woken hourly. It felt alien to be held all night. Even in his sleep he sensed my efforts to escape his grasp, guiding me back into his embrace each time I rolled into a more comfortable position. But as tired as I was I revelled in his want for me.

The answer had been simple when he asked me to stay: I wanted nothing more. How could I leave? And when I told him I would have to let my parents know he had replied, "Of course," and got up to fetch my phone, gracing my eyes with the full glory of his tattooed, naked being as he left the room. All of the images adorning his body perfectly complemented his dark skin. His dedication to the gym was evident, his body perfectly sculpted, yet there was no arrogance about this man who epitomised male beauty.

When I opened my eyes for the final time this morning, Faceless had been back, standing at the foot of Blaine's bed with a chilling and uncannily timed message.

"He's inside you now. You have been inside him since the first time he saw you and you must do what I cannot. Save him, Maya. Please. For me. For him."

Waking with a start, my eyes scanned the space Faceless had occupied. Blaine was asleep. He was sweating, his face twitching and his eyes flickering under closed eyelids. I touched his cheek and called his name. He woke, sitting upright in a split second, looking panicked.

He touched my face, kissed me lightly on the lips and thanked God I was okay. His dream had been about me, another film and I was the lead role, alone in a house as a boy watched me through a window. He could see a man inside the house, coming for me, but could not find a way in to protect me. Both the front and back doors were locked and none of the windows would open. I had screamed as the man inside entered the room I was in. The boy had turned to look at the TV screen, as though talking directly to Blaine.

"You don't need to see this, look away."

But he couldn't look away because it was me and he needed to know I was safe. The boy picked up a rock from the ground, hitting and shattering a windowpane. As Blaine watched him climb through to save me, the TV screen began to flicker, distorting the scene. That was when I had touched his face and woken him. We laid in silence for a while, processing the relevance of our dreams. I could not tell him what Faceless had said.

He got up, pulled on some sweatpants and disappeared to the kitchen. I contemplated joining him but sat up to take in the details of his room instead. No photos in here either, but the bed really was quite magnificent and when Blaine re-entered the room with a tray of coffee and croissants I questioned him about it. He told me how he made it himself, with some help from Rob, how the wood was reclaimed timber and how the project took them more than a week of evenings to complete. It was a bed to envy and looked significantly more impressive while sitting in it.

Breakfast was good; having it delivered to me by a gorgeous man was better. Knowing I was no longer a virgin and that my first time was probably what all girls dreamt of felt heavenly. He had not been appalled at the sight of my body, nor had he been put off by my lack of experience. He was honoured that I gave it to him. And that was exactly what I wanted to feel.

I wondered if he was prepared for today; he looked too relaxed, laying there in bed, and I doubted if he would appear so when we got to the house. I contemplated how Dad might behave knowing I spent the night here; I didn't want Blaine to feel uncomfortable. He had not asked me to go to him after dinner with Rebecca; he certainly would not have seduced me had I turned up with innocent intent.

No more am I Maya the immature or Maya the singleton. I am Maya who does the walk of shame after spending the night with her boyfriend. Her devastatingly handsome boyfriend. It was the first time I had thought of the word "boyfriend", and I said it aloud. Blaine looked at me askance. He said he preferred the term "lovers" but I am not sure how Dad would feel about that and so suggested he did not announce that today.

## Blaine

She'd made her way into the dream, turning it into a nightmare. I thought I was scared of moving too quickly and losing her, but that wasn't it. This was what I was scared of; her being so deeply inside me that I can't go back. Because there was no going back now. How could I think about anything else now I'd been inside her?

She was naked and beautiful and smelled more enticing than I could bear. I wanted to be inside her again but didn't know if I could control myself in a way that was appropriate for someone who only lost their virginity last night, so I left the room to make breakfast, hoping with all my might that she'd be dressed when I re-entered the bedroom.

A ball of anxiety tightened in my gut at the thought of facing Richard today. He took the time to warm to me and I repaid him by taking his daughters virginity a week after gaining her trust, just days after gaining his. How could I look at him now? It'd be guilt in my eyes not integrity or honour. I was going to move mountains, and I couldn't even control myself when she tempted me.

She was still in bed looking around the room when I returned with breakfast. The quilt was tucked tight under her arms, her shoulders small and inviting called me to them. I knew if I kissed them there'd be no going back. She asked questions about the man-bed, as Rob called it, distracting me for a few short moments before I disappeared to the shower, leaving her to eat.

When I returned she was sitting on the edge of the bed, half dressed, just her legs exposed, asking if she could shower. I used the time to iron a shirt, all the while thinking about her standing naked and wet in my bathroom. When she came to me she was dressed and apologising for using my shower gel, so I suggested we get her some bits of her own to leave here. Looking at me all dewy-eyed she asked if I really wanted her stuff around the place already. I couldn't think of anything nicer than entering a room and seeing reminders of her.

## The Elders

"Her love is powerful, maybe even enough to awaken him. All we can do is observe and be ready."

"I thought the same thing once upon a time. I believed that loving a beautiful woman was all I needed, that her purity would cure my pain. Maya's love alone will not be enough. She has to know she can save him. I can show her."

"She can do no such thing. We will protect her the same way we protected Angela."

"You did not protect her; you punished her for protecting the one she loved most."

"It has been her lesson in selflessness, compassion, in the purest form of love. Angela is succeeding where you failed. That is why she too will be one of us."

## Blaine

She didn't have the same beauty about her and her eyes didn't bore into your soul, but Sissy was every bit as pure as her sister. I was a fish out of water amongst these unscathed people who welcomed me into their lives like they trusted Maya to pick someone worthy of them. And no one mentioned her staying with me last night; not even Richard.

Maggie led me to the kitchen to get started soon after we arrived, excited to cook with me. Maya had disappeared upstairs, reappearing at the kitchen door in a soft grey jumper and blue jeans with ripped knees, hair pulled up into a high ponytail, exposing the full beauty of her make-up free face, the most casual I'd seen her since we met. It suited her, proper Sunday clothes.

Sissy and Henry joined us in the kitchen. Sissy made tea while Henry asked questions about my job. I couldn't tell if he was genuinely interested or attempting to make me feel better about my menial role. He played his own job down, attributing his success to nepotism; it was his father's company and he was on his way to being CEO. He was humble about it, like he needed me to know he hadn't worked hard for it. He was a nice guy but different to the ones I knew. I tried to picture him sitting with me and Rob, certain he'd feel as out of place as I did right then. But they couldn't have tried any harder to make me feel at ease; any discomfort was mine alone.

Maggie shared stories about Maya, who flitted in and out of the kitchen, half-listening and wholly embarrassed. Stories about how she'd always been a kind girl, putting others before herself. She said how good we looked together; how happy she is that Maya found me and how she just knew we were meant to be together. Sissy agreed, smiling at me with real warmth.

Maya laid the table while Maggie and I dished. She'd already warned me not to clean up the mess, that was Sissy and Henry's job. It was a family effort here. Richard didn't join in, but it seemed their roles were traditional. Maggie didn't work; Richard was the bread winner and I assumed it was his entitlement to relax and be waited on at the weekend; after all, he'd kept everyone in this lovely lifestyle.

Sissy told me she and Henry had been trying for a baby. Maya overheard and suggested they'd benefit from a dirty weekend away but both Sissy and Henry looked horrified at the thought. Maggie nudged Richard, telling him they could probably benefit from one too. He rolled his eyes and Maya pretended to gag at the thought.

Everyone complimented the dinner and Richard decided I should help Maggie every Sunday. I suggested they come to my place for a meal so I could return their kindness. Maggie looked thrilled and Richard agreed; he'd love to see what I'd done with the place. I told him about the photos I took following the process from the day I moved in to completing the renovation. Henry asked who'd done all the work and was impressed to hear I'd done most of it myself, with a little help from Rob and the occasional skilled tradesmen.

Maya revelled in telling them all about it, going into detail about the bespoke bed. Richard's face turned serious, but everyone else was listening intently, Maggie even suggested I make bespoke furniture as a side-hustle. Richard didn't offer anything to that conversation, presumably wishing the subject would change so he could get the image of his daughter in my bed out of his head.

After everything was eaten and cleared away Richard suggested a swift one or two at The Dog and Ferret and Maggie invited me to spend the night rather than driving home. With that, a cab was ordered and off we all went. The barman greeted Richard, asking him about work and acknowledging the family had grown by one. He didn't ask what he wanted to drink, just poured a whiskey and put it on the bar in front of him. Maggie was given the choice of red or white wine, plumping for red after a moment's deliberation. Sissy requested a lemonade, raising an eyebrow or two, and Henry and Maya both chose a glass of white before he turned his attention to me, asking what the new man of the family drank. I joined Richard in a whiskey; he clinked the side of my glass with his and said, "Welcome to the family, Blaine."

Chit-chat turned to talk about a forthcoming family holiday to some Christmas village in Scotland. Discomfort rose in my gut; a week without seeing her and it was only a couple of weeks away too. I tried suppressing the feeling but it quickly overwhelmed me.

Why hadn't she mentioned it? When was she planning to tell me she'll be gone for a whole week? It took a concerted effort to hide what was going on inside my head; I didn't want these lovely people to think badly of me. I'd never felt like this about Hannah, I didn't care where she went, that was why it was easy with her. I never had to come to this place. Yet here I was, feeling something vile in the pit of my stomach. Maya was smiling at me with adoration; surely I had nothing to fear. I just needed to put this down and not worry about her being away from me.

When last orders were drunk we returned to Richard and Maggie's in a taxi. Richard refused my offer to pay for it but I'd managed to get a round in at least. We all headed straight for bed and I felt as on edge as a teenage boyfriend staying over for the first time. I knew nothing could happen under this roof but I needed to feel Maya against me. And I needed to know how I was going to cope without her for a week. I needed to know why she hadn't told me.

## Chapter 20

## Monday 21st November 2022

### **Maya**

Dad had acted with the utmost decorum all day, despite not being as elated as I at the prospect of Blaine staying the night. After The Dog and Ferret we all made for bed, with the exception of Mum who headed to the kitchen to potter. Blaine gripped my hand as though he feared getting lost on the way to my room. Shutting the door, he pulled me into him, whispering how he had been dying to hold me all day. He pushed his lips against mine, gently backing me up against the closed door. The kiss was long and deep; I wanted more, but he was going no further. Just holding me, kissing me, looking into my eyes and kissing me again.

 Stepping back, he kept hold of my hands and asked how he was going to live without me for a whole week. His face was pained, his eyes sad. I have been so swept up in us that I had completely forgotten to tell him about the holiday. He had consumed my every thought, leaving little room for anything else. Next year, if he could stand it, he could come with us.

Coaxing him down onto the edge of my bed I straddled his lap and unbuttoned his shirt, already certain he would not accept my advances. His chest was beautiful: muscular, tattooed, mine. His skin smelled divine and as I slipped his shirt over his shoulders my lips were drawn to his neck. But he interrupted my hunger for him by asking for a glass of water and reluctantly I climbed off his lap.

Mum was extracting wilting flowers from the vases on the windowsill when I entered the kitchen. She thought Blaine was perfect and said if she were to pick me a man from a line-up of candidates she would not choose the best dressed man or the highest earner, she would pick the man who looked at me the way Blaine does. Then with a devious grin she added that the fact he is a living Adonis is just a total bonus. Apparently she felt his arm when she led him to the kitchen this morning and wished Dad had arms like that; she could only imagine what was going on underneath his shirt. We giggled like schoolgirls as she made me promise not to tell Dad.

I returned to a waiting Blaine; how odd to open my door and see such a gorgeous man lying in my bed. I told him what Mum had said then, picking up my phone, saw that Sissy had messaged. Well, Blaine just seems to have every woman's attention.

*Good god, Maya, he's bloody gorgeous (Don't tell Henry I said that!). And you look fabulous together... Not at all jealous of course xxx*

I turned the phone towards Blaine, showing him the message. He swore he had never had such an effect on women before, although I was certain he must have done. Pulling me onto the bed he peeled off my jumper, undid my jeans and slid them down my legs. I wanted him again and didn't care about Mum and Dad being so close by. But he simply pulled me into his arms and held me tight against him, the fingers of one hand lightly stroking my skin as the others teased through my hair.

"I want to, Maya, but I can't, not here. Your parents have been so gracious, I couldn't betray their generosity."

The next thing I knew was my alarm signalling morning from the bedside table. Blaine was awake, lying in the same position we had fallen asleep in with his arms tight around me. Somehow, I had slept like that the whole night; maybe the wine had helped. His fingers were still stroking my skin and when I asked if he had been doing that all night he replied, "Maybe."

Breakfast became a family affair. Mum prepared an impressive spread of croissants, pancakes, cereals and fresh juice, enough to feed an army. She stopped what she was doing as we entered the room and gushed with pride, telling us how beautiful we looked together. Blaine blushed; Dad turned to Sissy and Henry, assuring them they looked beautiful too, but Sissy reminded him they were old news now, conceding that they probably didn't look as hot as us. Henry eyed Blaine from head to toe before agreeing with her, and everyone, including Dad, dissolved into fits of giggles.

The sky was clear and the air cold and wintery when we stepped outside. I shivered and Blaine wrapped me in his arms, the heat from his body instantly warming me. Holding me tight he asked if he could take me to dinner tonight. Of course I agreed, but didn't want to wait that long so he promised to visit me at work; after all, how could he stay away knowing I was just across the road? I thought of Ruby; she was sure to want to hear about my eventful weekend.

I thought about the holiday too. The more time we spent together the less I wanted to be apart. If only we had met a little sooner he could have come with us. For the first time I was not looking forward to our family holiday quite so much.

## Blaine

Resisting her was the hardest thing; undressing me, kissing me like a temptress. But I wasn't about to make them regret inviting me to stay the night. She'd fallen asleep in my arms, but each time I drifted off I woke with a start and a sick feeling in my gut, fear about her being away.

Richard and Maggie were generous hosts, feeding everyone well before work and it was nice being part of a real family, even if I was the outsider again. I was sure in time that this would feel as normal to me as it looked for Henry. He shared the story of how he and Sissy met, how Richard and Maggie welcomed him into their house and treated him like one of their own. They seem to be doing the same for me.

Their warmth towards one another made me think of Rachel and Warren, of how much they'd love meeting Maya. I reached out, giving her leg a playful squeeze under the table. I just needed to feel her and remind myself that she really was mine. She stroked the back of my hand, sliding her fingers in between mine, and her touch sent shivers through my body.

Light-hearted chatter flowed around the breakfast table, including the revelation that Maya and I looked hotter together than Sissy and Henry. I remembered the words of both Maggie and Sissy last night and felt myself blushing. It was nice to be popular but I'm not entirely sure it's appropriate when it's your girlfriend's family. "Girlfriend"; it's a funny word, not a strong enough description. We felt more like souls with an indefinable connection, lovers brought together by a twist of fate, never to be separated, unless fate had other ideas.

*\*\*\**

Rob looked a mess when he crawled into work; I've no idea how he stayed upright on his bike all the way here. Too much tequila last night, Hannah's influence no doubt, secured him an appointment with the toilet bowl just moments after arriving. I left him to it and went to fetch coffee: merely an excuse to see Maya but he looked like he needed it.

My goddess, a picture of perfect beauty, stood beside Ruby. They were deep in conversation and I had a feeling I knew what they were discussing. Maya blushed when she saw me and Ruby's response only confirmed my suspicion. Shooting me a knowing smile, she raised an eyebrow in an "I know what you've been up to" kind of way. Maya mischievously nudged her out of the way, demanding she stop flirting with her man. That sounded better than boyfriend.

An image of a diamond heart sitting in the recess at the bottom of her throat, small and delicate like her, flashed in my mind's eye again. Taking the coffees back to work, I made my excuses and disappeared into town. I knew just the jewellers I needed; there were a few in Woodbridge but there's this little one with a good reputation for quality. The window was full of sparkling pieces and the perfect necklace winked at me from a purple velvet tray. It wasn't exactly as I'd pictured, but I could picture it on her. I'd imagined yellow gold; this one hung on a white gold chain, the diamond heart set in a white-gold surround. Neither too big for her delicate features nor too small to say what I needed it to. It was perfect and she was worth every penny of the price tag.

## **Maya**

Listening intently, a gleam that suggested she might like to be romanced herself occupied Ruby's eyes. Blaine caught us in the middle of my rundown of the weekend, ordering his usual and a black coffee for Rob who'd arrived hungover. He scribbled on his receipt, folded it neatly and pushed it back across the counter and, with one last smouldering look, turned to leave. A small yet perfectly neat heart sat at the bottom of the receipt.

Sometime later he messaged saying he had reserved a table for two in his kitchen this evening; the thought of us being alone again made my head spin. I didn't want to repeat the mismatched underwear ensemble he had to suffer on Saturday. No, something matching tonight: the pink lacey set. What I really needed was something more alluring. Ironic, considering that just a few weeks ago I had feared dying a spinster.

The thought of my life pre-Totally Coffee, pre-Blaine, overwhelmed me, so I replied telling him I couldn't wait until we were alone and how I hated the thought of not seeing him or feeling him ever again. He replied immediately, asking why I would I say such a thing. I confessed how deep my feelings for him had become in such a short space of time. Another instant reply: he felt exactly the same. I thought about Blaine all afternoon. I thought about the man in my dreams too; not intentionally, he just kept appearing in my head.

During a lull in customers a man in an oversized coat, maybe forty-something, entered and sat at a table. He did not place an order yet sat not far from the counter, watching me, a look of pain on his face that reminded me of Blaine. I smiled but he looked away and shortly after left, with neither a word nor a smile. Right outside the shop he stopped to speak with none other than the elderly couple from the park and as they spoke they all looked through the window, directly at me, as though it were me they were discussing. Feeling somewhat self-conscious I busied myself cleaning and when I looked back all three had gone.

Mum was cooking beef cobbler when I arrived home. I hoped she wouldn't be too disappointed about my absence this evening. She shot me her sad look; she had rather hoped Blaine might come here again so she could feed us all. I promised we would do that soon but I wanted him to myself after sharing him with everyone yesterday. Suddenly she looked proud, asking if I would be coming home tonight. But I couldn't answer because I didn't know; I hoped not and assured her I would inform her if that were the case.

After showering and thinking of little else but tonight, I put on the pink underwear. It was more pretty than sexy, but it was the best I had. I chose the floaty black dress with the tiny pink flower print and angel sleeves, finished with a pair of pink, low-heeled sandals and my hair hanging down in soft curls. The "staying in but hoping to get lucky" look.

It was cold outside but there was little hope of getting a coat over the dress sleeves. For the first time since spring every exhale of breath hung in the air. The trees on the driveway looked bare and the damp lawn had a covering of fallen leaves. The gardener must have been due soon to take care of that.

Blaine answered the door looking and smelling amazing. Beyond him I could smell something cooking; it too smelled good but all I wanted was him. Still in the open doorway he kissed me and as he pulled away said, "Don't ever think about not being with me, Maya; I can't bear the thought of it either."

Is it too soon to be falling in love? Is that what he had implied when he drew the heart on his receipt this morning? Had I asked him, he would most likely have said, "It is never too soon," only I couldn't bring myself to say it. It was most likely infatuation, the brain releasing chemicals because you met someone new, chemicals that made you feel as though you couldn't live without them. In time, the chemical release reduced and then you knew whether you really loved them or not. I guess that was what Sissy meant.

Just like on Saturday, the chemistry was undeniable. We kissed again, neither able to stop. I didn't want to eat; I wanted to feel like one connected entity. Kicking the front door shut, his hands lifted my dress and stroked the bare skin of my legs before sliding up to my waist. I breathed him in and lost myself to the feeling. He picked me up, my legs around his middle, kissing me as though his life depended upon it, and carried me to the bedroom once again. I succumbed to his lead.

We made love for the second time; he was just as gentle and loving as the first, and as we lay comfortable and satisfied I could not shake the feeling of not wanting to lose him. The fear made me hold him tighter, stroking his skin and locking the memory in my mind.

Prising me off of him, much to my obvious dismay, he said he had something for me and left the room in his beautiful naked glory. Moments later he returned, climbing onto the bed, pulling me into a sitting position and handing me a small, silver-grey box. Staring intensely at me, that pained expression once again, he motioned for me to open it, observing my every movement. Inside, a diamond heart hung from a white-gold chain. Blaine reached into the box and took out the necklace, placing it around my neck, kissing my skin as he fastened the clasp. I pressed the heart against my skin with the tips of my fingers; I could carry him with me every moment of every day. When our eyes reconnected I knew that was his intention.

For a long moment he sat looking at it and never has so much been said in complete silence. Raising his hand, he gently slid his fingers through mine, joining me in holding the heart against my skin. Wrapping his other hand around the back of my head he pulled me into him, kissing me, still holding the heart against my skin. My confidence swelled and I rose up, pushing him to the bed and climbing astride him as though I had done this a hundred times before. He obliged my control and we made love again until the loudest noise, an alarm, tore through our ears, killing the moment. Blaine looked horrified as he shouted over the racket, "Shit, dinner's burning."

The most passionate of moments was ruined by the ensuing chaos and the smell of burnt pastry. How had we not smelled it sooner? Following Blaine to the kitchen I waved a tea towel frantically at the smoke alarm in a bid to stop the noise, but after a minute of flapping and continued noise I realised he was staring at me, not moving, just transfixed on me. I was naked, stark-bollock naked. My cheeks glowed with embarrassment. His expression softened as he strode towards me, lifting me off my feet and placing me gently down on the kitchen table where he finished making love to me, despite the noise.

It was in this exact moment that I no longer felt like a girl. I was a woman. A woman who, in the face of chaos, had kitchen sex with her gorgeous man!

## Blaine

The noise was thunderous in my ears but I couldn't move for the sight of her. The heart around her neck looked just as I imagined, familiar and connecting. Only this time the heart was mine, no doubt about it.

Frantically flapping my tea towel at the smoke detector, completely in vain, she hadn't realised how dumbstruck by her beauty I was. Dinner was ruined but it didn't matter; I had her heart, who needed dinner anyway?

Eventually she realised the futility of the towel flapping, suddenly embarrassed at being naked in my kitchen with me gawping at her. Ignoring the noise and the smell of burning beef wellington, I picked her up and finished making love to her on the kitchen table.

# Chapter 21

## Tuesday 22nd November 2022

### **Maya**

My hand reached for the heart, my fingers holding it against my skin. Blaine was awake, lying on his side, smiling at me. Brushing the hair from my face he leaned over to kiss my cheek. "Good morning, beautiful," he whispered softly.

His words and expression stirred something that made me pull him towards me. There was something inexplicably beautiful about his eyes. Not just their colour or shape, but something indefinable in the way he looked at me. As though he saw something that lured him, or maybe scared him. Whatever it was, it was beautiful. We kissed in a way there was no coming back from and as he slipped inside me he looked hard at my face and I was lost in him once again. Two separate beings becoming one. This had to be my forever; I couldn't be without him now.

*\*\*\**

Leaping from the bed enthusiastically and holding out his hand he led me to the shower. Another defining moment: I was also the woman who showered with her gorgeous man after breakfast sex. I had not thought it possible for him to look any better, yet under the flow of steaming water he looked as though he belonged in a pin-up calendar. I thought of Rebecca and how proud she would be. I had to tell her I'd taken her advice to throw caution to the wind, but it would have to wait until later.

Blaine reminisced about how good his wellington might have been while I dried myself, and when he boasted about his homemade pastry an idea came to me. I wasn't sure how Mum would feel, given her aversion to pastry, but it would be great if he could teach her how to make it. Blaine was up for the challenge; I just needed to convince Mum.

She was waiting for me in the kitchen, staring expectantly, wanting the juicy details, and although we share everything I felt uncomfortable about telling her the particulars of my new sex life. I started gently, describing the way he looked at me. She suggested that what I saw in his eyes was a deep appreciation of me, then asked what I knew about him, but the truth was I knew very little. He did not volunteer anything about himself or his family and lived quite a solitary life. I recalled that Rob had said the same thing: he had known him a while yet knew little of his history or personal life. But men do not chat the way women do and I had not read too much into it. There must have been more to him than just work, working out and cooking.

Mum looked deeply offended when I suggested Blaine could teach her to make pastry but admitted it was her only Achilles heel in the kitchen.

I was not sure if it was the thought of being able to successfully make pastry or being able to cook with Blaine again that won her over, but she agreed on the condition they do it at his place so Dad could inspect Blaine's handywork.

## Blaine

I woke at four a.m. Another film dream. A woman in need of my help; I didn't know what for. Her face was close to the screen, her eyes pleading with me, her mouth moving, her expression desperate, but I couldn't hear her. The screen flickered and went blank, and that was it. A fleeting thought to sneak out and smoke crossed my mind, but I wasn't willing to risk it. Instead, I laid in silent awe, not taking my eyes off her until after six when she woke, my mind torturing me all the while over this impending holiday. Visions of her meeting someone else or realising she didn't want me after a few days without me played over and over, and once a train of thought was in motion I was powerless to stop it; I just had to let it free-roll out of the station until it ran out of steam. Each pointless barrage of thoughts ended with the same conclusion: not Maya, she wouldn't do that. Then within minutes another pointless destructive scenario began playing out in my head.

The relief when she finally woke up, her fingers reaching for the heart, making sure it was still there. All that worry for nothing. I wanted to be inside her again, to really feel her, and as she looked over at me it was suddenly clear: that's what it was, I could feel when I was with her. The numbness that blighted me wasn't there when she was here. Her eyes acted like a power button; that was why she paralysed me that first time I saw her. She switched something back on inside me.

Today felt like the right time to introduce her to Rachel and Warren; they'd love her and she'd love them. She'd ask questions but it wasn't like she could never know. I was hardly the first person it had happened to and maybe Rachel would answer some of the questions for me, then I'd only have to explain why I didn't tell her myself. But instinct told me she'd understand.

Rachel was thrilled when I rang to say we'd call round later and Maya looked as excited as Rachel had sounded when I suggested taking her to meet them. Rachel had offered dinner but I didn't want to be stuck there just in case. I wanted to test the water, start getting things out in the open.

## Maya

When I messaged Rebecca, inviting her to lunch tomorrow, I didn't anticipate needing to see her quite as much as I do now.

After making love and showering together, Blaine had suggested buying a toothbrush and whatever else I needed to leave at his place, adding that we could do it on our way home from visiting the people who raised him. I sensed the discomfort as he talked about his family. Who referred to their parents as "the people who raised me"? But I was happy he wanted us to meet and eager to know what kind of people parented this intense, gorgeous man.

In Ruby's absence I spent the day serving with Amber. She noticed the heart around my neck and, guessing it was from Blaine, asked countless questions. We chatted and laughed all day; she imparted endless anecdotes about Rupert, including his new obsession with Father Christmas and being on his best behaviour to ensure a place on the nice list.

She reminded me of our mutual agreement to double date again, so after messaging Drew and Blaine respectively and arranging a sleepover for Rupert with his nanny, it was arranged for Saturday night. Amber booked a table at The Orange Tree, assuring me the food there was to die for, and decided we could go back to the bar on the high street after.

The day flew by and soon enough we were locking the doors of Totally Coffee. One of the barista boys had informed us today that the name of the place had been decided following an argument between the owners, Julian and Ralph. They were brothers who, as young men, had dreamed of owning a tea shop, a hangout for the locals, somewhere they could socialise themselves. It would serve a broad selection of teas and cakes and play music.

But as the years rolled by, trends evolved and coffee shops became more fashionable than tea houses. Ralph still fantasised about a tea shop but Julian, the more astute of the two, wanted a business that would make them enough money to retire comfortably. During one of their arguments Julian demanded, "Get with the times, Ralph; what do you think is going to sell more by the cup, tea or coffee?" to which Ralph had conceded, "It is totally coffee," and that apparently was that.

The irony of the story was that neither brother had ever worked here. One of them was rumoured to have ended up in prison, and the other, Ralph, rarely visited, leaving the running of the place to the very competent Ruby.

Blaine was waiting at my car, watching me walk towards him, his expression softening with each step I took. His hand reached for mine and, pulling me into his chest, he kissed me softly on the forehead and said, "I'll miss you every second until I pick you up. Is seven o'clock okay?"

He assured me that Rachel and Warren would love me and suggested grabbing food after as we wouldn't be there too long.

## Rachel and Warren

"Did you notice the heart, Warren?"

"The heart?"

"Around her neck."

"No, I missed it. Do you think he bought it for her? Bit more than a coincidence if he did."

"That's what I thought. Beautiful though, isn't she? Not how I pictured her at all; I assumed he'd end up with someone more like him."

"Like him?"

"You know, someone who's lived a bit, who's seen things. I saw the way he looks at her though, like he's never letting her go."

"I noticed that. And I saw the way she looked at us and all the pictures when she came in. Didn't take more than a few seconds for the penny to drop."

"She didn't say anything though. Do you think he's getting the Spanish inquisition now?"

"Probably. I'd be curious if I were her."

"I wonder how he'll cope with the questions. He's not one to justify himself, but I think he just might with her. Don't you, Warren?"

"I think you might be right, love."

## Chapter 22

### Wednesday 23rd November 2022

### **Maya**

"So, how's it going with Mr Hot?" Rebecca asked no sooner had we sat down to eat. Had we lunched yesterday my response would have been entirely different. Gushy, proud of my new sexually active status, I would have imparted every last detail and attributed it all to her candid advice. Instead, I was unsure how to respond. I still feel those things, but they didn't make as much sense as they had. How could you share such intimacy with someone yet omit to tell them a fundamental part of who you were? I let him take my virginity, but he couldn't tell me who he really was.

Rebecca pressed for an answer and, when I still could not formulate one, said, "What is it, Maya? What's he done?"

The truth was he hadn't done anything, but I felt he had become a little out of reach. I explained how I took her advice, arriving at Blaine's unannounced after having dinner with her, pouncing on him in his own doorway. She beamed from ear to ear, asking questions so quickly I didn't have time to answer before the next one came.

"What was it like? Was he as shocked as I am right now? Did he even know you were a virgin?"

As I told her all about it some of the excitement returned. He had turned my life upside down in the best way possible; he had made me feel and want things I never had before. Rebecca looked delighted, saying she would forever take the credit for the vixen I had become.

We caught up to last night, to meeting Rachel and Warren, who were the nicest people. Rachel hugged me warmly and Warren told me how thrilled he was to meet me. I was drawn to the wealth of family photos in their hallway, a contrast to the minimalist style of Blaine's flat. Pictures of the five of them taken on family holidays, at Christmas and some beautifully timed natural shots of the three children hung on the walls. My favourite was a picture of Blaine and Rachel cooking together; he had flour on his cheeks and a look of deep concentration on his face, that same intense look he wore now. Rachel was looking at him adoringly.

But as we stood there in that hallway, all eyes were on me, watching me look from them to Blaine to the photos, waiting for me to acknowledge the obvious. Rachel was as pale skinned as a vampire, her curly auburn hair strikingly long. Warren, while not as pale skinned, had a mop of blonde hair. And Luke and Lucy were both pale skinned with curly, auburn hair like Rachel's. All four of them had deep brown eyes. My mind fought to make sense of this with various possible scenarios. He couldn't be either Rachel or Warren's from a previous relationship because he was younger than both Luke and Lucy. Perhaps one of them had an affair and Blaine was the result. Could they have adopted him? It had become painfully evident how little he had shared about himself.

The moment was excruciatingly awkward, but I said nothing. Warren and Blaine cast glances at each other as Rachel ushered me through to the kitchen and put the kettle on, probably hoping a cup of tea would relieve the tension and make me unsee what was right before my eyes.

Rebecca motioned impatiently with her hands and raised her eyebrows for me to get to the point and appease her curiosity. Well, the rest of the hour we were there was pleasant; Rachel and Warren were accommodating hosts, chatting about Blaine and how happy they were for us both. About how he had so much love to give and just needed to meet the right person. He appeared embarrassed at their compliments and reached for my hand, agreeing that he had met the right person at last. And, despite the enormous elephant in the room, there were no awkward silences, making it easier not to think about Blaine's parentage. But soon enough he suggested we leave as we still had some shopping to get and had not yet eaten.

Rachel and Warren hugged me as we departed, insisting we come back again soon. But in Blaine's car the silence was deafening, the awkward anticipation of wanting to ask questions filled me; he offered nothing of an explanation voluntarily. Only once we were parked outside the shop did he mention that I was quiet, so I took it as an invitation to ask the question.

"They're not both your birth parents, are they?" There was silence, as though he was deciding whether to explain. I repeated the question. "Blaine, they are not both your birth parents, are they?"

His response was rushed and tense. "No. They fostered me when I was a boy. They stood by me when they could have passed me onto another family or left me to enter the care system; they made me one of their family. And still do now."

He offered nothing more, no explanation as to why his own parents couldn't take care of him. I was heartbroken for him but also annoyed he would not tell me more. Seeing my reaction he reached for my hand, only I pulled it away and he looked devastated; I had made this about me instead of him. What did it matter if he was not ready to tell me why his real parents had let him go? I apologised and suggested we get the shopping we had come for, but with his head down and his eyes fixed on his lap he replied, "Another time, maybe," before starting the engine and pulling back out onto the road.

Blaine had only ever looked at me with the sincerest warmth and there he was, unable to look at me at all, let alone talk to me or shop for the things he was so keen for me to have in his flat. And worst of all, he drove me straight home. I could not bear to leave things like this so invited him inside for some food, but he made his excuses about not being hungry and said he would see me tomorrow. I leant forwards to kiss him but he remained motionless in his seat, his head bowed. He had told Rachel and Warren he had finally met the right person and now he did not want to be near me. I didn't understand, and I certainly didn't know this version of Blaine.

Rebecca thought I was too expectant; this was obviously a difficult subject for him. It certainly explained why he had not been open about his life and family. She could not imagine anybody being immediately open about something so personal. She thought I should be patient and give him time. No relationships were always plain sailing, especially when they started as intensely as ours did. Well, that was not something I had a great deal of experience in.

Knowing me well she asked how much I cried last night. I had at least managed to wait until I got to my room, but Mum knew all was not well as soon as I walked through the front door and followed me up the stairs, her words echoing Rebecca's.

"Give him some space, darling, this is clearly difficult for him. There is no question of how much he feels for you, but this is completely unrelated to those feelings. This is about his whole life and probably a whole lot of questions he may never have had answered himself."

Mum was the kindest and wisest person I know; I had no doubt she was right. She kissed my head and told me to call her if I needed anything before disappearing back downstairs. I checked my phone every few minutes in case I had somehow missed his call or a message, but each time my screen was blank more tears came. I hated this, I wanted to lay next to him and feel him holding me like he never wanted to let me go. I wanted to feel anything but this. Holding the heart between my fingers I prayed this was not the end.

It was almost eleven when a message arrived; my hand grabbed for my phone and my heart skipped several beats when I saw his name. *I'm so sorry Maya. I know I didn't handle that very well. I promise to make it up to you, I just need to get my head around a few things first.*

Mum was right, of course; this was about Blaine and about things I could never truly understand. I had no choice but to give him the space he needs, what was the alternative? Putting pressure on him to tell me everything and risking losing him? That awful feeling lurched in my tummy again, the thought was more than I could bear. Was that normal after just a week and a half? Rebecca thought it was indicative of a love that was written in the stars. After staring at his message for far too long I typed my response.

*Take all the time you need. I will still be here when you are ready.*

His message must have allayed my fears because shortly after replying I had fallen asleep. When I woke this morning, instinctively clasping the heart in my hand, I felt a connection that could not be broken by this. I messaged him again.

*I missed you when I woke up.*

But he did not reply.

## Blaine

I knew the questions would come and I'd anticipated handling them better. I tried desperately to recall the answers I'd rehearsed but they failed me when I needed them. I panicked and shut her down. I wanted to get away before I said something I'd regret. I didn't want to leave her like that, but I had to.

Back at home I smoked until my head was fuzzy and my mind stopped working overtime. I didn't want her to worry or think I'd had a change of heart so I messaged her, I needed her to know we were okay.

There was no choice but to let someone in when you felt this way about them. Of course she'd want to know who I was, about my life and my family. But I felt shame, and fear that she might not want to see me again. Only she did, and she told me to take all the time I needed.

I smoked until I fell asleep and woke up this morning to the phone ringing; it was Rachel, she was worried. She'd seen the questions brewing in Maya's eyes as soon as we'd walked through their door and wondered how I'd handled them. She did her best to console me, but I was pissed at myself and shut her down too, told her I needed time to get my head straight. She understood and didn't put any pressure on, just reminded me they were always there for me when I need them. But then she mentioned the necklace. I hung up.

## Maya

After leaving Rebecca I drove to the park and sat on the bench where Blaine and I had eaten lunch little over a week ago. It was cold; thick clouds filled the sky and fog was forming, obscuring the view of the bridge. I was sad and alone. Why had he ignored my message this morning? I wanted to send another but could imagine what Mum and Rebecca might say.

I closed my eyes and wished he would come here in the hope I might be waiting for him. But when I opened them the only people I saw looked like the old couple again, although in these conditions it was difficult to tell if it was really them. They seemed to be watching a man who was exiting the park ahead of them, and a few moments later they had all faded into the thickening fog. A sense of eeriness was growing but I did not want to leave just in case he came.

Pulling my phone from my bag I hoped he had replied, but only Mum, Sissy and Rebecca had messaged. Mum had spoken to Sissy, reporting that I was upset and that she should ring me to make sure I knew everyone was there for me. Only Sissy couldn't ring because she was working and messaged instead.

Mum was letting me know she had spoken to Sissy and hoped I did not mind; she thought it might help if everyone was supporting me. And Rebecca was worried about Blaine. She was making sure I wouldn't do anything silly like put more pressure on him to talk. Honestly, I only left her half an hour ago.

I loved them all dearly, but I just wanted to be alone and put my phone back in my bag without replying to any of them. Well, I actually wanted to be with Blaine, but it seemed that was not an option.

Moisture from the bench seeped through my trousers; it was cold and uncomfortable so I walked to the bridge, recalling that first day we connected, and as I stared into the murky water below I remembered how it felt kissing him for the first time. I wanted desperately to kiss him now and see the candles in their jars bringing the bridge to life. Tears flowed again and I was grateful for the fog and the emptiness of the park. My heart ached and I so wanted it to stop.

Cold to the bone, I made my way back to my car. I knew Mum would be home when I got there but for the first time in my life I did not want her to comfort me. She had two mugs of hot chocolate powder ready and waiting for the milk that was heating on the stove. I would never know how she knew when we are coming and in need. She filled the mugs and topped them with whipped cream and marshmallows, setting them down on the table. "Have you heard from him, darling?" was all she asked.

I told her I had not and we sat together in silence, sipping our drinks, which were rather tasty and defrosted me nicely. Getting up from the table she kissed the top of my head and began pulling things from the fridge to cook for dinner. I did not feel the need to go and hide in my room; it was comforting being there with her. She must have known I didn't want to talk because she put the radio on and hummed to the songs as she cooked, glancing over every now and again.

## Chapter 23

## Thursday 24th November 2022

### **Maya**

Mum and Dad were oblivious to me listening to their conversation from the landing last night. Mum was worried about me, about us. Dad thought I couldn't possibly understand what Blaine had been through. How could I? I had never been rejected nor had to struggle for anything, least of all love. And he was right, I had no idea of the trauma Blaine suffered, being taken from his parents for whatever reason, and yet he was loving and thoughtful.

Sleep had been fitful after. Faceless returned, talking as though my dreams were advising me, asking me to be patient. We sat across from one another at a white table in a small, otherwise furniture-less room with bare white walls. He had said so much more but I could recall nothing else.

There had been nothing extraordinary about this morning; the sky was still a mass of thick clouds, my heart was still heavy and pining for something, anything, from Blaine. There was not a single notification on my phone and Mum's breakfast spread was as accommodating as ever. I feared spending all day at work gazing at the door, waiting for Blaine to enter only to be bitterly disappointed. Mum sent me off with a big hug. "Don't worry, darling, he will come around when he is ready," she whispered. Only I would have swapped that hug in a heartbeat to be in his arms.

Outside, the thick blanket of cloud did nothing to stave off the falling autumn temperatures. Mum watched me walk to my car through the kitchen window, smiling like a Cheshire cat. It was a change from her sombre expression of a minute ago when she was hugging me, but I had no idea what had caused the change of mood. Until I pulled my car forward from behind the tall hedge towards the entrance of the drive. From the kitchen window she had seen what I could not: he was there, with flowers in one hand, a gift bag in the other, and a look that burned through my windscreen and into my heart. That pained expression and the indefinable something in his eyes, something deep and sincere. I wanted him to always look at me that way.

Frozen in my seat, I glanced back to the kitchen window, but Mum had gone. When I turned back, Blaine was walking the few paces to the car, his eyes unfaltering from mine. Dropping the gift bag to his feet he opened the car door, took my hand and pulled me into his arms. For the longest moment nothing was spoken. Awash with relief, I could do nothing but breathe him in and squeeze him tight. His warm lips kissed the top of my head repeatedly before he spoke.

"I'm sorry, Maya. Sometimes I just don't know how to handle things. I didn't know how to answer your question but it doesn't change how I feel about you." I held him even tighter; the day of absence had changed nothing. For me it had strengthened something. He loosened my arms from around his middle, just enough to press the heart softly against my skin with his fingertips and, with the most pleading look, said, "Be patient with me, Maya. Please?"

I'd experienced moments of déjà vu before, vague feelings of familiarity triggered by a place or a person, but never anything like that. Something in Blaine's tone transported me back to last night's dream. His words and voice echoing Faceless's. The way he said, 'Be patient," like it was the same voice, the same person. But there was no time to linger on it; he kissed me with such heat and affection that nothing outside of him existed in that moment. All the tears and the worry that I had lost him were all for nothing.

His lips broke from mine and he presented me with the flowers he had been holding the whole time. Stunning red roses, too many to count. He was smiling but his eyes told a different story. I saw fear, the same fear I felt when I thought my questions had pushed him away.

Handing me the gift bag full of shower gel, shampoo, deodorant and a box with a razor in it, he pulled out a toothbrush and, holding it aloft, asked if I would stay at his tonight to arrange all these things wherever I liked. He would take me to dinner first by way of an apology, somewhere nice with no expense spared; he knew he had some making up to do.

Suddenly my day looked much brighter and the anticipation I felt about going to work had vanished.

# Rachel and Warren

"Do you think he's okay, Warren? He usually rings back when he's shut me down like that, but I've not heard a peep from him."

"He'll be fine, love. He's never been a talker, he's not about to start now just because he's met someone."

"She's not just anyone though, is she? He's been the master of avoidance and suddenly this girl puts his head in a spin. I'm worried about how he'll handle it. For her sake as much as his."

"I'm not criticising, love, but you've always made these assumptions about him, that he'll do something bad. Some people just get over stuff and it never catches up with them. Besides, we don't know the full picture, only what his mum said, and no one even knows if she was telling the truth."

"You see it though, people keep that stuff down for years then something happens and bang, they do something no one saw coming. What if that happens to him? What if she's on the receiving end of it? Especially after Angela's claims."

"Rachel, stop worrying. He's a good man. He's been kind and respectful for as long as we've known him. I know he got into some scrapes at school, but he was never the instigator, he just stood up for himself so people knew he wasn't to be messed with. That's not a bad thing."

"If I ring him again he'll only get the hump with me."

"Leave him, love. He knows where we are."

## Blaine

I reached for her in my sleep, only she wasn't there and her absence woke me. I thought of nothing but her for the rest of the night, and by daylight I knew what I needed to do.

It was oddly reassuring when Rob walked into the kitchen. He was not my first choice of companion, but this morning he was better than no one. He stayed last night after the gym; we smoked and drank and I numbed what I didn't want to feel. There was this weird moment, probably whiskey induced, when Rob asked me what it was like sleeping with Hannah. It was fucked up to even ask and I wasn't entertaining him with an answer. Neither of us said much after that. This morning I rustled him up some breakfast and left him to it; I needed to get to Maya's.

Maggie waved enthusiastically from the kitchen window. Standing just out of sight I heard Maya's feet crunching on gravel as she walked to her car, then the door shutting and the engine starting, albeit a little sluggishly in the cold. The car rolled slowly forwards, her eyes meeting mine, and she came to a halt in front of me. She froze, not smiling, not moving, then looked back at the house and I wondered if she was planning to get out of the car and run.

But there was no need for worry; she hadn't disconnected from me at all, my wobble hadn't caused any lasting damage. All I could ask for was her patience and to let me take her to dinner tonight to make up for my stupidity. She looked up at me, her eyes exposing all my weaknesses. Maybe she already knew; maybe she saw it when she looked at me.

Her angelic face beamed when I showed her the roses and the things for the flat; I hoped she knew how much it meant to me to feel her presence there when she wasn't. She disappeared up the drive to take the flowers inside, appearing at the kitchen window a moment later with a vase and setting them down. Then she was back, standing in front of me with the most serious expression, saying, "I thought I had lost you."

## Maya

The unextraordinary day was revealing itself to be anything but and the early-morning reunion had left me glowing from the inside out. At work, Ruby had been explaining how Blaine seemed like his old self yesterday, ordering two coffees and leaving with neither a smile nor conversation. I had barely finished playing down the truth, suggesting it must have been a bad day at work when he walked through the door, winking at me, sending my heart into a flutter.

He had booked us a table at a perfect little restaurant just out of town and requested I pack a bag with work clothes so he could bring me straight here in the morning. Taking his receipt from my hand he ran his fingers over mine, holding my gaze before scribbling something on the receipt. Folding it neatly he pushed it back across the counter and under my hand. My eyes followed him to the door where he turned around to look at me one more time. I couldn't fathom that expression.

Ruby peered over my shoulder, waiting for me to unfold the receipt, but I was concerned his message might give away that yesterday was more than just a bad workday and disappeared to the toilet to open it alone. Another heart, this time the words "always yours no matter what" written beside it. I could only assume the "no matter what" referred to his distance and wondered if that was how he always dealt with things, hence his asking me to be patient. Was my heart strong enough to cope with that? When I returned, Ruby said that if Dale were to come over and leave her suggestive notes she would be a very happy lady.

I would have sacrificed dinner to be alone with Blaine. Only when he picked me up at six-thirty sharp, smelling like a god and wearing the white shirt that clung to every contour of his chest and arms, I was very happy to be spending time together in a public place, observing the eyes of jealous women laying heavy on him. All the while he noticed nobody but me, his eyes virtually unwavering from mine.

The restaurant really was perfect, the cream walls decorated with beautiful paintings of woodlands and rolling landscapes. Ivy garlands draped along and hung down from thick wooden beams. White tablecloths covered each of the tables; small vases of white flowers and tealight candles in ornate holders sat at their centres. Not one of the tables seated more than two people, this was a restaurant for intimate dining and I could tell at a glance that the food was going to be expensive.

In the corner of the room stood a smaller table with just one chair; I noticed it when we entered and wondered who might sit alone in such a place, quickly becoming too caught up in my handsome date to notice the table again until I felt the eyes of someone sitting there upon me, the man who watched me in Totally Coffee that day before chatting to the elderly couple outside. And here he was, watching me again, still wearing the big coat that made him stand out in a room full of people dressed in dinner attire.

In a whisper I explained how the man had watched me while I worked, and now he was here. Blaine turned to look but could see no one. As I looked up the man shook his head, looked me straight in the eye, then rose from his seat and left the restaurant. Blaine insisted there had been nobody there. He must have been looking at the wrong table.

The food arrived by the hand of a pretty young girl who smiled and lingered on Blaine a moment too long, not that he noticed. Despite talking about work and the food and how happy he was that he had found this gem of a restaurant, he spoke nothing of the visit to Rachel and Warren's and I dared not bring it up. I couldn't bear another twenty-four hours like the last; my body wanted only to be spending the night with him. He did however apologise for his absence, without going into any more detail, several times as we ate, regret visible on his face each time he mentioned it.

After refusing my offer to pay half the bill he held out his hand to help me from my seat and then, under the gaze of everyone in the restaurant, kissed my lips just long enough to make my body tingle from head to toe.

Outside the heavy clouds of the day had given way to a clear, star-filled sky, leaving the air chilly and crisp. I could wait no longer and asked him to kiss me. I had missed him terribly and wanted only to feel as one with him. He obliged, before insisting I get in the car and out of the cold; after all, we had all night for that.

Home felt so far away. By home, of course I meant Blaine's flat, but that was where I longed to be. No sooner had I got out of the car than he scooped me into his arms, carrying me effortlessly up the steps and through the front door. Inside his hallway we became a tangled mess of body and arms, kissing and tearing at each other's clothes. We got no further than there and were against the wall when I felt him slide inside me, and everything else slipped away. There was only Blaine and I, moving in perfect time with one another until we both climaxed and sunk to the floor.

I thought it might happen again. He was holding me, telling me how he couldn't bear to be away from me, not even for a day. That he was sorrier than I could ever imagine for staying away for all of yesterday. I thought if I mentioned the holiday being little more than two weeks away he might shut down again, but I couldn't ignore it. He made me promise to ring him every day and to bring him back a souvenir, something festive for the flat.

Pulling me up from the hallway floor he led me to the bedroom where a new grey dressing gown waited for me on the bed, fluffy grey slippers on the floor beneath it. He didn't want me to hide the new toiletries in cupboards, he wanted to see them and be reminded of me every second I was not here and suggested bringing some clothes over too so I could stay on a whim. When I reminded him we'd been together for less than two weeks he pulled me onto his lap, slid his hands into my dressing gown and around my bare waist, and told me that time was irrelevant. His heart already knew this was his forever. Of course, my heart knew that too, and there we sat for some beautiful silent minutes just holding one another.

He was first to break the silence, asking when Mum and Dad were coming for a pastry lesson and dinner. I suggested tomorrow and messaged Mum to ask her. *Absolutely, darling. Cannot wait*, she replied.

## Chapter 24

### Friday 25th November 2022

**Blaine**

We woke to the sound of my alarm, bleary eyed from a night of indulgence, making love in three different rooms, falling asleep shattered. Maya's toiletries on top of the chest of drawers were the first things I saw, then her lying next to me, holding the heart. She looked worried, but said nothing was wrong when I asked.

Perhaps this impending week of absence played on her mind too. My stomach twisted and my lungs tightened when I thought of it, but I couldn't let her see my weakness, this holiday was planned before we met, she was hardly likely to betray me while she was with her family.

I messaged Rachel, reassuring her Maya and I are fine; she'd have worried after the last phone call. In fact, we were so fine her family were coming here for dinner tonight. She replied saying she hoped they'd receive a similar invitation soon.

Maya asked what I'd planned on cooking, reminding me that Maggie wasn't just coming for dinner but a pastry lesson too. I suggested a remake of the beef wellington and with a wry smile she climbed on top of me, kissing my neck and chest. I was hard and inside her, lost in those breathtaking eyes. In those moments there was only her, and something in her stare overwhelmed me. I was enveloped in what I felt for her; I was completely and utterly hers. Tears formed in my eyes but I didn't want her to see them or stop. Pulling her down closer to me, chest to chest, I held her face against my neck so she wouldn't see the rogue tear running down my temple. Then out it came, as freely as the tear. "I think I love you," I said.

Only I didn't think, I knew. She pushed against my hand, lifting her head to look at me, and wiped the tear gently away with her fingertip before kissing me deeply. We rolled and I finished making love to her the way a man should make love to the woman he's in love with.

As we lay there motionless, her arms wrapped around me and her fingertips tracing patterns on my back, she whispered, "I think I love you too."

## Maya

Blaine's alarm startled me awake. I had been with Faceless at the side of a road; people panicked and blue lights flashed. Standing amongst muted chaos, he was telling a story that made no sense before pointing to the scene around us and saying, "This is what it will come to if he does not remember." Whatever was happening felt personal.

Faceless continued, "You should know he cannot see me. He won't allow himself to look into that mirror. The only way is to make him remember." As he faded from view I refocused my eyes, but it made him no clearer. He just kept repeating, "He cannot see me." Then the alarm had sounded, waking us both.

Blaine was studying my face and I was seeing something I had not seen before, something as unclear as Faceless's message. His face was the same, the intensity of his stare unchanged. But something was different.

Sensing my confusion he asked what was wrong and just at that moment I realised: Blaine could not see him, the man sitting at the table for one in the restaurant. His view of the table had not been obscured, yet he could not see him. I did not share Faceless's message and could not ask who Faceless was because it made no sense. He was a figment of my dreams. Instead, I reminded him of Mum and Dad's impending visit.

He decided they would recreate the beef wellington burnt in the height of our passion. The thought of it made me want to lose myself in him again, despite making love three times last night. First in the hallway when we arrived here, then again in the bedroom. Neither of us could sleep afterwards, so Blaine made hot chocolate and we sat in the lounge to drink it, but we were soon wrapped in one another on the sofa. It was somewhere after two a.m. when we collapsed into bed exhausted.

As I had drifted into sleep my head was consumed with his earlier words: he thought he loved me. It was soon, I knew, but I loved him too. This was not simply infatuation.

# The Elders

"The time for decisions is approaching. Do we agree that his presence is counterproductive to her growth?"

"I agree that to leave her in his wake risks undoing much of what she has accomplished. And Thomas now poses an increasing risk."

"I believe he poses the greatest risk of all. She is not a part of their journeys, but it seems he is willing to pull her into something in which she has no part. There appears to be no warning he will heed."

"Her journey is all but complete, her love is unconditional, her compassion boundless. We must decide before it is too late."

"We must weigh the benefits and disadvantages for both parties first. She is an asset to us in her highest form, but we cannot ignore the value of his journey."

"His value is undeniable, but he is early in his journey."

"We have time yet, but I fear it is short."

# Blaine

Rob insisted we sit in for coffee today, he wanted to talk about what it's been like since moving in with Hannah, only it was hard to focus on him with such a beautiful distraction floating from table to table, looking at me like I was her everything. All this time I'd felt numb and now my heart turned cartwheels when I looked at her.

She arrived this evening with Richard and Maggie, a bag of clothes in hand. Richard's eyes darted around, checking out my handywork, and he complimented everything and was even more impressed when the before and after photos came out. Maya gave him a second tour of the place with the photo album so he could compare every change in every room. He joked that he'd never need to pay another tradesman now he knew what I was capable of.

Maggie was the perfect pastry student. She told me about the disastrous strudel and how they'd never let her forget about it. And she forbade Richard and Maya from telling Sissy and Henry about tonight's lesson so she could blow them away at dinner on Sunday, which I was invited to, by remaking the strudel and finally shedding her title of "worst pastry chef known to man".

She spoke of the holiday and that vile feeling returned to the pit of my stomach; she sensed it even though I tried hiding it. "She'll be back before you know it, and we'll take good care of her," she said, placing a reassuring hand on my arm. But I wasn't reassured. I had no doubt they'd look after her. I had no doubt she'd be back. What I had was a sickening feeling at the thought of her being somewhere I couldn't see her. What if she changed her mind about me? Or met someone else, or realised her life was better before me. I just didn't want her being away. "I know. I'll just miss her," I replied, suppressing the words that wanted to escape.

Maya and Richard entering the room were a welcome distraction. His endless questions about the renovation lightened the mood and eased my stomach. By the time he'd run out of questions the Wellington was in the oven. Maya led them to the lounge, pouring some wine while I finished prepping the veg.

It turned out well, Richard cleared his plate and asked for a second slice of Wellington. Maggie was pleased with the pastry and couldn't wait to wow with her strudel on Sunday. She asked Maya if this was the first time she'd had my Wellington and after an awkward silence I admitted I'd attempted to make it for her earlier in the week but left it in the oven too long and spoiled it. I didn't think the whole truth would be appreciated and it wasn't exactly a lie. They left around ten-thirty, thanking us for a lovely evening and making no attempt to coax Maya home with them.

## Maya

He had violated another receipt, tucking it under his coffee mug before leaving with Rob. Another perfectly drawn heart with "you" written beside it. I had felt his eyes watching me for the duration of their visit and felt brighter with his attention upon me. And when they were gone I was happy in the knowledge that the receipt, along with his love, was in my pocket as I served the rest of the comparatively insignificant customers.

His car was gone when I left; I knew he would have rushed home to prepare for tonight and I did the same, getting ready at lightning speed for an evening of watching Mum cook with Blaine while Dad inspected the flat. Blaine must have thought Dad was exaggerating his appreciation of the work, but really it was genuine.

Mum was very happy with the pastry, swearing us to secrecy so she could surprise Sissy and Henry on Sunday. The whole strudel catastrophe was a big thing for her and I knew deep down it upset her that she couldn't do everything perfectly for her family. Blaine teaching her this was the gift that none of us could have given her.

# Chapter 25

## Saturday 26th November 2022

### **Maya**

I trialled as a barista today, preparing orders and enjoying brief conversations with customers, under the watchful eye of Harry, my mentor for the day. Some of the customers chose not to engage, staring at phones, avoiding eye contact. Blaine, however, lingered. He informed me over breakfast that he would be working for a few hours, long enough to finish a job and catch a glimpse of the beautiful girl at the local coffee house.

Ruby served tables, colliding at one point with a customer, neither paying attention to their surroundings. Ruby had been giving instructions to one of the boys and the customer —well, she was staring at me. After the incident and the apologies that followed, the customer turned to me and said, "Wow, your eyes." I must have looked surprised because she assured me they were "quite something". It looked as though she was about to say something else, only nothing came; she simply stared for a moment before walking away, looking back again as she opened the door to leave.

Ruby looked put out again when I told her about tonight's double date. I liked her very much but could not imagine Blaine getting along with David the way he did with Drew. And he did so again tonight, chatting easily about work and Rupert as though they had been friends for years, until Drew asked Blaine if he wanted children himself. He fell silent, worry spread across his face, and his head jerked slightly in an uncomfortable motion. I had no idea what was wrong and did not want to put him on the spot asking in front of Amber and Drew.

The following minutes played out awkwardly. Drew looked embarrassed for having caused him discomfort. Amber stumbled over her words, attempting to change the subject, and all I could think was to ask Blaine to help me get more drinks. He was silent and staring at me, or maybe through me. I repeated his name only louder, gaining his attention, asking him again to join me at the bar. Without a word he stood up and followed.

I played it over in my head while lying in Blaine's bed, wondering what on earth was behind his reaction to the most natural question one might ask. Wondering why he held me so tightly while we stood awkwardly at the bar. Wondering why he whispered, "Maya, you have to let it go," when I asked him what was wrong. I did not risk asking more and not seeing him for another whole day, or worse.

Then he had kissed the top of my head and pulled away, taken my hand in his and asked what I was drinking. He ordered the drinks as though nothing had happened, paid for them and returned to the table and to chatting with Drew. Amber glanced at me questioningly, but I had no more of an idea about the reason for his response than she did.

The rest of the evening was as normal as any other, at least on the outside, ending when Amber called time on the date. Rupert would be back first thing in the morning and she would need her energy for him. Blaine thanked them for a lovely evening and now here we were. I knew he was awake despite his back being turned. What was he thinking? Was Drew's question a reminder of his own parents giving him up? Did he fear having children and not wanting them the way his parents didn't want him?

I wanted to wrap my arm around him and feel him against me. But I wanted answers too. Answers I knew would not come had I asked.

## Blaine

I tried carrying on as normal, but back here, just the two of us, it wasn't so easy. I thought if we slept we'd forget about it. But she was restless, she didn't want sleep, she wanted answers. She must have thought about having children one day; her experience of family having been so wholesome. Only for me that day wasn't coming, the risk was too great. She could walk away from me if ever she needed to, but a child… it would be stuck, defenceless. The trouble was I couldn't go back now; I couldn't be without her. I'd have given anything to keep her, anything but answers.

## Chapter 26

## Sunday 27th November 2022

### **Rachel and Warren**

"He had Maya's parents round there for dinner on Friday, Warren."

"Yes, you've mentioned it a few times. It's not hard to tell when someone's put your nose out of joint."

"It's not out of joint, I'm pleased he's making the effort with her family, but he's got family here too."

"You know it's not personal, just complicated, look what happened when he brought her here. He's already told you he didn't handle it very well. What he needs is time and nobody pestering him. He's taken a big leap letting someone in."

"Has he really let her in though? I don't think he knows how to. He loves us, I know, but we've always been stuck on the outside of him, even after seventeen years. He wants to bond with us, he gives that away with the little things he does, but it's like he just can't make that leap and let go.

Do you remember what he made us for Christmas that first year he was here?"

"Oh, I do, Rachel; the bird house, made it from bits of wood he'd collected because he knew I liked watching the birds in the garden. Did his best to make it look like a little cottage. It was crude, but he was only ten, it showed potential. I treasured that thing until it fell apart. I don't think a single bird nested in it, but it was a triumph for such a young boy. I remember him saying he wanted the birds to have somewhere safe to live."

"It's funny how he never caused us any problems, he was never anything less than thoughtful and considerate. The night he came to us that social worker told us to prepare for the worst and said if it was too much she'd collect him and place him somewhere more suitable. But he turned up, that quiet boy who barely spoke a word. Just sat there not knowing what to expect any more than we did."

"You could tell he'd seen something bad. You could see it in his eyes. Of course we had no idea how bad at that point."

"Oh, Warren, we couldn't have done any more for him, could we?"

## Maya

Sleep was fitful; each time I woke in the pitch-black room Blaine's breaths were slow and steady, his body motionless. That was how the night continued until three-forty a.m. Faceless had me pinned against a wall, shouting in my face, his hands pressing into my shoulders, my physical weakness no match for his strength. His voice was full of anguish, his breath filling my nose with a stench that could only be described as death.

"You must make him talk, Maya. You must make him remember." He was shaking with rage, I with fear. When I awoke that final time Blaine was leaning over me, whispering my name and pleading with me to wake up. They were just dreams, but Faceless was the same in each one. The black tee shirt, the gold chain around his neck. Jeans and black loafers. His voice was always the same, everything clear apart from his face.

Blaine scooped me into his arms apologetically, believing last night's behaviour had triggered the dream; he had known a relationship would raise issues he could not discuss. Faceless's words played over in my head: "You must make him talk, you must make him remember."

It was just a dream, yet so pertinent, so timely, again. I told him about it, about Faceless. He was still as he listened and then laid me back down on the bed and without a word left the room. I waited, unsure whether to follow him or give him the space he wanted. There was nothing but silence and darkness. I wanted to find him and reassure him he did not have to talk if talking was too difficult, only I dared not move.

It wasn't long before he reappeared with a tray bearing two cups of tea and a glowing tealight candle, illuminating his chest and face. He was beautiful and I meant to tell him so, but when I opened my mouth, "Who is he?" came out instead. He sat down on the bed, passing me a tea before replying.

"One day I'll tell you about my other life, but not yet. Right now, I don't even know what to tell you. This life started the day I met Rachel and Warren and anything before that is a time I haven't revisited since I lived there."

As we sat, facing one another in the candlelight, I remembered to tell him how beautiful he was, but even that seemed to trouble him. So, taking his tea from his hand and setting both cups down, I pulled him onto me and kissed him. It felt like the time for words was not now. It felt like the time to connect. He did not take any convincing and reciprocated my kiss. His bare chest against mine was all I needed to feel and I was there again, two energy fields merging into one.

***

Dad said I looked tired no sooner had we walked through the front door. Mum jumped in, saying, "You look as beautiful as ever, darling, don't listen to him." Blaine headed for the kitchen to cook with Mum, who insisted the strudel was on her and that he must leave the room whilst she made it. She had listened to everything he taught her, but when it was time to take that strudel from the oven it was a disaster. Blaine leapt from his chair, rushing gallantly to her aid, but it was too late; everyone had seen it. The soggy pastry and hot bubbling apple were stuck to the baking tray in a mess that did not resemble strudel.

No one had expected Mum to cry, and no one knew quite what to do. Sissy and I rushed to hug her and as she fought back the tears she exclaimed, "I just wanted it to be perfect this time." Poor Mum. Clearly feeling guilty, Blaine told everyone it was his fault, he had not reminded her to keep the pastry cool or it might not hold its shape. The rest of dinner had been a triumph, but the disappointment of her disaster was evident.

Dad plied her with extra wine to soften her mood, but the damage was already done.

Sissy tapped the side of a glass with her redundant dessert spoon, garnering everyone's attention, announcing that now seemed like the perfect time to tell us. She glanced at Henry, looking for his approval at the change of plan; he nodded and agreed that of everyone here, Mum probably needed this right now.

"Henry and I are… well, we were going to wait until the holiday to tell you but… this will definitely be the last adults-only family holiday we will have."

Silence fell for a few short seconds while pennies dropped all around the table. Mum resumed crying, this time with joy. Dad leapt from his chair to shake Henry's hand and Mum, Sissy and I were locked once again in a three-way hug, the strudel seemingly forgotten about. Blaine was following Dad to shake Henry's hand and the room was suddenly filled with happiness. A perfectly timed intervention from Sissy.

I was going to be an auntie. They were going to be super parents. And Mum and Dad would be the best grandparents. This little one would be so loved and, as if echoing my thoughts, Blaine reached out to touch Sissy's arm, telling her the baby was one lucky little human to have us all.

It was shortly after this that Blaine thanked Mum and Dad for their hospitality and announced his departure. It was only four-thirty. We had not discussed staying together tonight but still it left an uncomfortable feeling in my tummy. Nobody else batted an eyelid, all bidding their goodbyes.

I walked him to his car, where he held me tight. I wanted desperately to go with him, but when he was done hugging me he looked hard into my eyes and suggested we both get an early night after this morning's early start. Of course, I knew it was more than that. Last night's awkwardness, his reaction when I told him about Faceless and now the baby announcement. All had left him unsettled and it felt as though whatever had brought us together in the first place now wanted us not to be so blissfully happy. He took my face in his hands.

"I just need to get some sleep. You do too," he reassured. "We've both got work tomorrow and I'll be over to see you first thing, just try and stop me." I could not imagine a scenario in which I would want to stop him.

## Blaine

She whimpered and shook in the darkness. All I could do was wake her and hold her to end the distress. But the darkness was soon mine. A man she described in dress but not in face had her pinned against a wall, shouting at her to make "him" talk, to make "him" remember. How could she possibly have seen him in her dream?

I left the room to compose my head. Messy stuff was creeping in, stuff I promised myself she'd never see. In the dark kitchen I put on my headphones; the gym playlist was loud and heavy; it drowned out the sounds and switched off the images in my head like a TV having its plug pulled.

I thought I could carry on as normal when I went back in, but I hadn't imagined she'd ask who he was. What else could I say but that maybe one day I'd tell her about my other life, the one before Rachel and Warren.

There were no more questions; she simply pulled me down onto her, an angel in the flickering candlelight. To feel her flesh against mine and to make love to this beauty who dared to be mine was everything I needed. Each breath she breathed onto my skin warmed every cell in my body. Every sigh and sound she made heightened what I already felt. I existed in a different world all the while I was inside her, a world I could have lived in indefinitely.

But our bodies could only sustain for so long. Her back arched underneath me before sinking back down with a final sigh. There was no doubt, I was in love. Only that didn't stop things happening inside my head every time I thought I'd got a handle on it.

*** 

Dinner had been going so well right up until Maggie pulled that bloody strudel out of the oven. If only I'd reminded her not to leave the pastry at room temperature too long, she wouldn't have cried, and Sissy wouldn't have made that announcement until they were all away together, when I wasn't around.

For the second time today I had to leave, remove myself from the celebrations before the questions came back on me again. This time the playlist came with me to the gym, the perfect antidote to the angst in my head. Back at home I put on a film and smoked so I wouldn't have to think about anything else. Only the more stoned I got the more I thought about Maya, and the more I worried about losing her. What if my repeated distance made her realise she was better without me, that someone else might treat her better? I wanted it to be like the beginning again, just the two of us losing ourselves in each other. No questions, no plans, just us in the here and now.

## Maya

Going back inside had been the hardest thing to do, all of them still reeling with the happiness of Sissy's announcement. I poured a glass of wine, drinking it quickly to numb the void his departure had left inside me. None of them seemed to notice; they were all preoccupied, talking babies, dates and names.

For the second time in twenty-four hours I lay staring at the ceiling. This time alone and in my own bed, all the receipts Blaine had drawn on unfolded on my chest, my fingers holding the heart against my neck. Sissy and Henry were long gone and Mum and Dad were still downstairs, most likely discussing the baby. I was happy for them, but a gaping hole plagued my happiness. What had been easy now felt troubled.

Mum came in and sat on the edge of my bed. She had noticed how soon after Sissy and Henry's announcement Blaine had left and wondered if the events had been connected. Had I told her I did not want to discuss it she would have left my room graciously, but I wanted to tell her, maybe even needed to. She listened to how the date with Amber and Drew had panned out, from the perfect evening to the awkward moment when Drew asked him if he wanted children himself. Then the dream and Blaine's reaction to Faceless. And finally, today's announcement and Blaine running away, I assume, before anyone could mention him and children in the same sentence again.

"You know, darling," she said thoughtfully when I had finished, "he loves you dearly, we can all see that, but he experienced things you never had to endure. Imagine your mummy and daddy having given you up when you were little. Imagine the fear you would harbour of becoming a parent yourself and not being good enough for your own children. Who knows how he must feel or what the specifics of his situation are. Time will answer your questions, but you must be patient with him, let it come naturally. Don't force him or you might cause ruptures you cannot repair."

She kissed my forehead and instructed me to sleep because she was certain things would feel better in the morning.

## Chapter 27

## Monday 28th November 2022

### **Maya**

Only nothing was better when I opened my eyes. I should have been happy after Sissy's announcement: a baby on the way to love and spoil. Had I been told the news two days ago I would have burst with happiness. Instead, a dull ache surrounded my heart, tainting the joy.

Blaine had at least messaged by the time I left for work. A heart and the word "later". That was all. I was cross he was not concerned whether I was okay, or apologetic for yesterday's departure, but suspected I was being melodramatic. He had not left in anger; he had reassured me that he would see me first thing today. I had just not anticipated him leaving at all, at least not without me.

Work brought no relief. I watched the door, waiting for my handsome prince to come strolling through with that look that left me weak at the knees. But he did not. Twice I made my excuses, going to the toilet to check my phone, only to be disappointed by the absence of contact.

Mum had messaged, checking I was okay, but that only made me want to cry. I lied, telling her everything was fine, I did not want her to worry when she had a grandchild on the way to be excited about.

Lunchtime came and went still with no sign of him. "First thing," he had said. "You just try and stop me." Like a fool I spent my lunchbreak at a table in case he appeared. The clumsy girl who liked my eyes came back, but no Blaine. I noticed her as she entered, mostly because I looked at everyone who entered in case it was Blaine. Her eyes seemed to scan the place, checking out each member of staff as though looking for someone specific. I stood to return to the counter, inadvertently catching her attention. She smiled and did a half-hearted wave at me, as though her body had acted before her brain censored her hand movement a moment too late. I responded only with a strained smile.

By the time she had made her way to the front of the queue I was back behind the counter, but instead of ordering her coffee she said, "Are you okay? You've lost your sparkle today." Her question caught me off guard, but she was right; my sparkle was waiting by the door for a prince who never arrived. I lied, assuring her I was fine, grateful for her concern and asking what she would like. She asked for a cappuccino to go and a smile. I did my best to muster one up, but she said she hoped whoever had run off with my sparkle brought it back or she might have to sort him out. What an odd thing to say to a stranger.

The entire afternoon passed with no sign of Blaine and when six o'clock came and we were locking up the shop it was dark outside. I turned to face my car and the dark silhouette standing beside it with eyes fixed on me. My heart skipped in my chest. I did not want to be happy to see him, I wanted to be angry with him for leaving me hanging all day, but I wanted to kiss him more.

He moved first, making my heart dance a little more. A white shirt clung to his chest beneath the casual black jacket; charcoal grey trousers hugged his thighs. His eyes were unwavering from mine. His breath left his mouth in white whisps on the cold wintery air. I could smell his cologne on every cold breeze that graced my face and by the time he was close enough to take my hand in his any trace of annoyance had dissolved.

"Come with me," was all he said as he led me down the road and past both of our cars.

"Where are we going?" I asked. But I already knew the answer.

## Blaine

I messaged Maya to tell her I'd see her later. The last thing I wanted was her waiting all day and getting mad. I'd told her I'd be over first thing, but I was going to work straight through, no breaks so I could finish early and have enough time to get home and change.

Rob agreed to help me set up once again, so at half past four I popped home to shower and put on my best shirt, then loaded the boxes of candles and jars back into the car and headed back to work for Rob, then to the park and the bridge.

Maya looked stunning, but in the glow of streetlights sadness was visible in her expression. I'd impacted her mood over the last few days, but that was what this was for, redressing my stupidity and getting us back to where we were before the questions started coming.

The park was empty, just the two of us and Rob until he walked away. The bridge looked magical illuminated in the dark. I wondered what might have happened had it been this dark and desolate the first time I brought her here; she would have run a mile. But now this girl just follows me into the darkness, away from anyone who could help her, trusting me without question. It sent a ripple through my body, heightening what I already felt. She was delicate and fragile, yet safe with me.

## Maya

I could not take my eyes off that beautiful bridge and the candle flames dancing in hurricane jars. The water beneath was a still black expanse but for the dancing fiery reflections. The only sounds were the rustling of trees and the faint hum of traffic from the high street. It occurred to me again how safe I felt with Blaine, how ludicrous it was to imagine anyone harming me in his presence. I was certain he would fight until his last breath to protect me.

As we stood on that bridge he expressed his regret at shutting down when he couldn't answer a question, and with a face as serious as any I have seen, explained how he wanted us to start again, to be carefree and happy together. That was why he had brought me back here, a reset back to the beginning. Because everything moved too fast; meeting each other's families, double dating with Amber and Drew.

Pulling me into him he kissed me with the heat and passion I had craved. His body felt good in my hands; I wanted him. I had no care for anyone who might see us in the candlelight. I pushed myself against him, aroused beyond self-control. But being the chivalrous man he was he scooped me up and carried me back across the damp grass, out of the park, setting me down on the path to walk the distance to our cars. I didn't want to be apart from him for a second but got into my car to follow him home.

Those moments on that bridge had been cut short both times; how nice it would have been to enjoy the effort he had made for longer. How nice it would have been had he taken me on that bridge.

## Blaine

I couldn't allow my beautiful Maya to reduce herself to sex in a park where anyone could see us. Carrying her back across the wet grass she looked up at me with those damn eyes and asked, "Your place?" It already felt like we were back at the beginning.

Picking her up outside the car, her arms tight around my neck, I carried her to the flat. This time I didn't put her down until we reached the bedroom. She was silent, looking at me as though what she really wanted was for me to take control. I wanted it too and quickly returned to my new happy place, disconnected from everything.

# Maya

He was impossible to resist, looking at me with those green eyes, smelling as good as he did. I felt once more like the innocent girl of a few short weeks ago. He led and my body demanded I follow. We made love on his bed, holding one another in perfect silence afterwards. His lips kissed my neck, his breath warming my skin until he rolled off the bed, handing me his hoodie to put on. It swamped me but was warm and soft against my skin and smelled deliciously of him. He was smiling, a glint in his eye as he pulled at my hand until I followed him to the kitchen. "Let's cook," he said.

Suggesting we start with something simple he took steaks from the fridge and, under his guidance, we cut vegetables into shapes, prepared minted butter for potatoes, drank wine and kissed at every opportunity. I rolled his hoodie sleeves up to my elbows repeatedly, only for them to fall back down my thin arms again. At one point he picked me up and guided my legs around his waist, setting me down on the worktop and pressing himself against me, kissing me deeply. Had the steaks not needed to go on when they did I think we might have made love again right there on the worktop.

The finished meal looked as good as if he had cooked without my interference. We ate in the lounge with plates on our laps, perfectly informal and perfectly placed to fall back into one other after eating. It was like being back at the start again. None of that silly awkward stuff seemed to matter; he was relaxed and happy. He was connected to me in the present without the weight of his past. I wanted to stay here like this.

But every relationship must move forward to survive, must it not? So how did we move forward if we couldn't discuss the very things that moved us that way?

## Chapter 28

## Tuesday 29th November 2022

### **Blaine**

I was sleeping on the sofa, only this time with Maya. The TV spontaneously switched on. In the dream I opened my eyes and saw the flickering lines on the screen. A face in the lines stared back at me, screaming suddenly, "HE HAS TO DIE!"

I jumped, waking myself, in bed not on the sofa. Maya was awake beside me, stroking my forehead, asking if I'd had another dream. Pulling my head onto her chest she held me, and it was perfect. My cheek against her bare breast, her fingers tracing patterns on my shoulder. I loved the way she did that. But eventually my alarm declared time to get up and begrudgingly I went to the kitchen to make pancake batter and chop fruit. She joined me, looking effortlessly beautiful, and together we ate breakfast and drank tea before leaving for work.

Ruby smiled warmly when I entered Totally Coffee and the spotlights above the counter made Maya's heart sparkle almost as brightly as her. She didn't ask what I wanted, just rang it through the till and handed me the receipt with an expectant look on her face. I scribbled on it, folded it and passed it back to her. She slipped it into her pocket, smiling a killer smile, melting me on the spot.

I spent every moment at work thinking about her, wanting to show her how serious I was. I messaged to tell her I'd meet her from work and take her to mine, where I hoped she'd wait for me to return from the gym. She was on board with the plan and by the time I got home she was settled on the sofa watching TV. As I handed her the roses, her eyes went straight to the key chain around one of the stems. I asked her to come here whenever she wanted; there was no need to announce herself. I could think of nothing better than hearing her key turn in the lock, seeing her face and knowing she wanted to come here to be with me.

She kissed me quickly on the lips before disappearing to the bedroom, returning with today's receipt and setting it down in front of me. "Do you really want me forever?" she asked. How could I consider anything or anyone else now?

## Maya

Waking up together and sharing breakfast was a heavenly way to start the day, but sadly work beckoned. The morning was damp and cold, thick clouds hung low, but the kiss before getting into my car made it feel as warm as a summer's day. I had hoped to be on tables; I needed time to process where Blaine and I were and to understand what I was feeling, only Ruby had me behind the counter with her.

When Blaine entered there was no need to ask what he wanted. Ringing his usual into the till I handed him the receipt, hopeful that he would scribble on it, another for my collection. Obliging, he passed it back, neatly folded, that intense look on his face. Part of me hoped it was something naughty, an exciting promise, but it was another heart and the words "you, me and forever". No one would have looked at Blaine and assumed he would write such things. And I suspected no one would look at me and assume I would hope he had written things such as I had.

At lunchtime he messaged asking me to go home with him, inviting me to wait for him while he visited the gym so he could come home to me, promising to return with dinner. I did not mind waiting for him one bit; it was nice being in his space. I had that feeling again, that Maya had finally grown up. She had a boyfriend who had his own place, where she could hang out.

Mum phoned while I waited, inviting us to join them for a takeaway tomorrow, adding that it would be only the four of us. A shiver of discomfort ran through me; Blaine felt we'd moved too quickly; what if he was reluctant to be around my family, or people who might bring up the subjects he seemed intent on avoiding? But the addition of "it will only be the four of us" made me think Mum had already thought that through.

Blaine returned, clutching a beautiful bouquet of roses, sitting down next to me on the sofa. A door key on a chain hung from one of the stems. He wanted me to come here whenever I chose, and I must never doubt arriving unannounced. It seemed a big step for such an early stage in our relationship, especially when he wanted to keep things in the here and now. But he said there was not a single thing that would stop him wanting to hear my key turning in the lock, knowing I wanted to see him.

Over dinner I tentatively told him about Mum's invitation. He paused for a second then said, "Yeah, sure," before changing the subject to his obsession with the gym, explaining how a free taster session had lured him in and he had never looked back. He felt clear and calm when he left the place, as though he left his stress there. I could not help but remark on how incredible he looked for it. He blushed, insisting it was just a happy side effect.

I asked about the tattoos; which was his first and what they meant. The eagle on his chest came first, representing freedom to be whomever he chose. I questioned his pain tolerance and he insisted it was mind over matter; some parts of the body hurt more than others, but he took himself off to a happy place in his mind, a remote cottage he dreamt of owning someday, and spent the sittings there. He said maybe we could own that cottage together.

I wanted to ask how he could consider buying a property with me when he couldn't even think about us having children. But I knew what might happen if I did, so I nodded and asked about his other tattoos. I was not really interested in his answers; my head needed clarity. I wanted a family of my own someday; how could we continue if he did not want the same thing? But how could I walk away and risk never feeling this way about someone again? Would I even want to have children with someone who did not make me feel the way Blaine did? Would I sacrifice having a family for the love of my life?

It was at this moment, quite out of the blue, that he announced with conviction and that now-familiar pained expression, "You know I'd sacrifice my life for you, right?"

## Blaine

She asked questions while we ate, about my tattoos and how I managed the pain. I told her about the cottage, how we could own it together one day, but she'd drifted off in in her head, like she didn't want to think about that. Images of losing her flooded my mind. I wanted her back in here with me and in my panic I told her I'd sacrifice my life for her.

"Why would you say that?" she replied. Because I would. What would life be worth without her anyway? She got up from her chair, straddled my lap and looking right into my soul with those ice-blue eyes, said, "Well, let's hope it never comes to that."

## Chapter 29

### Wednesday 30th November 2022

**Maya**

High on the memory of last night I drifted from table to table, my head full of things I would not have shared with Ruby or Amber had I been behind the counter with them anyway. Between flashbacks of making love in the kitchen I thought of Blaine's inability to discuss things that mattered, drawing no more conclusions than I had last night. I wanted to spend forever with this man, but that might have meant making sacrifices. Sacrifices that would be easier to make if they came with explanations.

*** 

We'd leave for Scotland early Monday morning; soon I had to pack and would need to buy a few things. My collection of jumpers was more suitable for southern winters than Scottish ones, and a pair of warm boots might have been a wise purchase. I had just messaged Rebecca, asking if she was free for shopping on Friday, when Blaine entered the shop looking gorgeous. His eyes shone as he smiled cheekily, clearly remembering the same images that had danced around my head all morning. Placing his order, he walked to a table, looking at me all the while, and when I set down his tray he took my hand, pulling me gently down towards him.

"I'd do anything for you, Maya," he said. The words felt reminiscent of last night's declaration, leaving me with a feeling of uncertainty. I was beginning to hate this internal place at which I had arrived. Why could I not accept his compliments without this anxiety? Why must I question his words and reactions? Mum made it clear I should give him the time and space he needed to open up, but I could hear Faceless's warning to make him talk, to make him remember. I realised how ridiculous I was being; Faceless is a fabrication of my dreams, Mum's advice is worth a million of whatever my subconscious could dream up.

He invited me to go home with him from here so we could arrive for our date with Mum and Dad together. I would have very much liked to watch him transform from grease monkey to hunk and told him to meet me outside.

## Blaine

Going home together would never grow old. She watched TV while I showered, so normal yet so novel, and her face when I re-entered the room with just a towel around my waist, eying me from head to toe and giving me that look… but there wasn't time for that; her parents were expecting us.

Richard was a gracious host, insisting I choose the food. Maggie opened a bottle of wine while Richard handed out plates and rummaged through the drawers looking for serving spoons. She insisted I stay again tonight, promising to make an early breakfast so I'd have time to eat before going home to get ready for work. Maya suggested I make the pancakes while Maggie prepared the rest. Maggie seconded the idea.

Conversation was easy; the wine helped. Richard made it clear how impressed he was with what I'd done with the flat, asking questions about specific bits of the renovation, how I did it and how I knew how to do it.

It was Maya who called time on the evening, claiming to be tired. In the privacy of her room she pulled me into her en-suite shower, the wine clearly having gone to her head. But it had gone to mine too, so who was I to argue when she switched on the water and began pulling at my clothes.

## Maya

Giddy from the wine I pulled him into the shower to make love. His strength made it effortless, sweeping me off my feet and holding me around his waist, my back pressed against the cold tiled wall. Several times his finger pressed against my lips to silence me. I knew we must be quiet, but it was hard not to make a sound.

By the time I had finished drying my hair Blaine was already asleep in my bed. I climbed in next to him, still naked and warm from the shower and the sex. Pushing my body against his back I slid my arm around his middle. Without stirring from sleep his hand reached for mine and held it tight.

# Chapter 30

## Friday 2nd December 2022

### **Maya**

Yesterday we woke warm and naked, my arm around his middle, his hand still clutching mine. The wine and sex had been good sleep inducers but waking gave rise to new and uncomfortable feelings. I had told Blaine about today's shopping trip but found myself compromising the truth about what I would be shopping for. I was just days away from leaving for Scotland, yet I neither want to mention it nor go. Holidays had always been a thing of togetherness and happiness, but this one felt like a thing of separation and anxiety.

He asked what a girl with as many clothes as I had could possibly need and with a twinkle in his eye suggested buying something for him instead. I decided that new sexy underwear would be a good parting gift; Saturday would be our last night together for a whole week so why not make it unforgettable?

Last night we stayed at his, eating dinner before snuggling up in bed with a film. Conversation was scant; we cuddled and watched, then made love before going to sleep. It was nice, but the holiday felt like an elephant in the room and I wondered if he still felt as uneasy about it as me. I had no desire to ask.

He seemed happy getting ready together and making pancakes and coffee this morning. Before parting he wrapped me in his arms and kissed me. I had noticed this thing he did sometimes after kissing me: he leant back, an arm still around my middle, holding me against him but distancing himself just enough to really look into my eyes. He swept hair from my forehead with a fingertip as though to get the best view of my eyes or face. It was mostly in silence; it was always intense and always made my heart flutter. Then he kissed me again before he let me go.

Shopping was a triumph, with me finding the perfect boots, warm winter leggings, jeans, jumpers and a hoodie that reminded me of Blaine. Rebecca enquired about my new life as a promiscuous woman, her words not mine, so I told her how I wanted to surprise him with something sexy. All the underwear I owned was cute and I had progressed beyond cute. We searched several shops and found the perfect set in a boutique lingerie shop: red and lacey with not really a lot to it; Rebecca was confident it would have the desired effect.

Halfway home from dropping Rebecca off I turned the car around and headed to Blaine's to use my new key and wait for him. It was four o'clock, plenty of time to review the day's purchases before he arrived.

Leaving the jeans and hoodie in a bag to show him, I put the holiday attire in the boot of the car and let myself into his flat.

I wondered how he might react but had not contemplated him noticing my car outside so my presence was not quite the surprise I anticipated. Still he beamed when he saw me, throwing his greasy self at the sofa, landing not so elegantly next to me. Apparently, it was his favourite homecoming in all the time he had lived there.

I made no bones about the smell of grease and my concern about him wiping it all over the sofa, so after giving me his best puppy dog eyes he disappeared to the shower. I made coffees while I waited and this time it was I who was happy at his arrival, fresh from the shower with just a towel around his middle. And now there were no time constraints. Who needed coffee anyway?

## Blaine

Yesterday we came home together, cooked dinner and watched a film. So normal yet so exceptional. I thought about her shopping with Rebecca all day and was still thinking about her when I arrived home to the welcome sight of her car parked outside. She banished me from the sofa like she owned it already, shaming me for wiping my dirty overalls on it, and demanded I shower immediately.

This was the best homecoming, and I had no doubt I'd have her before anything else occurred tonight. I wanted her to look at me the way she did on Wednesday before we left for her place. I wanted to give her exactly what she needed to stop her looking anywhere else while she was away. In truth I wanted to ask her to not go, but I mustn't be that person.

But I was the person who made her stand to attention by walking into the lounge in just a towel. Eyeing me from head to toe she reached out and pulled the towel away. Suddenly the mood was intense; not a word passed her lips, but her eyes told me she was just as in love with me as I was with her. Those eyes told me that no matter what, I was the only living, breathing thing she'd ever want. Her hold was tight and possessive, eager to have me, but I wanted to give her what she needed, even if she didn't know she needed it.

Working every part of her body until she begged me to make love to her, we finished on the sofa, me kneeling between her legs, her back arched, pushing herself against me. Her eyes closed, there was pure satisfaction on her face. The view up her body and over the curve of her breasts was priceless perfection. Perfection tainted only by me. She opened her eyes and, using my hands for leverage, pulled herself up to face me, smiled a mischievous smile, and said she'd bought something for me today, only I'd have to wait until tomorrow for it.

# Chapter 31

## Saturday 3rd December 2022

### **Maya**

Of course it was Hannah; who else would have been so fascinated with me than the girl he dumped for me? Her previous visits and interest now made perfect sense. How she must have hated me and yet been polite and complimentary, even concerned.

The moment she entered Totally Coffee with Rob today I had known it was her. I wanted them to leave and spare me the awkwardness, but I also wanted to interrogate her about Blaine. He claimed he never wanted her the way he wanted me, but how would she tell their story? I wanted to know if those questions he couldn't face had ever arose. Did he shut down on her the way he shut down on me? Of course, I asked none of those questions.

I tried picturing the two of them together, the image coming all too easily because they were in fact more visually suited than he and I. She was sexy both in looks and mannerisms. And I would defy anyone not to notice the cleavage bulging from her top. How was he not attracted to this girl?

Both made polite conversation, clearly trying to ease my discomfort, and when they left I made my excuses, retreating to the toilet to message Blaine, telling him I had met Hannah. After several minutes he had not replied and I returned to the counter before Ruby came looking for me. And there he was, pleading with Ruby to excuse me so we could speak. She shooed me away with her hand and a worried looking Blaine led me to a table.

I explained what had occurred, about her previous visits and fascination with both my eyes and my mood. His expression changed to one of relief; he had not assumed Hannah would consider the feelings of the girl who won over the man she wanted. His words warmed me: I had won him, and I had to trust that in time I would know him. He decided it was probably good that we had met, given her connection with Rob, although he did not foresee us all socialising together because I was different to them.

Ruby was keen to know what Blaine had wanted so urgently, eyeing me suspiciously when I told her he simply could not bear being away from me. Today was the first time she had seen Rob's girlfriend and said she was the very opposite of how she pictured her. When Rob has shared snippets of his life with her he described a woman who dressed in suits and worked in the city. I did not correct her that the woman he had talked about was not the one he was with today. What did it matter to Ruby anyway? Explaining would have opened a can of worms I would prefer remained sealed.

Blaine's words stayed with me long after he left Totally Coffee. What did he mean by "different to them"? Unworldly perhaps. Innocent. Naïve. All the things I did not wish to be. Even though he was right.

## Blaine

And just like that she was gone. What had I done? Everything I feared I became. Why couldn't I run after her and tell her how fucking stupid I was? In two days she'd be gone, where I couldn't see her for a whole week, and like the genius I was I pushed her away then sat here paralysed, unable to move or fight for her.

# Chapter 32

## Sunday 4th December 2022

### Maya

It felt right to please him in a way I believed he would like, only it did not go as I imagined. He was intrigued when I said I would go home first to pick up his present, telling him not to plan anything for our evening. I showered excitedly, curled my hair and put on make-up, framing my eyes with black eyeliner. Not over the top but considerably more than I would usually wear.

Putting on the new underwear I studied myself in the mirror. I felt confident and sexy, ready to show him I could make him feel as good as anyone else could. I wanted him to be happy, to want only me, not to look at girls like Hannah and wonder if they might be more fun. It had been passionate and tender from the start, but eventually he would want more than that.

When I entered his lounge he looked at me with wanting eyes so, wasting no time, I slid my arms from my dress, letting it fall to the floor, exposing the underwear I had hoped would please him. His expression changed, became unfamiliar. I thought he was buying into the game so I held his gaze, waiting for the smouldering look to return, or anything to tell me this was working, but it didn't come. He just had a poker face that gave nothing away.

I stepped towards him, painfully aware of the inferiority of my cleavage by comparison to Hannah's, but trying to look sexy and confident no less, willing him to look as though he was turned on. Only the closer I got the more confused he looked. Then he stood and with a raised voice said, "Stop, Maya. What are you doing?"

My confidence crashed; he looked angry and I couldn't process what was happening. All I had wanted was to please him. I stood in silence like a scorned child; he looked at my body, at the underwear, with a contempt I had not seen in his eyes before. My cheeks were hot, I was embarrassed and upset, but all I could utter was his name, just once, softly as though pleading with him to see this for what it was. I only wanted to please him.

I tugged at my dress, pulling it quickly back on, but my haste made me clumsy. He was coming at me, his face snarling, his hand grabbing at my wrist.

"I asked what you're doing. You look like a whore. Is this what you'll wear when you're away?" I was pulling away from him and his apparent disgust and heading for the front door. Tears welled in my eyes. The dress was barely back up to my shoulders but all I wanted was to be as far away from his anger and disgust as I could get. He shouted after me.

"IS THIS HOW YOU'LL BE BEHAVING FOR THE LUCKY MEN OF SCOTLAND NEXT WEEK?"

Tearing my coat from the hook by the door I ran for the car, shaking with cold and the fear and uncertainty of what had occurred. Sitting bewildered in my seat I hoped desperately he would come to tell me he was sorry, that he didn't know what had come over him. But when he did not and I could stand the torment no more, I drove home, tears free flowing down my cheeks, feeling as sad and confused as I had ever felt.

My heart ached. He had not come after me full of regret. He neither called nor messaged and I could not fathom what he must be thinking or feeling. Mum came straight to my room, wondering why I was home. Only I found myself lying, telling her Rachel was unwell and that Blaine had gone to her as Warren could not be at home this evening. She would not have told me to give him space and time for reacting as he had. She would tell me that people do not react like that just the once, that an apology would not be a reason to tolerate such behaviour. Worse than telling the lie was watching her face. Lying was not my forte; she saw straight through it but was gracious enough to not question me.

I lay awake, repeatedly checking my phone, convincing myself each time that he must have messaged by now, only to be bitterly disappointed. I must have drifted off somewhere after four a.m. and when I awoke late this morning there were missed calls and a string of messages.

*I'm an idiot. I'm in love with you and I behave like that. Maya, please forgive me.* Eight a.m.

*Please answer my call. I'm terrified that I've made you hate me.* Eight-thirty a.m.

*Maya, please, can we just talk. I understand if you hate me, but I have to let you know how sorry I am.* Nine a.m.

*Please, Maya, I've been awake all night, hating myself for being so fucking stupid. What must you think of me? Please don't hate me.* Ten past nine a.m.

*Please answer your phone,* was the final message at eighteen minutes past ten.

Tears flowed as I pictured how frantic he must be. Relief surged through my body but caution filled my mind, and before I had a chance to decide my next move he was ringing again.

## Blaine

"I'm so, so sorry. I'm an idiot and I hate myself. I can't lose you, Maya. I love you."

Pausing for breath I waited for a response, but only silence came. A faint noise like a stifled cry told me she was still there. I gabbled on, hoping that something I said touched her heart, made her realise she still wanted me, then paused again, longer this time.

"You scared me last night," she whispered.

There it was; I'd scared her. Paralysis tried taking over, I fought it and begged for forgiveness, but my words sounded pathetic, even to me.

Why should she forgive me? I wanted to stop, to hang up and hide. My head hurt and things I didn't want to feel filled my body like ants crawling inside me. She said my name, but I was out of words. Worse still my cheeks were wet. Repeating my name softly and without waiting for a response she said she was coming over and hung up.

I felt sick and weak but her face looking down at me, her fingertips wiping the tears from my face, her breath in my ear when she wrapped herself around me made everything hurt less. I needed to offer some sort of explanation for my idiocy, some reassurance it wouldn't happen again. What I would have given to see her slip out of her dress and reveal her most vulnerable self to me right then. But I'd be lucky if she ever did that for me voluntarily again.

## Maya

It was odd to see a strong man so broken. His sadness and vulnerability made him all the more attractive. We sat in silence a while, Blaine holding me as though he might stop breathing had he dared to let go. His face was buried in my neck; he was unable to look me in the eye, undoubtedly ashamed of what he had done.

When he was ready he pulled back, his head hung low, still holding one of my hands with both of his and explained how my going away scares him. How he feared me having a change of heart in his absence. The fear had been building and when he saw me in that underwear being something I was not it came flooding out. He had no desire for the girls who put on a show; he wanted me, "Pure and beautiful Maya." He does not want the Hannahs with the cleavage and swagger. He wanted me, like this, forever.

I assured him that not only will I not have a change of heart just because I could not see him, but that I would miss him terribly every second I was gone. I had been dreading going away for the first time in the history of our family holidays, all because I would miss him.

His eyes searched mine as though looking for the truth in my words; he must have found it because I could see my Blaine returning, his face more relaxed than broken. Until I told him I needed to go home, I still had to pack and would need an early night ready for tomorrow's early departure. Scooping me up he carried me to the bedroom and undressed me, all the while looking into my eyes with a sorrowful expression, making love to me slowly and purposefully. It was so emotional and passionate and connected it felt as though he believed it might be the last time we would ever make love.

I had struggled to leave him behind, and the sadness in his eyes only increased the weight in my heart. Mum and Dad were busy preparing the house for a week without us when I returned so after packing my case I gave in to my tiredness and laid on my bed, my eyelids blinking one last long blink before giving up the struggle, only to jolt awake sometime later after a visit from Faceless. It had begun calm and civilised, walking together along the high street, talking as though we were acquainted. It was beginning to feel as though we were.

"He knows the truth, Maya. But it hides under the layers of denial he created to keep himself safe from the very thing that can free him. He wants to stay in the present so he doesn't have to look either backwards or forwards. But he must look both ways to avoid making the mistakes I made."

His words were crystal clear but his entire self was hazy this time, there but not quite there. I had taken my eyes off him for just a moment and was looking ahead when he lunged in front of me, his demeanour changing suddenly to upset and angry, his voice raised and shaky.

"They're coming for him, Maya. I don't know if I can stop them."

# Chapter 33

## Monday 5th December 2022

### **Blaine**

She'd messaged already, sharing pictures of Hamlet-Noel. There was snow up there; all we had here was dank mist and rain. The work heater broke and it got so cold we couldn't feel our fingers so Bob sent us home. Only I didn't want to go home to dwell on how much fun she was having without me so I broke my tradition of not decorating the flat for Christmas. I had nothing against it, just didn't see the point. After arranging a gym date with Rob I headed into town to buy lights, decorations and a tree.

It turned out there was a knack to dressing a tree with lights, top to bottom in neat rows worked better than winding them round and round. The lounge filled with a festive glow and instant regret for not doing this with Maya filled me. I sent her a picture of my masterpiece with the words *Christmas has landed here too.* She thought it looked beautiful and hoped I had decorations to put on it. Oh, I had decorations, more than I knew what to do with, but she'd have to wait until the next picture for them.

I'd bought red and gold tree decorations, garlands and extra lights that I'd need to find room for. Wrapping said lights around a thick holly garland, dripping with pinecones and berries, I laid it on the top of the kitchen cupboards — it almost reached from end to end — then set about decorating the tree.

As I stood admiring my handywork she FaceTimed. Aiming the camera at the tree for her perusal she admitted she hadn't realised I had such creative flair, that it was as good as the professionally decorated trees at the hotel they're in. Her words hit like an unwelcome reminder of the distance between us, and an uncomfortable feeling twisted my gut. I became aware of the room around her, the oversized four-poster bed she was sitting on; it looked expensive and beautiful, it looked romantic. I knew being able to picture it would only make it worse. So I told her I still had decorations to put out before meeting Rob, blew her a kiss and hung up before something stupid came out of my mouth.

## Maya

Sleep had evaded me; napping yesterday afternoon did me no favours and the thought of Faceless shouting at me made it impossible. And Blaine would not leave my thoughts, the last couple of days churning around in my head. We left for the airport at five, early enough to avoid the busy morning traffic, and there in the back of Dad's car I fell asleep, waking with my head on Sissy's shoulder to the sound of Mum announcing our arrival at the airport.

The flight was short, one hour and forty minutes, but allowed me another whole hour of sleep. An hour that would keep me going until bedtime. We had thought it was cold when we left home, but that was nothing compared to the bitter chill that stung our cheeks when we stepped off the plane in snowy Inverness. A car waited at the airport, driving us to the village fifty minutes away. The snow steadily increased in depth as we travelled until everywhere looked like a beautiful winter wonderland.

Hamlet-Noel was a sight to behold. Iron gates adorned with lights and holly framed the entrance and swung slowly open as we approached, revealing a narrow lane lined with charming cottages, each dripping with Christmas lights, a well-lit tree in each front garden. The only things not covered with a blanket of snow were the well gritted roads.

Mum had booked us an all-inclusive hotel closer to the village square. It was small and intimate looking, as though it would hold ten families at most and, like everything else we had seen so far, was festively decorated to within an inch of its life. Lights, wreaths, garlands, trees and Christmas ornaments covered every surface. I took photos to send to Blaine who was quick to remind me I had promised something festive for his flat. He seemed happy and I was confident that as long as we maintained regular contact throughout the week, he would be fine.

After comparing our rooms, each as gloriously decorated as the rest of the hotel, we all rested to recover from the journey. Sissy had struggled the most; morning sickness combined with motion sickness had left her feeling dreadful. Poor thing.

I was lying alone on my generous four-poster bed, wishing Blaine were here with me, when he sent a picture of an illuminated tree in his lounge. It was a good start but looked a little bare without decorations, so he promised another picture when it was finished.

Rested and recovered we left the warmth of our rooms to explore. The village square was just a short walk from the hotel and at its heart was possibly the biggest Christmas tree I had ever seen. I could only guess at how many hundreds of decorations and lights were on it. There were small shops: a Christmas decoration shop, a sweet shop, cafés, restaurants and gift shops, that made up three quarters of the square's perimeter, the buildings all quaint and old looking. Between the shops and the tree at the centre were stalls selling hot chocolate, mulled wine, roasted chestnuts and hot winter-spiced popcorn. There were seating areas with patio heaters and carollers singing Christmas songs as beautifully as any professional choir.

The remaining quarter of the square's perimeter was the edge of a large ice-skating rink stretching away from the square towards a field, lined on its far side with woodland. Through the trees across the field I could just make out flickering lights, but it was difficult to see them in daylight. Mum thought they might be the woodland light trail.

Sitting under the warmth of a heater we drank hot chocolates and coffees, ate chestnuts and popcorn, and watched people whirling around on their ice-skates for what was left of the afternoon. The sights, sounds and smells were all we needed to get into the holiday spirit. I even found myself caught up in the excitement of Sissy and Henry's baby news.

Our table was decorated with candles and Christmas crackers when we returned to the hotel for dinner. A waiter arrived with a bottle of red and a bottle of white no sooner than we had taken our seats, placing them in silver buckets on the table. Poor Sissy could not take advantage of the limitless wine but made up for it with food.

After eating I made my excuses, retreating to my room to FaceTime Blaine. He looked pleased with himself and requested I close my eyes. When I opened them I was looking at the tree now full of decorations, everything matching in traditional reds and golds. Baubles, bows and bells were hanging from every branch. I was missing him terribly but knowing he was okay and getting into the spirit of Christmas made my heart glow.

The call ended sooner than I hoped; he still had more decorating to do and had planned to meet Rob so he said his goodbyes. Mum and Sissy came to my room shortly after, having left Dad and Henry at the bar enjoying a whiskey or three. Mum had attained a bowl of complementary chocolates from reception and wanted the three of us to watch a film together. It was going to be a good week. All that silly worrying for nothing. Blaine and I had the next and every Christmas to do this together.

## Chapter 34

### Wednesday 7th December 2022

## Maya

Blaine's distance since Monday had been somewhat unbearable. Something was wrong, I was certain. He sent more pictures of his decorations and I responded with a picture of the angel I bought, as promised, to add to them. He replied thanking me, only it was an underwhelming response. Yesterday I tried FaceTiming, but he messaged shortly after saying he was unable to answer, no explanation.

I had considered that I might be overthinking things, looking for problems that did not exist because I missed him. It had occurred to me that he could have realised he was better without me, that the fear he projected onto me before I left was his own. Mum had been all too aware of my worry and had done all she could to occupy me. Yesterday she entered us into the lantern decorating competition in the square. The prize was a fifty-pound voucher to spend in the Christmas shop, driving everyone to unleash their competitive sides.

Mum went all Kirsty Allsopp with her classically traditional design, while Sissy and Henry went modern and sparkly. I hand painted a gold angel on mine, glued holly leaves and red berries underneath her, and placed tiny gold trumpets above either side of her head, finishing off with clouds of gold glitter. I was not in the spirit of things but had to admit it did look rather good.

When the judges came to the table Sissy grimaced at Henry for going overboard with the glue gun and sparkly embellishments. Mum smiled adoringly at hers, as though she had already been declared the victor. Imagine her face when I was announced the winner, all due to my hand-painted angel.

But still I wondered why Blaine was quiet and sent him a picture of my masterpiece. His reply was short, *Looks lovely. Well done.* I rang again but he did not answer.

Tonight's entertainment was the woodland light trail, also chosen by Mum and very pretty indeed. A trail path edged with lights led through the trees; thousands of bulbs flickered in the canopy above our heads. In the long grass between the trees illuminated reindeers stood, and Santa even waved from his sleigh.

Yet despite all this my heart ached. I longed for Blaine to tell me we were okay. I messaged him again, meaning to tell him I missed him, only my fingers kept typing, explaining how I was struggling with his silence and that I knew something was wrong. His reply did not reassure. *I'm fine, just been busy that's all. You just keep having a good time.*

## Rachel and Warren

"I called Blaine to see if he's made plans for Christmas yet. He might not want to come here now he's with Maya."

"What did he say, love?"

"Not much, he was detached again. You know how he used to pretend things were okay, say the bare minimum, but it was obvious he wasn't okay."

"He's never really stopped doing that has he?"

"I know I said I'd stop worrying about him, Warren, but I can't let go of the fear that something will bubble up to the surface one day."

"And where's all that worry got you? What did he say about Christmas?"

"Just that they haven't made plans yet, so he doesn't know what he's doing."

"That doesn't sound detached to me, just sounds like he hasn't made plans yet and doesn't know what he's doing."

## Chapter 35

### Friday 9th December 2022

**Blaine**

I've lost count of the times I've pictured her in that huge bed with someone else, laughing at the pathetic guy she left behind. Then I pulled myself up because it was Maya; she wouldn't do that. But her beautiful face soon haunted me; I saw her with someone who deserved her, like the man she thought she wanted before she met me. I'd been to hell and back all week. She'd messaged every day, updating me on their antics, but the nagging doubts wouldn't stop.

Rachel wanted to know if she'd see us Christmas Day, but I couldn't see beyond Maya coming home on Sunday, although I was the last thing they'd want to see in the middle of the night after a long journey home. Truth was I'd love to take her to Rachel and Warren's on Christmas Day. They were good people who embodied the spirit of Christmas. They were the personification of kindness and everything they touched turned to gold. Apart from me.

## Chapter 36

### Sunday 11ᵗʰ December 2022

### **Maya**

I woke in the four-poster bed. Faceless was beside me, crying inconsolably, telling me he would have to bring me to him, that only I could change the outcome and thus far I had not. His words made no sense; I was already there with him, but he said it seemed I was out of reach. The only hope left was for me to ask about the night he was taken from his mother. Should that fail, he would have no choice.

That was when I truly woke, for the final time, in the four-poster bed, fully aware of who he meant. But Faceless was simply my subconscious chewing over what I knew versus what did not make sense. I knew he was taken from his mother; my dreams were not telling me anything new. He had not talked about it, I was aware of that also, but the advice was to give him time and space until he was ready to talk. My head seemed to be battling its own want to push for answers against the advice to give him time.

After breakfast we strolled to the square to spend my prize on a gift for Mum and Dad. The nativity scene Mum had eyed up earlier in the week was perfect and she was thrilled; the ideal gift to mark the impending arrival of the new addition to our family. For Blaine I chose a further gift; a tree ornament, lovers kissing under the mistletoe. All I wanted now was to see him and know once and for all if we were okay.

At our table in the square we reminisced about our week, about ice-skating and how terrible Dad was, even the second time. Sissy anticipated the journey home, hoping to fare better than she had on the way here. Henry said it had been his favourite holiday to date. He fared better than Dad on the ice but decided it had been his least favourite activity.

I was sure Blaine would love it here. Tears welled in my eyes at the thought. What if he no longer wanted me? I could not shake the feeling and Mum reached for my hand, assuring me everything would be fine, that we had just missed each other and by Monday we would be back in one another's arms where we belonged. I hoped beyond hope she was right.

I also hoped he would be waiting on the driveway when we returned, with that look on his face that said I was his everything. That he might wrap me in his arms and plead that we never be apart again. I wished to feel anything but this emptiness and messaged to tell him we would be starting our journey home shortly. He had not replied by the time we reached the airport, nor had he replied by the time we boarded our plane and switched off our phones.

As we touched down at Gatwick I switched it back on and my heart fluttered when his message flashed on the screen, only to be disappointed by the words *Safe travels*. The Blaine I left would have said, *Hurry home, I can't be without you a moment longer.* The Blaine I left would have been waiting for me at the airport because he missed me so much.

My eyes scanned every area of that airport, but the only familiar faces I saw were the old couple from the park. What were the chances of them being in an airport an hour away from home at the same time as me? Not impossible, I supposed. But then I saw him, the man from the restaurant. The one who came into Totally Coffee, watching me the whole time before speaking to the very same couple outside when he left. He was striding towards me at a determined pace, eyes fixed on me. My heart raced, but before I could wonder why on earth he was here and charging towards me, the old couple stepped in his way, stopping him dead. They looked cross with him and were saying something I could not hear. Just then a group of people stepped in between us, obscuring the three of them from view. Henry was closest to me, and I pulled at his arm, instructing him to look in their direction, but when the group moved on neither the old couple nor the man were anywhere to be seen.

The three of them played on my mind all the way home until we got out of Dad's car to nothing other than mine and Mum's cars on the driveway, illuminated by the security light. No Blaine, no romantic end to a difficult week. Just darkness beyond the safety of the light and the notion that he was out there somewhere, and that he did not want to see me.

## The Elders

"She makes allowances for his iniquities. Her ability to do so is not a weakness, it is borne from the depths of her compassion and unconditional love. She truly sees the good in people.

But her love alone is not enough. He has a long journey ahead of him and he must discover the way of his own volition. The lessons will mean nothing if he does not learn them. They cannot be handed to him."

"I think we are all in agreement we have waited long enough. To not recover him now leaves her vulnerable. Thomas is trying to take her; should he succeed our window of opportunity will be lost. Should she encounter Blaine in the after there will be little we can do either to return her or bring her to us. She will not leave him to suffer his own torment; her love is too great. Blaine simply must come first. It is the only way. We cannot take him if Thomas has her."

"Then it is decided. We come for him tonight."

## Blaine

Shielded by darkness I stood behind the hedge at the spot where the big tree broke the dense growth, leaving a gap big enough to see most of the driveway. The car's arrival triggered the sensor light, offering a clear view of the three of them. Richard must have dropped Sissy and Henry off on the way home. Her eyes searched for something in the darkness, for me, and I regretted my distance again. I'd make it up to her tomorrow.

When all three were safely indoors I headed back to the car. Dizzy from seeing her I stepped into the road. Someone called my name, making me spin around and step back onto the path to look for the owner of the voice. Screeching brakes rang out. A car skidded out of control on the icy road, barrelling towards me, clipping the edge of the path where I'd stood just a second ago, missing me by an inch before spinning one hundred and eighty degrees, coming to a halt the wrong way round in the road. Luckily for the driver the roads were all but empty at that time of night. Luckily for me I stepped back when I did.

My heart pounded as I scanned the street for whoever had called my name. It sounded like a man but I hoped Maya, somehow seeing me through the hedge, had followed me, only I could see no one. Well, whatever I had heard just stopped me getting hit that's for sure. My head filled with images of not having the chance to make things up to her, going to my grave without feeling her embrace or kissing her one last time. I just walked away; I didn't tell her I loved her. I couldn't leave it until the morning.

Turning on my heel I ran back to her house; Maggie was near the kitchen window. Looking up as I triggered the sensor light, she saw me running up the drive and her lips mouthed Maya's name followed by something I couldn't decipher. A second later the front door opened and there she stood, my angel, my goddess. Those eyes as captivating as ever. I had no words, just an overwhelming need to scoop her up and hold her.

# Chapter 37

## Monday 12th November 2022

### **Maya**

I neither asked nor cared how he knew we were home; he came to me and nothing else mattered. The separation had changed nothing; he still looked at me with eyes full of love and sincerity, but would not stay, promising instead to take me to the Dog and Ferret for a cosy, romantic meal tomorrow night, insisting I stay at his after.

My heart recuperated immediately; I was certain I would sleep well. Only I woke at three to Faceless again, screaming because they had tried taking his boy. I reached for his hand to calm him, but even though he was in front of me I could not touch him. He was screaming and fading both in sound and sight until he was gone and I was alone.

It had taken a while to fall asleep again, partly because of the dream and partly because when I checked my phone for the time Blaine had messaged, regretting his decision to not stay. He must have been asleep when I responded because no reply came until this morning when he suggested we visit Rachel and Warren on our way out this evening to discuss when we can join them for dinner over Christmas.

He bounced through the door of Totally Coffee this morning, gracing me with his best smouldering look, but the rest of the day dragged in impatient anticipation and when he picked me up this evening he swept me off my feet, kissing me as though making up for the entire week's absence in that one kiss.

I only wish the evening had continued as well, but here we were on our way to The Dog and Ferret and I had the sickest feeling inside me. All was fine until Warren invited Blaine to help make tea. The distant mumbling of their voices was barely audible from the lounge, but when Rachel pointed me to the cloakroom just past the kitchen I heard them. Blaine was cross at Warren. "It's nothing like that," he said, neither of them aware I was outside the door. Warren responded calmly.

"It's just like the heart Angela wore around her neck. Tell me you're not trying to replace her with Maya? It's been a long time."

"I'm not trying to replace her. I don't even want to hear the name Angela Farriner," Blaine retorted angrily.

I froze, listening to the heated exchange. Who was Angela Farriner? Was he married before? Perhaps he was still married. Warren's tone sharpened, matching Blaine's apparent annoyance.

"You're holding on to her, Blaine. I think Maya reminds you of her."

One of them was moving towards the door so I scooted into the cloakroom, closing the door quietly behind me. I could not unhear what I had heard, and I could not look at Blaine and pretend to be okay. I did not want to leave that cloakroom, ever. Reflected in the mirror above the sink was the very heart they discussed and I no longer understood its meaning. Had I been merely symbolic? A reminder of an old flame, or worse, a wife?

Mustering all my resolve I returned to the lounge where they all now sat discussing Christmas, Blaine and Warren unaware I had heard them. Rachel was saying how she would love to have us both there for dinner, even if it was on Boxing Day, reminding Blaine how Lucy would be distraught if she did not spend time with her little brother at Christmas. Blaine reassured her we would all have dinner together, his demeanour calm, as though the conversation with Warren had never taken place.

Then he said we should go to make our dinner reservations. I had not yet said a word, my mouth was dry and my stomach uneasy. Back in his car he explained how much Christmas meant to Rachel and how the whole family made a big deal of it. But all I could hear in my head was, *Who is Angel Farriner?*

Parking at The Dog and Ferret, Blaine looked at me, brushing the wisps of hair from my face with his fingertips like he did, and asked me what was wrong. He noticed my silence again since leaving Rachel and Warren's and was worried he had done something wrong.

"Who the hell is Angela Farriner?" I snapped.

Lowering his hand back onto his lap he took a slow deep breath as though composing himself. There was silence; painful, awkward, hellish silence. I repeated the question, only this time he shouted.

"DON'T SPEAK HER NAME. DON'T EVER ASK ME WHO ANGELA FARRINER IS."

His face was angry, his hands clasped tight around the steering wheel. Getting out of the car I made across the car park towards the road. What else could I do but walk away? There was too much he refused to share. How could we build a life together when I did not know who he was? I loved him but I couldn't trust someone who kept himself so hidden, someone who presented such anger when I questioned him.

I was too confused, too angry, to cry. Instead I took my phone from my pocket and typed her name into the search engine. Blaine shouted my name but I increased my pace. I should have been the one shouting, demanding answers. Instead, his refusal to speak had left me Googling her name in the hope of finding a social media profile that might tell me who she was. Only it was not a Facebook or Instagram profile that headlined the list of search results. It was a news article.

Blaine was shouting my name, anger still present in his tone, his footsteps closed in behind me. I stabbed at the link with a trembling fingertip. I was almost at the road. The article opened revealing the headline: *Angela Farriner: Sentenced to life for murder*. Everything inside my head went dark. Blaine Farriner had secrets that were too big, too dark to share with me.

He was behind me, his hand grabbing at my arm. I lurched forward to escape his grasp at the very moment I heard the roar of an engine. He screamed my name. Somebody else shouted too, a woman, a voice I did not recognise. Everything felt suddenly chaotic. It was too late to step back into his reach. The screeching of brakes rang out then THUD. The sound of the car slamming into my side, forcing me from the ground, was deafening. Then there was nothing but eerie silence as I sailed over the car, the flight momentarily freeing me from my imminent fate. Another sickening thud and cracks as my body hit the floor behind the now stationary metal assassin. Someone screamed, piercing my eardrums like a knife. Perhaps it was me. Pain was everywhere and everything.

A young boy, maybe eighteen, rushed to my side, crying and shaking, touching my face and pleading.

"I'm sorry, I didn't see you, you were just there in the road. Shit… shit, I didn't see you in time," he blathered, slumping to the floor beside me.

But I was not panicking. It was strange to lie in such pain and yet feel so utterly calm. No, not calm… acquiescent. An elderly couple approached us; it was them again, and now I was certain this was more than a coincidence. The man extended his hand, coaxing the boy back to his feet.

"It wasn't your fault, son, she just stepped out. "His face was kind, only it was not the boy he watched as he spoke. His eyes focused on the beautiful goliath of a man whose grasp I had been escaping when I stepped in front of this damned car. The man who looked at me now with as much pain in his eyes as I felt in my wrecked body. The elderly man continued.

"My wife and I, we were on the other side of the road waiting to cross. We saw you coming, but she... she kept walking, didn't even look up to check for cars. Too busy looking at her bloody phone. You couldn't have known."

His words had not reassured the boy. He was panicking, not for himself but for me. So, leaving him in the hands of a passerby, the old couple walked away to someone else who had been there the whole time. Someone whose clothes and face had become familiar. Was it... no, it couldn't be. Could it?

Voices were shouting and my heightened senses could hear everyone at the same time. A panicked voice instructed me to lay still, as though I could have moved had I the strength to try. Another recalled the accident, presumably to someone on the other end of a phone.

"Yeah, she's conscious.... Yeah, she's breathing but it looks labored. She's been hit by a car, went right over the top. There's blood coming from her head and her legs look bad, she's lying awkwardly. You've got to get someone here. Please hurry. We're outside The Dog and Ferret on the corner of Collingwood Lane..."

But the voices and the light were fading, the pain was fading. What a strange feeling; while the panic and the noise continued, quiet peacefulness consumed me, and as my final breath slipped into the ether all I could see was him. I acquiesced.

# Chapter 38

## Monday 12th December 2022

## 7.05 p.m.

### Pearl

"Thanks for seeing me at short notice. I almost didn't make it; the dog was sick and took a turn. My wife came home to sit with her, didn't want to leave the poor girl alone."

"I'm sorry to hear Willow's under the weather, Pearl. I hope it's nothing serious."

"She's probably just eaten something she shouldn't have. Your office turned out well. The new chairs go perfectly with the wall colour. Very calming."

"They're more comfortable than the old ones too; I was getting a numb behind after a full day of clients. I hope the smell of paint isn't too off-putting, I've had the windows open to air it, but it's lingering. What brings you for supervision earlier than scheduled?"

"It's my client, Angela."

"Sentenced for murder. You've had several sessions with her, but she hasn't given you much to discuss yet."

"That's her. Angela isn't like the other prisoners I work with. Most enter their counselling sessions with a clear voice, protesting either their innocence or their rehabilitation as though I might be a ticket to freedom if they say the right thing. Most have stories of abusive childhoods, getting in with the wrong crowds, addiction. But not Angela. She's balanced, rational, addiction free, warm. I could go on but you probably get the picture. She neither pleads her innocence nor her rehabilitation."

"So what does she bring to your sessions?"

"She's recalled her life from the idyllic childhood, born and raised in Barbados to loving parents, a mum who doted on her children and a father with a heart of gold, through to coming to England to where she finds herself now."

"Why did she come to England?"

"A holiday with her college friends brought her here initially. Back home she was studying a bachelor's degree in general nursing. She loved helping people. They wanted a holiday before commencing their final year of studies. That was how she met her husband. They fell deeply in love, and back at home she hated every second of being apart from him. Despite the pleas of her parents to remain in Barbados and marry someone of her own descent, she left."

"Did she maintain a relationship with her parents after leaving?"

"In the early days of the relationship with her husband she spoke to them regularly on the phone and travelled back to Barbados to visit them too."

"But the contact stopped?"

"Yes. But I don't want to jump ahead in her story. It's important you see it develop as I have."

## Maya

It *was* him, only he was both of them, and this was all very confusing. I was certain the car had struck me; I remembered the sounds and the pain. The same people were present, some panicking, some staring, but all silent. I found myself a short distance from the muted chaos this very man had warned me of.

Flashing lights appeared as an ambulance swung around the corner, a police car hot on its tail. Two paramedics and two uniformed police officers rushed towards something in the road; I could not see who or what for the bystanders obscuring my view. I had been certain it was me lying there, the feeling of fading into the darkness was still fresh in my memory. But the darkness had lifted, it was lighter than it had been just moments before. Turning to the man who had been there all along, the only person who seemed to notice me at all, I asked, "It's you, isn't it?"

"It is," he replied, offering nothing more.

A gap opened up in the gathering crowd, allowing me a view of the paramedic on his knees, pumping at the chest of who was now visible on the road. How could this be? A hand touched my shoulder as a dread of unrivalled measures filled me. It was not the weight of flesh and bones I felt, but warmth and reassurance that calmed me.

Across the road Blaine stared helplessly at the lifeless body. My body. Tears streaked his cheeks and more pain occupied his eyes than I had ever seen. His large frame was motionless amid the surrounding mayhem.

"How is this possible?" I asked Faceless, only now he wasn't faceless at all. And the big coat was gone, revealing the tee shirt and gold chain. How had I not noticed the jeans and black loafers before? Outside Totally Coffee, while speaking with the old couple, his legs and feet had been hidden by the wall below the window. At the restaurant they had been tucked under the table, and everything happened so quickly at the airport I simply did not notice. But I noticed now, and it gave him away.

Still he offered nothing. He watched Blaine closely and it struck me how they held the same expression of regret. "Please," I begged him, "tell me what is happening."

I needed something, anything by way of an explanation. Waiting no longer I moved towards Blaine, reaching for his arm, only he wasn't really there, I could not touch him. He was both in front of me and a world away.

"Am I dead?" I asked.

"Come. I will explain," Faceless finally said.

## Faceless

The weight of my mistakes crushes me. But now I hold in my grasp the one remaining opportunity; she is a gift to be held with the greatest of care, she is my chance to save him and leave this eternal hell.

Maya is beautiful, just as Angela is. Although opposite in appearance. Her skin porcelain, Angela's dark as the midnight sky. Her eyes soul piercingly blue, Angela's the deepest brown. But the depth of their love, that is what connects them. And what connected Blaine to them both.

The elders are displeased; she was not mine to take. But what choice did I have? I live my mistakes over and over, driven to insanity by my earthly depravities. I must leave but can only do so when he is safe, free to live, free to grow and recover and forgive.

She is both Blaine's and my recovery.

# Chapter 39

## Monday 12th December 2022

## 7.09 p.m.

### **Maya**

I could not say if we moved or whether the scene around us shifted, but we found ourselves somewhere vaguely familiar: a white-walled room, little bigger than the white table between us and the chairs we found ourselves upon.

Faceless was silent, lost in a reverie. If this was death then it was not as expected. I had considered at length how it might feel, where I might find myself, but had not imagined this. My thoughts drifted to the elderly couple; they too had been at the accident, and many other places of late. He knew them, I had seen them together more than once. Then to the accident itself. What a fool to have lunged into the road — what had I thought Blaine would do, had his grasp on me been successful? Did I believe he was capable of hurting me?

It struck me how differently thoughts occupied me here. They were not confined in my head as I was accustomed to, rather they *were* me. My body was no longer a solid and separate entity to the workings of my mind. My whole self was as light as the thoughts that defined me.

Questions overwhelmed me, spilling silently into the white room. Angela Farriner. Who was she? What was she to Blaine? And who on earth had she murdered? The necklace that bound us was still around my neck and, despite the new weightlessness of everything, it weighed heavily upon me. If only I had stopped instead of lunging into the road, I could have read beyond the headline. I would have known who she was. I would have been alive. Instead I was here, clueless, and with none of the heavenly expectations of death. Still he watched me until my patience wore thin.

"Look," I snapped, "it's time you started talking. Who are you and where exactly are we?"

## Faceless

How should I tell her she had not found herself here by accident? Two questions she asked but I heard many more. Nothing was beyond perception once you attuned to the environment. She asked where she found herself; her confusion as evident as mine the day I passed.

Explaining *here* was not straight forward. *Here* was different for each of us. For some it was the last stop before another chance at growth, new experiences, new lessons. For some it was a place to reflect before moving on to a final destination, neither here nor there but everywhere, all at once. Utter freedom from everything that restricted us. For me it was hell, an endless remembrance of the stain I bore upon those who loved me. Groundhog Day, my mistakes on repeat.

She asked who I was, who Angela was. I did not want her to read on and find out that way. My way was for the best. Angela could not have loved me the way she loved Blaine; with him her eyes exposed a love so powerful it was painful to watch. She loved him with every ounce of her being, until she went away. And her heart being so pure she simply accepted her fate. He loved her immeasurably too, but that love seemed to have dried up now, his attention turned to Maya. Of course, I knew she was perfect for him, there was no need to continue searching for Angela's replacement.

My arrival here had been unexpected to say the least. The life-taker's hand forced by those who hector me now. I did not blame as I had before, this time it was a necessity, to protect and survive.

But Maya, dear sweet Maya, the unwitting pawn. The elders would not allow me to hold her for long. This room would keep us safe for now, but in time they would find us and as I could show her nothing from here it would be counterproductive to stay. I must tell her of things before we left; our time would be short. The elders would not be far behind.

# Pearl

"Pearl, I feel you might have come to a conclusion about Angela and wonder if I'll make the same assumption."

"Indeed. Ordinarily you observe the finer details, possibilities I may have overlooked, connections I failed to make. This time I simply wonder if you'll arrive at the same conclusion."

"Then please continue."

"I'll spare you further details of her life in Barbados; I believe it's irrelevant, except for the references she made to how her father never struck anyone nor fell foul to the drink. And how she wanted to look after people, save them, as it were.

"Angela and her college friends stayed at a caravan park, travelling to new destinations each day, covering as much of the English southeast coast as they could in two weeks. It was the fifth day when they decided upon Woodbridge.

"Sitting outside a café on the harbour, enjoying an ice-cream and the late July sunshine, taking in the smells and sounds of the coastal summertime, she noticed a man standing motionless some twenty feet from her table, staring expressionless at her. She thinks if he hadn't been so handsome she may have found the experience somewhat intimidating. The boys back home had no trouble approaching her and telling her what they were thinking. But this man just stared at her, as though paralysed.

"Her friends laughed at him, but Angela felt something. Something she hadn't felt when talking to the confident boys back home. His focus shifted to her friends and, looking suddenly humiliated, he retreated into a pub a few doors along from the café. When Angela and her friends left their table they walked past the pub, and there he was, watching her from the window. Still expressionless.

"Angela couldn't stop thinking about the handsome stranger. Her sleep that night was fractured by dreams, his face appearing in each of them. By morning her mind was made up; she wouldn't join her friends to the next coastal destination, she would instead return to Woodbridge, alone.

"Heading straight for the harbour, Angela wondered whether she was of sound mind. Why would anyone return to find such a peculiar stranger? Especially alone. But she continued on, recalling her disappointment when, after three hours of sitting at a table outside that same café, he hadn't returned. The following day she headed to Woodbridge once again."

"I'm wondering what you thought about her leaving her friends to pursue this unknown male."

"I thought it both foolish and romantic. But it fitted with her ideals about falling in love. Her parents had experienced love at first sight and went on to have a long and happy marriage. I believe she thought the same would happen to her.

"After sitting outside that café for a third time, still with no sign of him, she entered the pub he'd retreated to, partly through curiosity and partly to take shelter from the hot sun. It was bright and cheery inside; people, mainly men, talked and laughed. It had warmth and character, the sort of atmosphere you might hope for when holidaying. And there at the bar was the man. As his eyes met hers he pushed away his whiskey glass and stood to face her.

"Apparently, the silent staring lasted longer than was comfortable and she feared he'd walk away again, so she introduced herself, telling him how she'd come looking for him. She told me it was love, right from that moment, maybe even from the moment he stood motionless, watching her with her friends.

"She believed God brought them together, that there could be no other explanation for a connection so strong between complete strangers. He wasn't religious and didn't share her opinion; he believed fate had intervened that day, lovers drawn together by an indefinable connection, never to be separated, unless fate had other ideas. His words, according to Angela.

"He was sad she would only be in England for one more week and, after kissing her passionately, vowed to spend every remaining day with her. Angela said her life changed forever that day."

## Chapter 40

Monday 12th December 2022

7.13 p.m.

### Maya

Snapping from the reverie, anguish heavy in his eyes, he apologised for bringing me here and explained how this room was the only place we could talk uninterrupted. He continued with another apology that I found myself here at all, that it had been a terrible way to die and would no doubt cause Blaine further suffering. Falling silent again he stared absently into my eyes.

I stood from my seat, unsure of what I planned to do or where to I might go. I found myself dead and in the company of this man; it was all a little too much. I wanted answers. He rose also, beckoning me to sit, promising to tell me everything — well, actually, to show me everything, but only after we had talked.

I sat back in the seat I could not feel beneath me. It supported me yet felt as though it could be a figment of my imagination. Perhaps all of this was a figment of my dying imagination. A hallucination as my senses and mind failed me. You read about such things in studies.

Then he started, recalling first how the elders had robbed him of his life and his chance to be happy with Angela, returning him to this place where every time he died he was forced to play out his mistakes, but was never given the chance to return and put things right. Every return was a different lifetime and a new set of mistakes. Every death he retreated to this room, the only place the elders did not look for him. But they would, if they knew he was here with me.

"Who are the elders?" I interrupted. But there were a hundred more pressing questions swelling within me. His expression changed.

"I'm terribly sorry, Maya." He looked at me with warmth as he spoke. "I expect so much of you. I told you to ask him what happened the night he was taken from his mother. It could have been the catalyst in making him talk. Why didn't you ask him? You wanted the answers so badly for yourself, yet you missed the opportunity." He wanted an answer, but I had only questions that so far he had ignored.

"Who are you? What is your interest in Blaine and me?" I demanded.

"I hear your questions, even those you have not yet asked, but our time is short. Let me try again, Maya." He continued, "I have been watching over you both, as have the elders. Blaine is a broken man and I must help him heal from the things he has done wrong. They were not his fault. I believed if I brought the two of you together you might save him, or at least help him remember the things he has buried so deeply.

"The elders watch for different reasons. They decide when it is time for people to leave their current lives and return here to review their progress. In each lifetime we evolve by means of failing and learning until our souls achieve their highest potential. Only then can we become one of them. Influencing who stays and who is recovered. They tell me such decisions are made only for the greater good and that until a soul has reached its highest potential one cannot comprehend the true meaning of the greater good.

"They are certain you are highly evolved and will soon be one of them. That is why they guard you so closely; they will not allow for the sins of others to set you back on your journey. You epitomise the greater good, all bar one small detail. That is what you are learning this time around.

"Matching you with Blaine was a risk for this very fact. But what choice did I have? No one else was going to open his heart the way you have, and without doing so the elders would have brought him back here to start again. But none of this is his fault. He should have lived a life full of love and hope and learned the things he was destined to learn in this lifetime. And until I help him back onto the right path I am stuck here. If they recover him now, what will become of me?

"This place in which you find yourself, it is both heaven and hell, and for you it is an in-between space."

"What is it for you?" I asked, certain of the answer.

"Oh, this is my own personal hell. I will not leave it until I have helped Blaine overcome his traumas and removed the risk to those he loves."

Memories of the anger in Blaine's face when I presented myself to him in new sexy underwear and his attempt to grab me at the roadside flooded me. Was this the risk Faceless referred to? How far would he have gone? Blaine would not have hurt me when he held me so carefully. Pain swelled from within, filling the room, pain that he would not hold me again, pain that I pulled away from the final opportunity to feel his hands touching me, wanting me. But I could not cry, and just as my pain had filled the room so too it dispersed, falling like mist to the ground.

"I still do not know who you are. I cannot continue to call you Faceless now you have a face. And still you have not told me about Angela, or her relationship with Blaine, or where you fit into all this."

He looked at me with doleful eyes. Whoever he was, I assumed him to be the victim of Angela's crime. "She was meant to save me, but she did not and here we are."

## Pearl

"They fell in love, or obsession, very quickly, spending the rest of the week touring the southeast together, he delivered her back to the caravan and her friends each night. She said his appearance defied his romantic nature."

"What did he look like?"

"Tattooed, toned, unshaven. Just not the typical romantic looking guy. Whatever one of them looks like. They didn't consummate the relationship. He was adamant he would wait and prove his love and commitment to her. That she was too pure of heart to be rushed into sex. She confirmed that she was a virgin when they met, a practising Christian, and despite her longing for her new man she preferred to wait until marriage for consummation. His honour only made her love him all the more.

"Parting ways was traumatic for both of them and back in Barbados she missed him terribly. So, each day, from the community college or her hospital placement, she would phone him. The distance between them did nothing to dampen their feelings and after just a few months he proposed. She abandoned her studies, so close to completion, and her family to come here. They forgave her of course and she promised them regular visits and frequent phone calls.

"They married without fuss at the local registry office and honeymooned at the very caravan park he had delivered her safely back to each night when they met. The relationship was consummated on their wedding night, and every night thereafter. He told her that when he was inside her he felt alive, in a way he hadn't felt before.

"She always enters my room with a photograph in her hand, a picture of herself holding her baby. In it she wears a necklace with a diamond heart pendant and for the entirety of every session she sits with her fingertip resting on the heart. She explained how she and her husband had exchanged necklaces as wedding gifts and how hers had been torn from her neck during an altercation. But she hadn't divulged how the relationship changed at that time.

"Angela fell pregnant soon after the wedding but her husband was shocked. He'd pledged his eternal love so she hadn't considered that children wouldn't be a part of that. Looking back, she thinks it was a warning that she missed, blinded as she was by his love. He distanced himself from her and when questioned he wasn't sure why. Angela offered ample reassurance about what a wonderful father he'd be and by the second trimester he'd grown accustomed to the idea of fatherhood, spending hours pondering baby names. Angela reported that they were almost as happy as they had been in the beginning. Although she stated that on several occasions, when something triggered him emotionally, he would shut down and distance himself for a day or two."

"What sort of things?"

"Another man. Jealousy. Angela worked in a care home. One of the other carers took a shine to her. She wasn't interested in him, she was a one-man woman, but he made his feelings for her clear. Towards the end of the pregnancy he even told her he would raise the child as his own if she left her husband for him. She'd confided in him as a friend about how her husband seemed distant after she announced the pregnancy, fearing he'd leave her to raise the baby alone. It seems the other gentleman got his hopes up too soon, only to have them dashed when the relationship healed. But he persisted right up until Angela went on maternity leave.

"Her husband saw him sometimes, waiting with her outside the care home when he arrived to pick her up. She assured him he was only making sure she was safe outside in the dark until her lift arrived. But he would anger, saying he saw the way the other man looked at her, that he thought himself more than just a friend and she'd have to be blind not to see it. Obviously she saw it, but that was a truth that would do more harm than good."

## Faceless

"I must show you who Blaine was before he fell in love, when he was just a boy. He experienced terrible things at the hands of his father. Things your precious heart could not comprehend, Maya. Things that made him the man he became. They are not wrong when they say history repeats itself; it does indeed. Blaine embodies everything his father was, destined to commit the same sins. But it cannot be too late for him. He can change. He must be saved. Come, watch with me."

## Chapter 41

## Monday 12th December 2022

## 7.16 p.m.

### Maya

The stark white walls faded and Faceless proffered his hand, lifting me from my chair. To hold a hand yet feel neither flesh nor bone, only warmth and love, was a strangely familiar sensation. His eyes laid heavy upon me; his expression between pain and fear.

Without moving we found ourselves in a bedroom where a woman slept in her bed. The transition had been smooth but all too quickly scenes flashed before us in fast forward, unsettling on the eyes, too fast to decipher. Faceless released my hand to clutch at his head, the palms of both hands pressing into his temples, eyes shut tight; he was not in control. Shaking violently, he let out a howling wail and the scenes slowed before us.

We were in another room, a scantly furnished lounge, a dado rail separating floral wallpaper from cream paint. The whole room was immaculately clean and tidy. A small boy, seated on the very edge of a brown corduroy sofa, wrung his hands. It was Blaine, no more than five years old. The boy who grew into the man I loved. You could tell, even at that age, how beautiful he would become. His small hand patted the sofa beside himself and without effort I crossed the room to sit with him. "Now ask him," instructed Faceless, "ask him what it was like."

But I did not need to ask him a thing because he glanced up at me, those beautiful green eyes with flecks of brown and gold, not as bright as in the adult version but present, developing, filled with tears that spilled on to his soft little cheeks, running past the dimples more distinct in youth than in adulthood.

"He's always cross with me," he said. "Daddy." He flicked his head back slightly as though to indicate Daddy's presence in another room.

Shouting erupted from somewhere unseen. Little Blaine covered his ears with his hands. "He's gets cross with her too," he said, "but he's always sorry after. I hear her sometimes, crying in the bedroom. Sometimes she cries when he leaves the room. Sometimes she cries when he's still in there. He always leaves after he's made Mummy cry."

"What does he do that makes Mummy cry?" I asked, but little Blaine shrugged his shoulders; he was not allowed in Mummy and Daddy's room so how could he know?

"Why do you think Daddy is always cross with you?"

He shrugged again before answering. "I try to be good, but I always get it wrong. He just doesn't like me."

"That cannot be so. You are just a boy." But this seemed to upset him even more. Recoiling away from me, he pulled himself back on the sofa until his back rested upon the over-sized cushions and his socked feet reached barely over the edge of the seat.

"No one believes me," he replied with his head hung low, "that's why I don't tell anyone."

"Who doesn't believe you?"

"You, the lady at little school. And Daddy told me how I made the lady cross with my made-up stories."

I pictured adult Blaine and his inability to discuss the things that matter. The small boy trapped inside the adult form. The scene shifted again. Everything seemed to happen around us here. A different lounge, the same sofa, the same little boy, just older, maybe a year or two. On the coffee table in front of him, dregs of whiskey sat abandoned in a glass. Blaine watched it as though deciding whether to drink it.

"I wouldn't," he said, looking up at me. There was a new maturity in his tone, not the kind you want to hear from someone as young as maybe seven. "He'd kill me for sure if I took even a sip."

He was sat further back than when I first saw him perched on the edge of the sofa and his feet touched the floor comfortably now; he was visibly taller. Turning to face me fully I saw the bruises on his forearms, big and purple. Lifting his sleeves higher, he revealed fading yellow-brown bruises, the type left behind by fingers squeezing young flesh too hard.

"Did Daddy do those?" I asked, pointing to them. But a voice rang out in the background.

"You better not be talking to anyone out there, Blaine, telling them our business. Telling them your dirty little lies."

## Pearl

"Angela described her husband's behaviour as being a bit Jekyll and Hyde during the latter stage of the pregnancy. He was mostly loving and attentive, wanting her by his side, but distant and withdrawn when occasionally triggered. Nothing alarming, just average jealousy for an obviously insecure man according to her."

"What's your interpretation of that, Pearl?"

"Oh, a red flag for sure. He couldn't accept that other men might find her attractive without her needing to run off with them. But it's clear how besotted with him she was. I don't believe she could have left him had she tried. She still spoke to her family at that point. The pair of them travelled to Barbados during the pregnancy and the whole family adored him; they could see how much he loved her and believed she was safe in his care. Before they returned to England her parents made them promise to return with the baby as soon as they could. But the trip never materialised.

"The birth itself was troublesome and by the time the baby was born Angela was haemorrhaging and needed medical attention. She was thankful her husband could take the baby and start bonding straight away. Only it didn't work out like that. The bond didn't occur. Even at home he never offered to help her with feeding or changing. She said everything changed again the day of the birth. I'd say it developed rather than changed, that it was there all along, she just hadn't wanted to see it.

"She'd hoped he would love their son the way he loved her, but he resented sharing her attention. Everything the child did seemed to anger him and as time went on he began drinking, sometimes heavily, and his contempt grew. She said the drink made him lustful towards her but also emotionally disconnected. There were times when she didn't want sex because she was tired or because he was drunk, but this became another trigger. If she turned him down when he was sober he'd withdraw, but when drunk he became angry, took what he wanted whether she wanted it or not."

"You mean he raped her?"

"Repeatedly. She'd tell him she didn't want to, that he stunk of alcohol, but it wasn't up for negotiation, he wanted it and that was that. He'd tell her he loved her and hold her gently afterwards, but the damage was done. He didn't even notice if she cried during the ordeal. She never went to the police because she was ashamed; he was her husband and it was her duty to be available for him. She made less phone calls to home because she couldn't lie to her family, but also couldn't tell them what was going on; it would have broken their hearts.

"He forbade her from returning to work at the end of her maternity period for fear of the other man hitting on her. But after five years, when the child started infant school, he seemed to have forgotten about him, mainly because he was drinking most nights, and allowed her to return. The other man still worked there but she didn't tell her husband about him until his name slipped out accidently. That was the first time he struck her, across the face with the back of his hand. She said it was the most shocking thing she'd experienced, even more so than the rapes.

"He demanded she ignore the man and never be alone with him, but the nature of the job meant they'd have no choice but to work alone when paired together by the senior in charge. The man became her confidant and still had feelings for her. He was kind and compassionate; he never judged her or made her feel anything less than she was. He held everything she told him in confidence.

"In time he confessed his love for her; she felt something for him but wasn't sure if she loved him or whether he fulfilled a need that her husband was no longer able to. Nothing happened between them, but an absent-minded comment from one of her colleagues in front of her husband escalated the situation."

"What was the comment?"

"Something like 'Oh, here's your other husband, got them falling at your feet.' Well, the husband lost his mind, shouting at her in front of everyone and back in the privacy of their home he struck her violently. He was sorry, promised it would never happen again, and she forgave him even though she knew it would repeat itself.

"The other man noticed the bruise on her cheek a few days later. He held her and cried, begged her to leave her husband and move in with him, child and all. She said if she'd taken him up on that offer things would never have turned out the way they did. She wouldn't have ended up in prison.

"The violence continued and the rapes became more aggressive as his jealousy grew out of control. The contempt he showed their child escalated too; he would lash out, only he didn't apologise or show any remorse to him afterwards the way he did with her.

"She said the child would look at her with tearful eyes while his father was hurting him, but she didn't dare intervene, such was her fear of her husband. She saw a flash of something cold and vicious across his little face once when his father was beating him. His eyes had pled for her intervention but when she didn't respond his demeanour changed and he glared back at his father in defiance, no tears, no fear, just hatred. She said her mother would have called it wickedness."

## Maya

Another shift, the same lounge, a bigger Blaine, a woman crying hysterically in another room, only this time I could see her, both rooms visible at once. Blaine told me she was his mum, that Dad had gone out after making her cry. She was curled up foetal position on a messy bed. Blood spatters on the white sheets. She held her face with one hand, the other rubbing gentle, circular motions over her tummy.

"I heard him screaming at her, calling her a whore. What's a whore?"

Faceless was beside me, remorse leaching from every line on his tired face. "This isn't even the worst of it," he said. "When you looked into his eyes, Maya, when you held him in your arms, did you sense the pain and the torment he had to suffer because of that man?"

I had felt it, in the way he held me like I was glass. Arms strong enough to break me but never did he dare squeeze any harder. And the eyes, the look, the pain. It was there every single day, every time he looked at me.

He would not have hurt me had I not escaped his grasp. He would never have subjected me to this because he knew how it felt. Faceless had to be wrong; this history could not repeat itself. I could not allow myself to believe that Blaine would repeat the terrible behaviour displayed by his father.

Another shift; he must have been nine or ten now. Another flat; we were in the kitchen, all was silent. Blaine had marks on his face, scratches, a fading bruise on his neck that looked like fingertip impressions again. He told me he wore a scarf to hide it, and Mum no longer cried as much as she used to even though dad shouted at her more frequently now.

His features were changing, becoming more masculine, more recognisable as the Blaine I knew. But his changing appearance only made his father angrier. His mother could not get near him for fear of being hit. She used to cuddle him all the time when they were alone, but he said Dad saw it in her face when she lied to him, and he asked her all the time if she'd been near "the boy". That was how he addressed him. As though he could not bear to say his name.

Young Blaine told me how his father pushed him around, how he hurt him if he so much as opened his mouth. How his mother watched but did nothing.

Faceless interrupted, "His eyes plead with his mother's; all he wants is to be saved. All he wants is for her to protect him, to stop the violence. He does not care how; he just wants it to stop. But she is too scared to protect him. We must never be too scared to save someone, Maya. We can help them if we just know how."

# Chapter 42

## Monday 12th December 2022

## 7.19 p.m.

### **Pearl**

"The other man stood close by as Angela got into the husband's car one evening after work, making eye contact as though warning him not to hurt her. They'd worked together all day, and she'd told him she feared for both hers and her son's safety and he'd pleaded with her again to leave her husband. Then he'd kissed her. That was how she knew she didn't love him; he was her friend and confidant, nothing more. She told him so too and broke his heart. Only she hadn't known it would be the last time she ever saw him.

"So angered was her husband at the sight of the other man he demanded Angela go straight to the bedroom to wait for him when they got home. Certain he would beat the boy before turning to her, she recalled praying to God for help. She described his eyes as those of the devil. He smelled of whiskey and smoke and aftershave. She couldn't see the man she married anymore, just the demon forcing her onto the bed, a slave to his own jealousy, snarling in her face about her being his wife, not the whore she'd turned out to be. She was crying but he didn't care, he just snarled even more, demanding she enjoy it. Then he pressed on her windpipe until she gasped for breath, tearing the chain from her neck as he released his hand, throwing it to the floor. He punched her face and bit her shoulder, all the while penetrating her forcefully. She showed me the scar on her shoulder: perfect teeth imprints.

"But in his rage, he had failed to close the bedroom door. Angela saw her son watching at the doorway with terror in his eyes. She made eye contact with him, silently pleading for him to turn around, to go to his room and not come out. She said he obeyed.

"Angela reported, as an afterthought, that her son had reached into the room to pick up the necklace from the floor before retreating to his room. She couldn't look me in the eye when she told me this but made eye contact when adding how she hoped it was still in his possession. It's her only connection to him. To her it symbolises giving him her heart the way she failed to as a mother.

"With her eyes fixed back on the floor, she said when her boy turned around to walk back to his room it was the last time she ever saw him too. Maybe it was sorrow that made her look down, or maybe it was an example of how she struggles to lie. Either way, that was when she said she reached for the kitchen knife, the largest one from the block that happened to be on the bedside table and thrust it into her husband's back. She described how he froze on top of her, unsure of what had just happened. She pulled out the knife, certain he would die quicker if she let him bleed out. He slumped to the bed beside her, still breathing, still conscious, whispering, 'What did you do?'

"Angela waited until his breathing had stopped before dialling 999. She didn't want him to be saved; she wanted him dead, where he couldn't hurt anyone else. The police arrived soon after and arrested her, and her son was placed with a foster family. She received updates about him; the family he was placed with took good care of him and he seemed to demonstrate no devastating effects of what she claims he witnessed that night."

"What she claims he witnessed? You don't believe her version of events?"

"What do you make of it?"

"Well, I found myself wondering what the knife was doing beside the bed. I could understand a smaller knife being there, one you might use to peel or cut an apple, say. But what would you use the largest one for in bed? Had she premeditated the murder?"

"That's what the police believed."

"But surely he would have seen it? And that would pose the risk of him using it on her instead. Or at the very least angering him into a more violent attack. And the chances of the boy accurately deciphering the intention in her look seem slim. How could he have known what she pled? I sense you debate the likelihood of him having stopped to pick up the necklace on his way back to his room too. Or indeed if that was the last time she saw him."

"It doesn't add up. There are flaws in the story. Angela's a gentle lady, I don't believe she premeditated the murder. I do believe much of her recollection of the events, especially the abusive nature of her husband. But unfortunately, with no previous reports of domestic violence in the family, they attributed Angela's injuries as likely to have been caused in the scuffle before she killed him. I think the jury made a grave mistake when they dismissed abuse as a motive. What they held on to was the evidence given by one of Angela's colleagues. She told the court Angela had been having an affair with a male colleague and most likely wanted her husband dead so she was free to pursue the relationship. The witness said the affair had spanned over five years and they had seen them being intimate.

"When the police questioned the son he offered absolutely nothing. Just sat with his eyes fixed on the wall, not looking at anyone. They tried child psychologists but he would say nothing of his life with his parents or of what happened that night. He'd been found with bruising, which was dismissed as insufficient evidence of physical abuse and it was deemed that she'd fabricated the abuse and handed a hefty sentence for murder. I just can't shift the feeling that had he spoken a different story may have emerged."

"Do you even believe Angela was the one who killed her husband?"

"I believe she's holding something back, the most crucial part of the story. Events that would have changed the outcome of her conviction. She was handed the longest possible sentence and treated like a cold-blooded murderer. Who would accept that if they didn't deserve it? Unless they were desperate to protect someone they loved."

"Pearl, your phone just lit up. I think you've got a call."

"Hello, love. Oh no, I'll be home as quick as I can. I'm leaving now. I'm sorry, I must go, it's Willow. She's deteriorated. But thank you. Angela's due for parole and I've been asked to feedback to the parole board about our sessions and how she presents. This has been helpful."

## Maya

The room remained the same, but the furniture was rearranged. Different cushions on the sofa, smaller, in better proportion, pale peachy florals that complemented the brown corduroy. Faceless said Blaine was ten, but Blaine was neither speaking nor looking at me. His expression was melancholy.

"He doesn't smile. Ever. He speaks rarely, either here or at school. His feelings towards his father now match his father's contempt for him," Faceless informed me.

Blaine reached forward, his hand stretching past the empty whiskey glass to the ashtray at the centre of the table. A half-smoked blunt awaited his fingers. He put it to his lips, then picked up the lighter discarded beside the ashtray. He breathed the smoke in deep, coughed and spluttered but returned the blunt to his lips to inhale again. His eyes rolled to the ceiling, perhaps in relief or maybe resignation. A man entered the room and I couldn't believe what I was seeing. Who I was seeing.

He loomed over Blaine to grab at his hair, rogue strands escaping between his man-fingers. I wanted Blaine to escape him too, but he was pulled to the floor, a knee resting on his stomach, a hand around his throat rendering him captive. His mother appeared in the doorway, the heart hanging around her neck. She was Angela and things were starting to make sense. She screamed for it to stop, which seemed to surprise all three of them. He let go of Blaine, who was neither crying nor reacting, and headed towards her. He snarled in her face, "You dare favour him over me?"

Then they were gone. He had pushed her into the bedroom but the door was ajar. Blaine had never seen what happened when his father made his mother, Angela, cry. But he saw now. She was beneath him, her clothes torn. His father's hand pressed her neck; he could see she was struggling to breathe. Faceless told me Blaine was panicked but knew he could not stop this man, this angry violent demon before him.

She was punched and bitten all the while his father was atop her, naked from the waist down. It seemed his penis was pushing into her, which sickened Blaine even though he did not fully understand what was happening. But he heard his mother's cries, he saw her pain and when she looked at him I could hear his thoughts. He knew exactly what she wanted: the same thing he had wanted all along, to be saved, for someone to stop this monster.

We watched as Blaine retreated to the kitchen and pulled the biggest knife from the wooden block on the worktop. He stopped for just a moment, inhaled deeply and released the breath, as though composing himself, making clear in his head what he was going to do. A scream rung out from the bedroom and with no further hesitation he left the kitchen, knife in hand, returning to the open bedroom door. Suddenly I knew; I knew what happened the night he was taken from his mother.

He entered the room unnoticed by either adult and, with the blankest expression and in complete silence, plunged the knife deep into his father's back. Angela and her husband both froze, both trying to comprehend what had occurred. She pulled the knife quickly from his back and he slumped to the bed, still alive, his lips moving.

I screamed Blaine's name but of course he could not hear me. None of this was real, Faceless was merely showing me what happened that night because I had failed to ask him myself.

Only he was not just Faceless; he was Blaine's father.

Angela instructed Blaine to pick up the chain with the heart from the floor, then wash his hands thoroughly and go to his room. She told him not to come out until a grown up told him to do so, and that when the paramedics and the police arrived she would most likely be taken away and he may not see her again. That he was to be strong, to never speak of what happened and that he must keep the heart forever; it would connect them.

I turned to Faceless, Blaine's dead father. "You're Thomas," I say.

"How do you know my name?"

"Because he cannot bear to hear it. He shudders at the very sound."

## Chapter 43

Monday 12th December 2022

7.24 p.m.

**Thomas**

"I feared losing her to another, Maya. Not just another man, but to my own son. The thought of waiting in line to receive what scraps of affection she had left for me killed me, quite literally.

"I could not have anticipated what I would feel for the boy, for Blaine, from the very moment of his birth. I named him, you know; ironic considering I came to hate the name. He was swaddled and passed straight to me. I received him with open arms, an attempt to dismiss my infantile jealousy, but his eyes, I knew them already, and I loathed them. Have you ever loved and loathed someone at the same time, Maya? No, of course not. But I already knew he would take everything from me.

"What Angela did was the most selfless act of love. He had saved her from me and so she saved him too, from a life of borstal and detention.

A life that would have created a very different Blaine. A Blaine that would have deserved recovery by the elders. But this Blaine, the one who survives despite everything, he deserves a chance.

"I deserve nothing more than the shame that consumes me, but him, he deserves to be saved, again, by you."

## Maya

We were back at the roadside, at the flashing lights and muted chaos. Blaine, the damaged survivor, who loved me with unequalled ferocity, was kneeling behind the paramedics, head in hands, sobbing at my loss.

Thomas recalled seeing Angela for the first time, how her eyes held him in a state of paralysis. He recalled with perfect clarity the hope in her eyes, the adoring way she looked at him. He was her everything. He knew Blaine and I would feel the same way because of the progression of our souls. He explained how the highly evolved soul was drawn to lesser evolved souls and vice versa. The highly evolved was compelled to help, guide, teach. The lesser evolved was drawn to the strength, wisdom and unconditional love they had yet to develop.

Only I had no interest in what he was saying. I was seeing Blaine with new eyes. I was interested in my lifeless body, unable to tell him what I knew or help him overcome what he had been forced to endure. Thomas continued, speaking faster now.

"I have suffered and sinned, I have loved and lost. But nothing compares to the pain of damaging the greatest offering you have made to the world. He deserved so much more, a father to equal the love and purity of his mother.

"Maya, you must listen to me: unless you help Blaine to remember and overcome, he will eventually do the same to you. The elders know this and will not let him hurt you. You are so close to joining them that they will protect you at all costs. They will come for him again. They will bring him back here, to the afterlife to await a new life, as a new person. He must break the cycle now, there is no other way.

"For Blaine to heal from his past he must first remember it was he who killed me, not his mother. He must forgive himself for that and he must forgive Angela for not protecting him. She lived in a state of terror every day, petrified of what I might inflict upon them next.

"He must realise that everything is my fault, not Angela's and certainly not his. Until he remembers the truth of that night he will be stuck, terrified of becoming me. But his fear and reluctance only serve to ensure he will make the same mistakes as I; he will always hurt the ones he loves. He knows this deep down; it is why he avoided love for so long. The greater his love for you grows the more he will hurt you.

"You know Angela has the purest soul, just like you. It is my belief that the elders twisted Blaine's fate that night, that they intervened, guiding him to kill me to spare Angela. Although they will neither admit nor discuss this with me. The sacrifice she made for Blaine, turning her life over to incarceration so that he might walk free, was the final act of her development. Her sentence is not one of punishment but one of growth."

More paramedics arrived in a car. One of them fitted paddles to my chest. Everyone but Blaine had cleared a path around my body. Thomas' voice became urgent.

"Maya, you must listen to me. Have you ever wondered why you never decided on a career path? It's because there is nothing left that any career could teach you. You are almost ready to become one of them, the elders. You see only the good in the most broken, you exist from a place of pure love. Your final act is to save him Maya; only then will you be ready to join them upon your true recovery."

I was listening but distracted by the elderly couple moving towards us, slowly, tentatively. "Are they the elders you speak of, Thomas?"

"They are watching us, guarding you. Ready to intervene. It was never my intention to hurt you, but they were going to take him without giving him a chance. I couldn't let them; none of this is his fault, it is mine alone. You did not act upon your dreams and they would not allow me close enough to you in your waking life. But I knew if I could just speak with you, I could make you understand."

A shock pulsed through my lifeless body; my shoulders jumped an inch from the ground. Faint voices were audible. Blaine's voice, pleading for my breath.

"We are running out of time, Maya. You must listen. Last night before Blaine came to your door the elders came for him; they tried taking him. I called him, made him step back out of the road. It was enough to stop him befalling this very fate." He was pointing to my body lying in the road. A paramedic resumed chest compressions.

"So, this should have been him, not me?" Thomas brushed off my question with a flick of his hand before demanding I do as he asked. Another shock, another jolt. Voices.

"I've got a pulse."

"Maya, just breathe. For god's sake, breathe. Please, stay with me." I could hear him, Blaine. His voice, his desperation for my return. "Stay with me."

Then a paramedic; I could hear him too. "We need to intubate." Thomas was becoming hazy, everything was hazy.

"You must not tell him you have seen me or spoken with me, Maya. You must not tell him what you know, it will be too damaging. He will not believe your source. He will not trust you and all will be lost. I will be forced to recover you once more if you fail him, and I will not allow you return again if it is the only way to keep him alive."

A peculiar sensation gripped me, an awareness of time being imperative, an awareness of Thomas. The elders were watching me. I could feel them as though they were connected to me. Perhaps what he was saying was true. That I was almost one of them.

"You have shown me Blaine's story, but what about you, Thomas, where do your demons hide?" They came from my mouth but the words did not feel like my own. He was almost invisible, a hazy outline, when his reply came.

"That is a story to be told another time, Maya. Now go back and save my son."

# Chapter 44

## Wednesday 18th January 2023

### **Blaine**

If we'd gone straight to dinner, if I'd just answered the question; the stupid simple bloody question, I wouldn't have had to endure watching the light fade from her eyes. Those excruciating minutes spent watching her broken lifelessness, willing her to breathe, willing her to stay with me. Making promises to myself that if she didn't die, that I'd be better.

I could have rung her parents from her phone, but I couldn't face the shame of knowing that if I hadn't chased her or grabbed for her, she wouldn't have lunged into the road. All this was on me and breaking the news to Richard and Maggie was on the police.

I'd kept pace with the ambulance en route to the hospital but when the paramedics rushed her through those resus doors, I had to let her go. A nurse had ushered me into a relative's room along with Richard and Maggie and Sissy and Henry, all distraught at the news but unaware of the extent of her injuries. I had to explain. Then the question I'd dreaded, "How did it happen?" Followed by, "She's such a careful girl."

They'd have had me kicked out of that room for sure if I'd told them the truth, scaring their precious girl and risking her life. I made another promise to myself that night: if she recovered, if she made it through this, I would never put her at risk, no matter what I had to do. She would not suffer again.

## Maya

I would have expected to feel myself re-entering my body, acknowledging the transition from light and ethereal to physically broken and pained. Only my next moment of awareness was a confusing one, voices coaxing me to open my eyes, a breathing tube being pulled from my throat. Stinging daylight forcing my eyelids back down to a squint, moving silhouettes offering little reprieve until Blaine eclipsed the sun that shone painfully through the ICU window.

His hand touched my face and a tear dropped to my skin as he leaned to kiss my forehead. This was the moment I realised Thomas had allowed me to return to Blaine. To save him. Not just for him but for me too, to perform a final act before joining the elders. But how was I to save him, even with the knowledge I now held?

Thomas' words rung in my ears, obscuring the jubilant voices around me. *You must not tell him you have seen me or spoken with me. You must not tell him what you know.* Was any of it even real? Then Mum and

Dad were over me, crying that I was awake, that I was alive. Mum's gentle hands cupping my limp one, Blaine gripping the other as though he might never let go.

The first few weeks were the hardest, before the injuries began to heal. Physios helped restore my mobility, small movements initially. My spine and one hip had been fractured by the impact of the car; the other hip displaced. My forearm was broken and my skull fractured. The driver was cleared of any liability; witnesses agreed he was not speeding and there was neither alcohol nor drugs in his system. Finally, it was internal bleeding from a rupture in my spleen that caused my heart to arrest at the scene.

But the most significant memory from those early days after waking up was looking at Blaine and seeing someone new. Not the Blaine I met, nor the Blaine I fell in love with; he was someone else now. Of course, he was the same person he had been all along, only now I saw the full version of him. Sometimes, when he caught me staring at him too long, picturing the horrors this beautiful man had endured, he would ask what was wrong. I would lie and say, "Nothing," but he knew it was something.

Dad once said I could not understand what he might have been through because I had never struggled for anything, least of all love. And he was right. This poor boy, beaten by his father, avoided by his mother as her only means of protecting him. There was so much to repair if I was to do as Thomas asked.

# Blaine

I told them only what the police would later clarify; she'd been too distracted by her phone to see the approaching car. Witnesses saw me grab for her and assumed I was trying to save her, having seen the car myself. They didn't know how I'd shouted at her, how I'd made her run from me in fear. I couldn't tell them what was on her phone when it fell from her hand. And I couldn't delete it from my mind, the headline periodically appearing in my head. If I didn't allow myself to repeat it I could let it go until its next involuntary appearance.

It wasn't long after she woke up, drowsy, different, that she told me she knew about Angela's heart. More words I didn't want to think about. I'd prayed in vain that the head trauma would make her forget what she'd heard, but it was there, fresh in her mind like she'd held onto it the whole time she was unconscious. But she didn't speak of that damn headline. Maybe the car hit her before she read it.

Something had changed now. She was more fragile than before and her eyes lingered on me differently, pitifully. Or maybe my paranoia wanted to believe she blamed me too and was looking for the right words to send me away without angering me again. Even her lips felt different against mine. The longing and electricity was replaced with fear. Not her fear of me, but my fear of her, of what she might say. My want to be with her every second was replaced by a desire to leave so I didn't hear when she told me it was over.

I believed her recovery was all that mattered. I hadn't considered how it might feel between us all the while she slept peacefully, full of lines and tubes.

## Maya

Christmas Day was a strange affair. Mum, Dad, Sissy and Henry all huddled around my hospital bed. Blaine arrived after lunch. A strategy to ensure I would not spend any of it unaccompanied and could spend time alone with him in the evening. That had been difficult since waking up, what with the endless stream of nurses, consultants, family and friends. Even Ruby had visited, instructing me to take all the recovery time I needed; my job would wait for me if I was able to return.

Not returning was a reality I may have had to face. My recovery was, according to the medical geniuses, on track, but there was no guarantee that things would be the same as before. I may have been unable to stand for prolonged periods without pain and although Totally Coffee was never my career ambition, I liked it there; I wanted very much to return.

Mum, Dad, Sissy and Henry brought the Christmas presents with them, along with Christmassy nibbles. The four of them donned matching festive jumpers and covered me in a well-coordinated blanket. They left the hospital around three p.m. to go home for Christmas dinner, promising to do another when I got home. They did and Blaine was invited, and although it did not compensate for missing out on real Christmas, it was nice to share our belated Christmas with him.

Rebecca had popped in briefly to bring me a gift and tell me she would take me shopping again once I am discharged, even if she had to push me in a wheelchair. I never told her how Blaine reacted to the underwear I bought the last time we went shopping. I pictured his face that awful day and saw traces of Thomas, as though his DNA had forced him to react that way.

Blaine stayed late into the evening, until the nurses appeared inconvenienced by his presence. Before leaving he told me with a heavy heart how he had looked forward to our first Christmas together and would not forgive himself for causing all of this. Thomas's words rang in my ears again. *He must forgive himself, and he must forgive Angela for not protecting him from me.* And I was expected to help him do so.

It was the night before I returned home to familiar surroundings and my comfortable bed when Thomas took me to the white room in my dream, his face still crystal clear. It was strange to be asleep and yet be so conscious. He was sorry for causing such suffering, confident it was the only thing he seems proficient in.

"I want you to know that I was not born with the urge to hurt people. My father was a mean man, full of rage. I am the way I am because of him, just like Blaine is the way he is because of me. If someone had saved me from his malevolence, maybe I would not have inflicted the same onto Angela and Blaine.

"I have spent my death in bitterness at this. Why did nobody save me? Worthless little Thomas. My grandparents, my mother, even my father were all here before me. Any one of them could have done something before the elders stepped in to end my existence. It would have been more than just me they were saving.

"But we must focus now on Blaine. Start gently, Maya; ask him about Angela. He knows you know of her. You do not need to reveal anything else you have learned."

## The Elders

"She is safe for now; hasty decisions are not necessary. Thomas believes she can save Blaine; I think he believes she can save him too. He put the same belief in Angela. Do you see the pattern? Instead of having faith in himself he leaves his fate in the hands of others.

"Thomas will not make a move for Maya until she fails him, which she will. It is an impossible task he has set upon her. And Blaine will not put her in harm's way again; he feels responsible for the accident that took her. It is possible that, should he need to, he might do the right thing."

## Chapter 45

### Wednesday 15th February 2023

### **Maya**

Ten weeks had passed since we shared a bed, since I had woken to his face and that smile when he saw me upon waking. So much had occurred and yet it felt as though nothing had happened at all. Laying there, revelling in the connection to him, I could be forgiven for thinking I could say anything without consequence. Mum had suggested he stay, it being Valentine's Day and all.

Until now I had mostly rested, with gentle indoor exercise restoring my mobility. I was walking unaided, but pain and unsteadiness remained. Blaine insisted our first outing should be to the intimate restaurant, where Thomas had watched us from the table for one. I could not tell him I feared Thomas being there again because he knew nothing of my time whilst dead.

Thomas had visited my dreams several times since I'd been home, urging me to act before he was forced to take me again. But my connection with Blaine had suffered and the fear of pushing him further away had been too great. Of late I had felt the connection returning, the heat of our kisses intensifying. Time seemed to be healing the guilt he felt and numbing the power of the knowledge I had gained. Of course, I knew I must try to make him speak of his past, but it only felt urgent when Thomas was haunting me. When I was awake it felt as though things were returning to normal.

We were leaving the restaurant; Blaine was opening the car door for me when I saw them, the elders, moving slowly towards us. I hadn't noticed before how effortless their steps seemed for such mature beings. I had no reason to contemplate such things. My heart raced at the sight of them and Blaine noticed my changed expression. Believing the cause to be pain he took my arm and helped me into the car, fastening my seat belt to spare me further exertion. Still, they moved towards us and I wondered if this was it, if they were coming for him. I told him to fasten his belt too and to hurry me home. But they simply watched us pass by, Blaine oblivious to their presence.

We retired to bed soon after arriving home; I was tired from the outing but wanted desperately to feel Blaine intimately. It had been too long, only he was certain my body was not ready and would not risk hurting me. Instead, I laid in his arms until I drifted into a sleep interrupted by Thomas, reminding me once more of my duty. He knew the elders had come to us; he knew they were deciding whether to take Blaine. He insisted I act or suffer the consequences.

# Blaine

I was beginning to trust she was not looking for a way out. Only it turned out she was looking for a way in. "Tell me about the heart," she said. But I couldn't; something happened inside me when I thought about it. It was like being asked a question that I was expected to know the answer to. But I didn't, so I panicked; my brain shut down and there was nothing intelligible to respond with.

Seconds passed and when nothing came from my mouth she spoke again, asking me to tell her about Angela. I could have gotten angry again, I could have got up and left, but I didn't want to lose her. After everything I'd put her through, I couldn't shut her down now.

# Maya

If they were contemplating coming for him then time was limited and the only way to save him was to, well, save him. It felt safe; we were reconnected, he was looking at me with eyes that said he would never look at another the same way. Just as he did before the accident. I still called it an accident, even though I knew my fate rested in Thomas's hands. But I had not told a soul; who would have believed me had I tried?

I started gently, a question about the heart to test the water, but even that seemed too much. He recoiled away from me, not physically but emotionally, the vacant look returning to his eyes like he did not want to go there. I changed tactic.

"Then tell me about Angela."

I felt his chest rise as he drew in a breath, bigger than any he had taken since waking. I feared what might come when he exhaled.

"It's not what you think. She's my… she was my mother."

He volunteered no more so I asked him to tell me about her, but he requested through gritted teeth that we save it for another time. Time, that thing we had little of.

Chapter 46

Thursday 16th February 2023

**Blaine**

It would be cold for sure, but I'd taken measures to keep her warm. There was something particularly beautiful about her tonight: a spark, a sure sign she was feeling stronger. Still, I carried her across the park so she wouldn't weaken too soon. Rob had been reluctant to help set it up this time; he was spending the evening with Hannah, but I talked him into sparing half an hour of his time. The night air was cold but not bitter, a perfectly timed intervention from the gods, and the bridge glowed in the candlelight. It looked quite something and Maya's delight was evident. "Let's stay longer this time," she said.

As I placed her back on her feet she swept her arms around my neck, pulling me into her and kissing me. Heat pulsed through my veins and that familiar spark ignited in my body, just like before. She wanted me and I wanted her but I still wasn't ready to risk hurting her.

Rob had lent me his fishing chairs; they were crude and a little muddy but she wouldn't have lasted long standing up, or sitting on that cold and wet bench, and I'd packed her a blanket and a flask of hot coffee to keep the cold out for longer. I felt on edge; I'd told her we'd talk about Angela another time, but there was no "another time". No good came from interfering with things best left in the past. All I could do was hope that now wasn't the time she'd bring it up again.

She told me she wanted to return to work, just a few hours a week to see how she'd cope. She was going stir crazy at home having read every book on her shelf. She missed chatting with Ruby, and she missed me walking through the door and leaving doodles on receipts.

We'd been there a while, swept up in conversations that flowed easily, when she thought she saw something in the darkness. Her demeanour changed; she was scared. She didn't think anything could happen while she was with me, surely? But when I questioned what she'd seen she clammed up, like she was embarrassed to say. Then out of nowhere she said, "What was it like, Blaine? Your childhood, before Rachel and Warren?"

## Maya

I guessed where he was taking me as soon as he parked the car. This handsome man carrying me across the grass, devoting his time and attention to pleasing me. The bridge looked beautiful once again; I had forgotten how it glowed through the darkness. Ripples of light dashed across the pond's surface, dancing yellow streaks from the candles and the milky white blur of the moon. Overwhelmed by the moment I kissed him and everything I have ever felt for him swiftly amplified by a million. My body longed for him again and I hoped he would give in to me here on the bridge, the place where it all began.

Only he was not for persuading, no matter how hard I tried. Instead we sat, I wrapped in a blanket, he looking irresistible and adamant he was warm enough in just his shirt and jacket. But something beyond him caught my eye, a movement in the darkness, figures in the trees. He looked around to where my eyes had focused but saw nothing. Thomas's words filled my head. *It was pointless trying to make him see me. He can't.*

What if he couldn't see *them* either? They could come for him and he would have no chance to save himself. Fear filled me. I had no choice but to do as Thomas demanded, to ask questions. If they could hear me easing his memories to the surface they might allow him more time. I thought if I started gently he might tell me something of his childhood, anything that might open the door to his past. But Thomas was right about history, about how it repeated itself. Blaine stood from his chair, taking hold of the bridge's balustrade, his face wild, looking anywhere but at me. I stood, placing my hand on the small of his back. His breath was erratic.

"I know it is difficult, but there must be something you can tell me."

He turned to face me, wearing the same expression of fear I had seen on little Blaine's face. Pushing my hand away he gripped my shoulders and shook me, shouting in my face, "BUT YOU DON'T

KNOW, MAYA! HOW COULD YOU POSSIBLY KNOW?" he raged as pain pulsed through my healing bones.

"You have to stop, Blaine," I pleaded, but he forced me back down into my chair, my hips and spine jarring on impact with the cloth seat. Pain seared through them.

The figures were visible again, emerging from the trees. Perhaps they had not been coming for him at all, perhaps they were observing, ensuring my safety. But now they were coming, moving swiftly closer. Blaine fell to his knees before me, tears streaming from his eyes, his head falling to my lap.

"Forgive me, Maya. What have I done? I'm so sorry. You know I'd never hurt you." The figures stopped twenty metres away, observing his movements, assessing my safety.

"They will come for you if you hurt me." I had not meant to say it aloud but it all happened so fast. Blaine looked up in confusion. The figures retreated; or maybe they faded, until I could no longer make them out.

"Who'll come for me?" he asked, not waiting for the answer, tripping over his words in his desperation to say them. "You have to believe I'll never hurt you." Only he had hurt me. "It's just too hard to talk about my life before Rachel and Warren. Angela did something terrible and I don't want to think about it. I only want to think about us, about what's ahead, not what's behind us."

He was full of fear and regret and, looking into his eyes, I saw Angela laying on her bed, crying, terrified, Thomas full of rage as he struck her. But then he kissed me with heat and love. I no longer felt fear, but a mixture of pity and love.

## Blaine

It was starting to happen the way it had with him, losing control piece by piece. I took her home and retreated to the flat where I could do her no harm, where I could smoke to numb the disgust steadily consuming me. Only it wasn't enough; it took whiskey too, glasses of the stuff, to block it out.

The process was cathartic; drink, remember the vile man, feel myself become him, loathe him, see Maya's face and fight what instinct wanted me to be. Then again. Drink, see his face, become him, loathe him, love Maya, fight to be free. Then again and again until the whiskey and weed muddled the thoughts; drink, love Maya, become him, be free... Become him, drink, loathe Maya, love him, be free.

What followed was a peaceful nothingness I would return to in a heartbeat. No thoughts, no regret, no guilt. Simply unconscious bliss. Then she was there, staring down at my pathetic form, foetal position on the sofa, stinking of smoke and whiskey, with nothing but pity in her eyes.

## Chapter 47

### Fridy 17th February 2023

### **Maya**

With a heightened sense of pain and exhaustion I had retired to bed with painkillers and a tumultuous head. How could I possibly save him? Thomas demanded I ask about Angela, that I make Blaine remember the events of his childhood, yet he was adamant that we only look forward; the past was not a place he would visit. And his volatile reaction made it too dangerous.

\*\*\*

Three am, that damned witching hour again. Thomas came with a stark warning; he had spoken with the elders who had dallied long enough, they were taking measures, now. He warned he would come for me before they take Blaine; I was failing and he would not allow his boy to be recovered. There could be only one outcome if we were both to live; he must be saved.

When I opened my eyes to escape the dream, Thomas remained, in my room, waiting for me to respond to his demand. "Now, Maya," he insisted. "You have so little time."

He must be saved yet I could not drag him to safety; he must be willing to save himself. If I was out of time then I saw no other way but to reveal what I knew. Thomas was fearful that telling Blaine would destroy any chance of saving him. I believed he was wrong, that his belief was born of fear. If I armed Blaine with the knowledge I held then it would be up to him to face it or run from it. He would not allow harm to befall me again. I was certain he would do the right thing; he would remember and be the man Thomas had failed to be.

My hips and back ached, my head felt weary, but this man had taken me once already. If he took me again I would not return.

## Blaine

Alcohol fog obscured the wall clock. It looked like three-thirty a.m. but what would she be doing here at this time? How had she got in? Moments passed and my eyes began adjusting; it did look like three-thirty. I remembered she still had a door key. With eyes bearing down on me heavy and silent, "We have to talk, there's something I need to explain," she said. I pulled myself upright, too stoned and drunk still to argue or send her away. She looked at the ashtray and the blunts within with none of the surprise or disgust on her face that I would have expected.

"When I died, while you were watching the paramedics fighting to save me, I was somewhere else. This is going to sound ridiculous but I swear on my very life I would not lie to you, Blaine." I was trying hard to focus, to stay with her words, ridiculous or otherwise, but my attention was sliding to the hands of the clock. Still trying to determine if I was seeing them correctly.

"I felt that car hit me and my body breaking. I saw the old couple help the driver to his feet; I saw the old man staring across the road to you. I also saw *him*, the same man I saw in Totally Coffee, and at the restaurant you took me to. He was at the airport too when we returned from Scotland. It was the same man from my dreams, the man you know. Then I felt all the sensations of slowly dying."

She had my attention now. The mention of that man replaced the fog in my head with the pounding of a memory trying hard to be seen. I fought it and reached out to her, taking her hand in mine.

"I know who he is, Blaine." The pounding moved from my head to my ears, noise like nothing I've heard, not ringing nor crashing, more like that noise when the TV screen distorts and flickers, only louder, harsher, deafening. I squeezed her hand and begged her to stop talking.

"You have to hear this. They will come for you." That threat again.

"Who will come for me?" But I didn't want to hear any more. I didn't want to hear her say the police. There was only one way to stop her from talking; I pulled her towards me. I needed her heat, the electricity, the connection. My lips pressed onto hers, a momentary spark dulled by her resistance. "Maya," I pleaded, "I need to feel you." But her hand was on my chest, pushing me away.

"You have to listen. In those moments while I was dead, I wasn't just there on the road, I was with Thomas." The noise grew louder. I kissed her again, holding her head, pulling her into me. I wanted to feel her, I wanted the noise to stop. I didn't want to think about him. She was trying to pull away but I held her still. She wanted me; she loved me. She had to want me.

## Maya

The man lying foetal on the sofa looked no different to the child who bore the weight of the abuse. The assailant being dead had only deepened Blaine's scars. Everything I saw in his childhood was depicted in this one scene in front of me. His substance-abused eyes blinked wearily at me.

I understood this would be a challenge, but he had to hear it, and not just hear it but believe it if it was going to work. He stared at the clock until I mentioned Thomas then, eyes on me, he begged me to stop and kissed me, not passionately, but desperately. I was pushing him away but he held me tight, pushing himself into me. Blaine, but not Blaine. He was not reading me or sensing that now was not the time for intimacy. I tried to continue.

"He showed me the things you've been hiding, Blaine." His face pushed harder onto mine, his lips pressing mine hard against my teeth until I was unable to speak further, the love this man showed me now all but absent. I pushed harder with my hands but my resistance seemed only to strengthen his grip. He was no longer my Blaine as he pulled me to the floor, covering me with his body, grappling at my chest with one hand, the other still holding my head while he kissed me. I did not recall feeling terror before, not even when lying utterly broken on that road. But now I felt terror. Now I understood just what Angela must have felt.

"Show me a good time now," he snarled, "like you wanted to before." He was lifting my top, the familiar tingling replaced with repulsion and dread. He was squeezing my breast when the tears began free flowing from my eyes. Catching his breath he pulled his hand from my top and stared down at me, a look in his now soulless green eyes that I could not decipher. I seized the opportunity and begged him to stop. This was not who he was.

Only he did not stop; his eyes glazed over as he lifted himself slightly, enough to unfasten his jeans. I knew what was coming; I had seen it in my death and I could not let it happen to me. I raised my hand and struck his face. The shock sent him backwards against the sofa, and seizing my chance I scrambled to my feet and ran for the front door and out to the street.

He followed, only this time I did not want him to.

## Blaine

"No, Blaine. Don't do this. Please, don't do this. This isn't you. This is him."

She was crying, and somehow she knew him, knew what he is... was. I felt myself become him, an involuntary response to her words, as though she had made me do this to her. Maybe Mum had done the same. More thoughts I didn't need. I just needed to be inside her, then all this would go away. She'd remember how much she loved me, how I made her feel. Only she was playing hard to get, playing the victim, but she had made me feel this.

Then the palm of her hand struck my face. My beautiful Maya; gentle, sweet Maya, slapping me before running away. This time I caught her and I caught myself in that exact same moment. What the fuck had I become?

## Maya

My eyes fell immediately upon them, their eyes fixed firmly behind me. Blaine's fingers locked tight around my arm. His time was up. My tummy lurched; he had made me fear him yet still I felt compelled to help him.

"In the car, NOW, they're here," I commanded. His eyes scanned the street before falling back to me. "There's no one here," he exclaimed, but there was no time to explain. Taking his hand I pulled him to the car. The elders watched from across the road, eyes now on me. I had no idea how they intended to take him but I had to give him the chance to hear what was happening.

"Where are they, Maya, where are the police?"

"The police? What are you talking about?" I asked.

"You keep saying they're coming for me. Who else would be coming for me?"

The penny dropped; he must remember, why else would he think the police might come for him? Once again the elders observed as we passed. I knew they would follow, their ability to move from one place to another an effortless manoeuvre. Wherever we stopped they would most likely already be present. This time in the car might be all the time we had to talk.

Besides the journey to Blaine's, this was the first time I had driven since the accident. Confused and ashamed he cried and apologised, only now was not the time to waste on what could not be changed.

"Do you trust me Blaine?"

"Of course I trust you."

"When I died, Thomas, your dad, was waiting for me." The roads were all but empty, allowing me to keep a steady pace without the need for frequent gear changes. My hip would not have allowed the leg movements. "I didn't dream it; I know it was real because of the things he showed me. If I am wrong then tell me. But tell me only in honesty." His head was hung, maybe in shame, maybe in fear of what I was about to say.

"I saw you as a boy; I saw what he did to you. And to Angela."

"This is impossible, Maya. How could you have seen any of it?"

"That isn't important right now. Right now you have to allow yourself to remember everything that happened, to face what he did, and what you did to him. If you don't…"

"ENOUGH. This is insane. Stop the car."

"If I let you out they'll take you."

"WHO MAYA? WHO THE FUCK WANTS ME?"

"Those on the other side…" They were there at the roadside. We had driven at least a mile and they were still observing. They could create an accident to stop us but that would put at me at risk. We just had to drive until he understood. "… those who need you to remember. But you do remember, Blaine."

"I can't do this Maya. I know you mean well but it's too hard."

"There is no choice. Tell me what happened. Or I will tell you as I saw it."

"Then tell me, what did you see?"

"Thomas showed me everything: the violence, the fear you lived in, what your poor mother endured. But there was more. And it will sound absurd, but there are souls, beings, I don't know what they really are, but they maintain order. They decide who stays and who is recovered back to the afterlife to await another chance to learn lessons and evolve as a soul. They were coming for you, Blaine, because you were living in denial, falling foul to the patterns of behaviour that gripped your father."

"You've gone mad, this is bullshit."

"I am not mad. I am scared. The night before the accident, you were almost hit by a car. You told me so yourself, but you did not tell me about the voice you heard, the man that called your name. How could I know that, Blaine? I know because Thomas told me; it was he who called you. These souls, the elders, had come for you. It was supposed to be you who was hit, not me. Thomas knew they were coming for you and did what he could to protect you. He called your name to distract you from stepping into the road; he saved your life. But to prevent them coming back for you he took me. It was no accident; he orchestrated it because he knew they would not take you if he had me. He knew if he had me he could show me everything and send me back to save you. Only I cannot save you, Blaine, nobody can. You have to save you, you have remember everything and you have to choose to be better than him. To fight for yourself every second that you are breathing." Another mile and they were there again, nodding at me as though in approval.

Blaine was silent, his head still hung low. "I did hear a voice; I knew it was a man but I'd hoped it was you. I'd waited for you outside your house, hiding in the darkness. I was desperate to see you and know you were okay. But my head was a mess, I couldn't come to you for fear of what I might say. When I heard that voice I just prayed that somehow you'd seen me and followed me. It saved my life."

"Thomas saved your life. But he took mine in return and promised to take it again if I couldn't make you remember. You must forgive your mother for not protecting you, and you must forgive yourself for what you did. If you hang on to all this pain and resentment and guilt it will destroy you and just like him you will hurt everybody you love... Me. Over and over again. Just like he did. But the elders will not allow you to do that to me."

"If this is true then why did they allow him to do it to her, to my mum? This is insane, none of this is true. It's just some hallucination you experienced while your heart was stopped."

"Then how would I know about the heart? Tell me how I know Angela wore a heart necklace that he bought for her. Tell me how I know you picked it up from her bedroom floor after he ripped it off her while he was raping her? Tell me how I know that you went to your kitchen to get a…"

"STOP! ENOUGH!"

"You know this is true. You never forgot; you just buried it somewhere in your head where you believed it wouldn't destroy you. But it is destroying you Blaine. Tell me how he died."

"ENOUGH, MAYA!"

"I saw it all. I already know. You did what you had to because you believed she wanted you to save her." I had been driving on autopilot, concentrating only on Blaine, and found myself heading to the spot above the town.

"She did want me to save her. She told me so."

"She wanted you to leave, to turn around and not watch what he was doing. She loved you and only ever wanted to protect you, she just didn't know how because she was so scared of him. She never asked you to save her, she pled with her eyes just the way you did, only you pled a different message."

"She wanted me to leave?"

"The elders have been following us since we left the flat. When we stop the car they will come for you because of the threat you now pose to me. You will only be safe if you are no longer a threat. Thomas will try to come for me first, to prevent them from taking you. He believes all of this is his fault and that he must undo the damage he caused. He won't let them take you. He will come for me first, he promised me so, and he will not allow me to return next time."

## The Elders

"Still she protects him, but she must learn to detach herself from the subject in order to allow their growth. She has only this and her lingering judgement of how others present on the outside, their clothes and their professions, to overcome. Although I believe Blaine himself has helped her begin pushing past this weakness. She simply must remain in order to develop these attributes. We will not allow Thomas to recover her again, he will not outwit us this time.

"Blaine's battle was never hers and I am certain he is not so lost after all."

"You believe he can still progress in this lifetime?"

"Oh, I am certain, but that does not negate our duty, we must continue as planned. He can threaten Maya's journey no more."

# Blaine

She didn't want me to save her. She wanted me to leave. I wanted him dead. I despised him. I blamed him for everything and resented her for making me do what I did. I've been hiding from the truth that was too much to bear, and all this time she'd accepted the punishment for my crime. She had protected me.

As we neared the spot I demanded Maya stop the car. Of course she was reluctant, but I was ready. Ready to face it all, to remember what a monster he was, what he did to us. I was ready to be the man he couldn't be.

We were out of the car, the town stretched out below us. At this time of the morning only the main road streetlamps were lit, stretching out like veins carrying blood to the vital organs. The capillaries were all shut down; the extremities not needed.

The beauty of the town, of Maya, of life, struck me all at once. After everything I had done to her she wanted only to save me and I would have gotten down on one knee and pledged my unwavering love and commitment to her if circumstances had been on our side. She said Thomas was there, the elders not far behind. He was coming for her to stop the elders coming for me and I couldn't allow him to take her again. I heard him, the same voice I heard that night at the roadside. I should have recognised it then.

"Blaine… No."

# Maya

The elders were there, unmoving, watching. But Thomas, I had told Blaine everything he told me not to and now he was coming for me.

"I killed him, Maya," Blaine said, holding my hands tight in his. "I killed him and she took the blame. She sacrificed her freedom to protect me because she was as pure as you. If things were different, if we could have a future, I'd marry you and have children with you. Lots of them. And we'd raise them in that cottage. I'd be everything you needed me to be. You'd be my forever. Never forget that."

His eyes, his beautiful intense green eyes, full of soul and love and something now definable, told me every word he spoke was true. Only there was no time to respond; Thomas was almost upon us, upon me. It was funny how I felt no fear, even though I knew what he had come to do. Blaine looked away, to where Thomas's voice rang out, "Blaine... No," then kissed me with the heat of a thousand suns. He was back, and not just back, he was free.

What happened next seemed to happen in slow motion. Thomas increased his pace towards me. The elders made their move towards not Blaine, but Thomas and Blaine pulled me into him as a tear escaped his eye, making its break for freedom down his cheek before disappearing into dark stubble. His fingertips brushed the wisps of hair from my face before his hands lightly cupped my head, turning it slightly as he whispered "Thank you" into my ear. His chest pressed into me; heat and electricity passed from his body to mine. Then, releasing me, he ran the few short metres to the edge of the road where the land fell away, not the gentle slope towards the town, but the sheer drop. Hell's mouth.

"You know I'd sacrifice my life for you, right?" His declaration rose from the depths of my memories to the forefront of my mind, ringing through my head, shattering my heart. He did not look back, he did not see me fall to the road, nor did he stop when I screamed his name. He simply jumped the barrier and ran the final two strides where the ground ran out beneath him and he was gone. And with him my promise of forever.

# Chapter 48

## **The Elders**

"We are wiser than to say I told you so, but… He did not only promise Maya he would keep her from harm; he promised himself. He just needed to rise above his denial in order to fulfil his promise."

"I must admit I did not believe he would open himself to the truth of his past in this lifetime. It would have saved him, but by sacrificing himself to ensure her safety above all else, he elevated his soul to an entirely new level. Such a big leap from where he was stuck. We will monitor him closely from here and observe how he adapts to this new ability."

"I had expected Maya to trust we would not have allowed Thomas to take her again. Perhaps in her anguish she could not see that we were protecting her from him. What puzzles me is that she stopped the car, she let Blaine go. I believe we may have connected with her, led her to act instinctively. If this is so, she may be on the cusp of loving unconditionally while detaching sufficiently to allow the independent growth of others. It is likely she will fulfil her final acts in this lifetime."

"We will continue to observe Maya also. Her perception of his death will undoubtedly impact her. She could come to view his passing as having been in vain, an unnecessary act of heroism. Grief can do peculiar things to a person's perception.

"Her final act is just as mine was; being selfless enough to let someone go, to make their mistakes and save themselves. It broke my human heart to watch my granddaughter suffer so, but when I had to choose between staying long enough to save her and leaving before I interfered and prevented her saving herself, there was only one choice to make. Lord knows she has struggled through her journey, but she seems to be battling her demons now. You know they set a dinner place for me at Christmas don't you?"

"Yes, I saw. She holds you deep in her heart and the memory of your unfaltering love undoubtedly guides her."

"I could not have stayed and watched her suffer, you know. It would have set me back; I believe I would have interfered out of love. Is that not a weakness? One that should have kept me from here. The same weakness Maya is now overcoming. However split-second that decision to let Blaine go was, she made it. As did I, and perhaps that was enough, perhaps I did not need to live that decision numerous times to prove my worth. Maybe Maya will not need to either. Although she is much younger than I was. I hope she will have time to live a full life as the beautiful soul she is before this stage of her journey beckons. She is heartbroken for now, but there is time still to find the forever she so desires."

"Blaine has passed over successfully. Thomas appears to have passed now, too. He had hung on to the notion of saving Blaine since his own death, caught up in the cycle of blame and regret, of trying to take responsibility for how others heal from the damage he caused. He has yet to see through his own denial, but he can start again now, a fresh journey in which to learn and overcome. I have no doubt their paths will cross once more as they have before."

## Hannah

It had really played on my mind; I didn't think it was her eyes. Or at least not solely her eyes. There was something else that had woken me a few times, hit me mid-sitting when I was focused on a client, made my heart flutter when she'd flickered through my mind. Something about her reminded me of Nanna. How was that?

## About Recovery

What began as a stand-alone story of 'broken-by-life boy meets naïve girl', quickly grew into a deeper story of what it means to be human, to love, to be broken. For the lucky; to recover. For the not so lucky; to be recovered, to start again with a new set of opportunities to heal and grow.

**Recovery** is the first instalment of a series of titles following Maya, Blaine and other characters in this title. The series will traverse friendships, relationships, lifetimes and recoveries in their various forms.

If you enjoyed Maya and Blaine's story and would like to continue the journey through future titles, you can keep in touch with me and hear when the next title will be released through the following links:

### Email

jmsinsauthor@gmail.com

### Facebook

https://www.facebook.com/j.m.sins.author

### Instagram

**@j.m.sins.author**

https://www.instagram.com/j.m.sins.author

### TikTok

https://www.tiktok.com/@j.m.sins.author

# Acknowledgments

Much love and appreciation to all of you who bought and read (and hopefully enjoyed) this, my first book.

To those closest to me who listened to my endless wittering about the characters and the developing story, who championed my ability to reach the end, and looked like they were interested even when they must have been sick of hearing about it! To those who proofread the awful early versions of this story, and were brave enough to feedback to me what didn't work. I am eternally grateful. You have all played a valuable part in my being able to hold a physical copy of this book in my hand.

Whether I wrote the story to a satisfactory level remains to be seen, but it is with the fondest regard that I release Maya and Blaine and all those associated with them into the world to see how well (if at all) they travel.

**J.M. Sins**

Printed in Great Britain
by Amazon